Show Me the Gold

Show Me the Gold

Carolyn Mulford

FIVE STAR
A part of Gale, Cengage Learning

GALE
CENGAGE Learning

Farmington Hills, Mich • San Francisco • New York • Waterville, Maine
Meriden, Conn • Mason, Ohio • Chicago

LIBRARY OF CONGRESS CATALOGING-IN-PUBLICATION DATA

Mulford, Carolyn.
Show me the gold / Carolyn Mulford. — First edition.
pages ; cm
ISBN 978-1-4328-2990-2 (hardcover) — ISBN 1-4328-2990-4 (hardcover) — ISBN 978-1-4328-2983-4 (ebook) — ISBN 1-4328-2983-1 (ebook)
1. Bank robberies—Fiction. 2. Intelligence officers—Fiction. 3. Missouri—Rural conditions—Fiction. I. Title.
PS3613.U433S54 2014
813'.6—dc23 2014026874

First Edition. First Printing: December 2014
Find us on Facebook– https://www.facebook.com/FiveStarCengage
Visit our website– http://www.gale.cengage.com/fivestar/
Contact Five Star™ Publishing at FiveStar@cengage.com

Printed in the United States of America
1 2 3 4 5 6 7 18 17 16 15 14

ACKNOWLEDGMENTS

As an editor, I learned that writers, including this one, rarely transfer everything they mean to say from their brains onto the page. To clarify the obscure and identify the chaff, novelists need feedback from skilled readers on the first draft and, quite likely, the first, interim, and final rewrites. My critique partners—Mary Ann Corrigan, Mary Nelson, and Helen Schwartz—gave me invaluable feedback on this manuscript. So did three other readers, Joyce Campbell and Blenda and Donald Marquardt.

A writer needs more than feedback. Mystery writers, particularly members of the Guppy chapter of Sisters in Crime, have advised and encouraged me as I made the transition from short nonfiction to novels. Friends, acquaintances, and strangers have provided information on a range of topics. Law enforcement officers in Maryland and Missouri have answered numerous questions on procedures, guns, and the attitudes of those who protect and serve.

Thanks to all who played a part in my completing *Show Me the Gold.*

Chapter One

I leaned back against a cool granite tombstone and gazed at the chandelier of stars faintly lighting the old country graveyard. The two-note song of crickets lulled me. Caution and the steamy heat kept me awake. The temperature had cooled from the low nineties—a typical August day in Missouri—to the low eighties, but the Kevlar vest Annalynn had insisted I wear over my black top kept sweat trickling down my back.

Achilles, my K-9 dropout, sneaked up and licked my face. That was his favorite joke. As I wiped off his kiss, he stretched out his long black and fawn body beside me and sniffed my paintball gun, Annalynn's preferred weapon against the young thugs who'd been vandalizing graveyards in northern Vandiver County.

"Phoenix, grab your spotlights. We have an emergency," Annalynn called from the squad car hidden behind an evergreen tree.

I sprinted to pick up the two remote-controlled lights I'd placed atop tombstones and stash them and the paintball gun in the trunk. I let Achilles into the back seat, slid under the steering wheel, turned on the motor, and stepped on the gas. "Did the kids hit Oak Grove?"

"No, the dispatcher got an all-hands call from Sheriff Towson." Her voice was tight. "Four men with assault rifles are holed up in an abandoned farmhouse five miles from here."

"Bloody hell!" I hit the brake. "We can't respond to a call like that from another county. You're not even supposed to be on a stakeout in your own county."

"Go, damn it, go!"

I hadn't heard her swear since sixth grade. I went. My adrenaline surged at the prospect of a real challenge.

"Turn right." She took a deep breath. "I have no choice, Phoenix. He has only two deputies there. No one else is within thirty miles. I can at least handle coordination to free up a trained officer."

Leaving me out of the game? No way. Skepticism intruded. "Who are these supposed desperados? How do we know these guys aren't our tombstone tippers drinking in an empty house to work up their courage?"

"Sheriff Towson had placed a motion-sensor camera outside the house to watch for meth cooks. He recognized a man who grew up here. The FBI identified him as one of the four people who robbed a bank in Cleveland, Ohio, Friday afternoon. They killed at least one person."

I pushed the Crown Victoria toward eighty, the max the blacktop road allowed.

"Turn right at the top of the hill. We report to a deputy two miles from there."

I slowed enough to slide around the square turn. Two miles later I braked to a stop ten feet away from the beige squad car blocking the road.

A decidedly pregnant officer came from behind the car holstering her gun as I lowered my window. "Please tell me you're Phoenix Smith and you brought an MP-5."

"I am, and I didn't." I'd never met this young black woman with corn-rowed hair.

Annalynn leaned toward my open window. "I'm Annalynn Carr Keyser, acting sheriff of Vandiver County. Phoenix is a *volunteer.*"

"A reserve deputy," I pointed out.

"Lieutenant Willetta Volcker. I'm coordinating the operation. Honored to meet you both." She peered past my shoulder. "You, too, Achilles. What weapons do you have?"

"Our Glocks and a deer rifle with a night scope."

"Damn. You're no better armed than we are. They have at least two AR-15s." She leaned down. "Sheriff Towson just texted me that they heard movement in the house. He thinks they're getting ready to leave. There's brush and tall weeds all around the place. He's afraid they'll get past him and Wolf to a car. Lord knows where they've got that stashed." She hesitated. "He'd like for you two to guard the back way out."

"Certainly," Annalynn said matter of factly.

I knew that her overdeveloped sense of duty had prompted that answer. Okay by me. I released the trunk lid and opened my door. "I'll get the rifle and our remote-controlled spotlights. We'll set those up to use if the robbers make a break for it. Are we sure enough of who they are to shoot to kill?" If we faced AR-15s, we had no other option.

"Well, give them a nanosecond to surrender before you fire. And hide behind the biggest tree you can find."

Annalynn turned off the dome light and maneuvered into the driver's seat. She prepared her Glock to fire. "We can't use our radios. How do we communicate, Lieutenant?"

"By texting. We need to exchange numbers."

I handed my mobile to Annalynn, made sure the rifle had a full load, readied my Glock and extra magazine, and slipped into the passenger seat.

"We're all set," Annalynn said. "Where do we go?"

"Halfway up this rise, douse your lights. At the top, cut your engine and coast down a long hill. Go past the driveway on your right that leads to the farmhouse. About three hundred yards after that you'll see a gravel road that runs behind the house. Leave the squad car across it and walk toward a dirt road—a track—that leads up to the house. Text me as soon as you're in place."

"Will do."

The officer stepped back from the car. "My sympathies for the loss of your husband, ma'am. He'd be awfully proud of the way you've taken over the sheriff's department."

"Thank you," Annalynn said, her even tone giving no hint of the grief that plagued her day and night. She closed her window and edged around the officer's squad car. "I'm sorry, Phoenix. I couldn't let a pregnant woman half our age take this risk."

"Agreed."

"You're in charge, of course. Did you ever face a situation like this in the CIA?"

"No." I'd crawled through fields to evade Hungarian border guards several times early in my career as a covert operative. Being the hunter scared me less than being the prey. "If the bad guys try to leave, we have to shoot them before they can shoot us. And from as far away as possible." If they got close with those AR-15s, we'd become sieves.

She shut off the headlights. "I'm terrified, Phoenix. I'll never forgive myself if you're hurt because I talked you into helping me try to catch some young hoodlums."

Always attuned to Annalynn's moods, Achilles whined. Before I rescued him, I hadn't realized a Belgian shepherd, a Malinois, could be so sensitive.

I reached back to stroke his dark head. "They're not expecting us. We'll be fine." My subconscious contradicted me. Once again I smelled the spices in an Istanbul bazaar, heard a submachine gun chatter, and felt a bullet rip through the flesh beneath my ribs. I blocked out the flashback. If I flinched, we'd be goners. "You won't have time to ponder the moral issues of killing, Annalynn. If these men don't drop their weapons the instant you say 'Police,' we both have to fire until they're not just down but dead."

"I understand." She turned off the motor.

"I'll fire from right to left. You fire from left to right. Just the way we practiced at the firing range."

"Okay." Her voice held steady.

I marveled at the nerves of a woman who had spent most of her adult life raising two children, organizing charity drives, and running her hometown's school board.

We coasted past the driveway to the gravel road. Annalynn pulled over to block it. "I'll carry the spotlights," she whispered. "Should we put the leash on Achilles?"

"No need. Quiet, boy, quiet." Free, he'd stand a better chance of escaping if we took bullets. I peered down the gravel road until I could make out the outline of brush and trees along the sides. Nothing to hear but crickets. The moon and stars provided just enough light that I could see nothing moved for fifty yards or so. "I'll go first. We'll walk by the undergrowth on the left side of the road until I find a place to set up an ambush." I had to ease the tension. "I must warn you: You may get your uniform dirty."

"Very funny, Pigpen." She took a deep breath. "It's really quiet out here. I don't think we should risk closing the doors."

I relaxed. Fear hadn't stopped her from thinking. "Right. Ready?"

"Ready."

I opened my door as quietly as I could and eased out with my finger on the rifle's trigger. Achilles landed on the ground beside me and pressed his shoulder against my left leg. As soon as Annalynn stepped out, I closed my door to within a finger's width of the latch and crept down the left side of the road. It was unfenced. On the other side, wood fence posts leaned like the Tower of Pisa. Probably barbed wire held them up. Thick brush and small trees on that side blocked our view of the farmhouse.

Annalynn nudged me at the same moment I saw the turnoff to the farmhouse ahead. I nodded, stepped deeper into the undergrowth, and moved forward gingerly until a thigh-high obstacle blocked my way. A fallen tree. Badly needed protection. "Wait," I whispered. I worked my way along the thick trunk about eight feet before a large limb blocked me.

I edged back to Annalynn. "Walk until you feel a limb. That's your spot. Find a place on a branch or sapling five or six feet high and at least that far to your left to set up one light. I'll do the same on this end."

She handed me a spotlight and remote and inched her way down the tree trunk.

Three long minutes later we knelt behind it, as ready as we could be. Achilles, quivering with fear, pressed against me.

Annalynn's iPhone glowed near the ground as she texted the pregnant deputy.

I shifted my eyes back to the grassy track barely visible among the weeds and brush, imprinting what I saw so that I could recognize the slightest change. Too bad Vandiver County couldn't afford night-vision goggles. I tested the night scope on the rifle. Junk. Still, better than the naked eye.

Achilles tensed and stood to stare at the sloping hill ahead of us.

I heard a faint sound. A car door?

Achilles grabbed the tail of my vest in his teeth and pulled.

"Let go. Stay."

He gave up on me and burrowed under our tree trunk.

I stared at the grassy track. A shadow moved in the farthest reach of my vision. I found it with the night scope. "A car," I whispered to Annalynn.

She texted the alarm. I focused on the car's left front unlit headlight and then the windshield. No head visible behind the wheel. They had opened the front doors to push the car down the rough slope. They moved slowly but steadily, but they'd turn on the motor when they hit the flat some two hundred feet away from us. I didn't dare let them get any closer to us than that. Besides, they'd be a much tougher target in a speeding car. I gripped the remote to the spotlight on my right.

"Yell 'Police' when I turn on the light," I whispered.

"Wait a sec." She punched in something on my cell and then on her iPhone. "Ready."

I hit the remote switch and moved my hand back to the trigger. The far edge of the light revealed a man behind each front door.

"Police. Put your hands on your head," Annalynn shouted.

The man on the driver's side stepped to his left and raised an assault rifle. He annihilated the spotlight as I put the first of three bullets into his chest.

Annalynn turned on her light, and the other man dove into the car. I put a bullet into the left front tire.

Bullets shattered the spotlight and showered us with leaves and twigs from the saplings behind us. The motor roared and the car leapt forward.

Annalynn and I both fired as fast as we could pull our triggers. The car turned onto the gravel road, skidded, and headed straight for our tree trunk.

Chapter Two

"Go!" I dropped the rifle, grabbed Achilles' collar, and dove to my right a fraction of a second before the car slammed into the tree trunk.

Out of the corner of my eye I saw a body fly past me. I drew my Glock and glanced back. The car flipped over the tree trunk and landed on its top. No one emerged, no sound came from inside.

"Phoenix?"

"We're okay." Except for scratches and bruises. "You?"

A moment of silence. "My uniform got dirty."

Surprised by her joke, I laughed aloud and kept a bead on the figure lying face down on the road, not moving.

Annalynn shone her flashlight into the car an instant and turned it back off. "There's no one in there."

So where were the other two men? A flashlight bobbed down the track. Another light moved up by the house. "Identify yourselves," I yelled.

"Sheriff Tiny Towson and Deputy Wolf Volcker," a baritone voice responded from the track. A light flashed on a bronze sheriff's star and then lowered and lingered over something on the ground. A moment later the voice said, "Orson's dead."

"Lights off," Annalynn called. "We've seen only two men."

Both flashlights went out, and the unseen deputy shouted, "The house is empty."

I crept toward the inert driver, straining to see his hands.

Empty at his sides.

Achilles jumped onto the man's back with a growl that would have chilled a grizzly. The man didn't move. Unconscious or dead.

Annalynn joined us. "His cannon is in the car, but he probably has a pistol. I'll keep him covered while you frisk him."

I started at his feet and worked my way up. I found a switchblade strapped to his right calf. He was a scrawny kid, probably too young to order a beer.

A car screeched to a stop on the blacktop. The pregnant deputy shouted, "An ambulance is ten minutes away. Need a first-aid kit?"

"Damn it, Willetta," Sheriff Towson yelled, "I told you to stay back."

I checked the robber's carotid artery. His heart was beating. His head was a bloody mess and his dark T-shirt was soaked. "He's alive. At least one bullet went through him. I can't tell whether lead or gravel did the other damage."

Sheriff Towson, service revolver at the ready, reached us just as his deputy did. "Since you're here, Willetta, check him out. I'll block the light with your blanket."

Still holding his weapon, the sheriff knelt and stuck one corner of the blanket between his teeth and stretched out one long arm with the other end. Annalynn knelt to shine a light on the wounded man's upper body while the deputy did a cursory exam.

Scanning the field, I walked toward the track with eyes and ears on super-alert. Nothing. Achilles kept his shoulder against my left leg and his nose in the air, but he no longer quivered, a sure sign the other two robbers were out of nose range. "Good dog," I murmured.

He licked my wrist.

The gravel crunched behind me. Tiny said softly, "I'm betting the other two took off before we got here, but we gotta be sure they aren't hiding somewhere close. Is your dog a tracker?"

"Not really. The DEA trained him—until he flunked out—as a narc."

"Let's try him anyway. I know nobody came out either door. Maybe he can find where they snuck out and pick up the trail. Will he work for me?"

I felt Achilles press closer. He distrusted strangers, especially men. "No. I'll go with you."

"I'd appreciate it." Over his shoulder he said, "Willetta, keep your eyes peeled and your weapon ready. Let Sheriff Keyser handle the first aid." He stepped around me to take the lead. He set a fast pace up the track, his long strides forcing me to jog to keep up. When he reached the body of the man he'd called Orson, he swung wide.

Achilles paused a moment to sniff and then attached himself to my leg again.

The track turned left toward a skeleton of a barn. Sheriff Towson plunged straight ahead beneath the overlapping branches of two trees. He paused as the silhouette of a sagging roof became visible through the leaves. "Wolf?"

A man holding a rifle moved from beneath the branches of a tree ahead on our right. His face showed as a white oval in the darkness. "I found signs they crawled out from under the southwest corner of the house and through the weeds into the trees. I reckon they heard us and used the floor for a door."

"Or somebody saw our squad car and tipped them off," the sheriff muttered. He switched on his flashlight, holding it high and far to his left, and shone it on the grass by the side of the house. "Let's see if your dog can pick up the trail."

I walked forward well out of the light's beam until I reached a two-foot-wide swath of crushed grass. Achilles dropped his nose and growled.

"Find." Nothing. I'd forgotten to say the magic word. "Find, please."

He turned and trotted back toward the gravel road.

"Achilles, come." I interpreted his move for the others. "He sees no point in tracking people he knows are down the hill. The only way he'll track the two unaccounted for is if he smells something with their scent on it."

"Wolf, you stay here while we take the dog inside," Sheriff Towson said.

I moved toward the back door with Achilles glued to my leg. He barked a warning and grabbed my vest in his teeth to jerk me back. "Take cover!" I ran with Achilles away from the house and flattened myself against the ground behind a tree.

The deputy dropped down near me and whispered, "I swear there's nobody in or under that house. There's no place to hide."

"An attic?"

"Barely a ceiling. Rain's come through and brought most of it down."

I looked up at the crumbling chimney's silhouette. Only a coon could fit in that. "Something's definitely wrong." What had Achilles learned to identify before being deselected? Marijuana and meth for sure. Probably other drugs. A chill rippled down my spine. I stood up. "I think I know what he smelled. I'm going around to the front door."

Achilles whined a protest but came with me. I walked slowly around the house a good twenty feet from it before heading for the front door.

He barked a warning, gripped the vest in his teeth, and pulled.

Knees weak, I backed away from the house. "Good boy, good boy." I knelt and hugged him and rubbed his chest. I even let him lick my face.

The two men stood on either side of me ready to fire. The sheriff whispered, "What is it?"

"I'm ninety percent sure both doors are booby-trapped with explosives."

The sheriff cursed under his breath. "The Cantree boys swore years ago they'd pay me back. Looks like they didn't forget."

An ambulance siren sounded nearby. We stood silently until it stopped and doors slammed down the hill.

Sheriff Towson punched a number on his cell phone. "New development, Captain. Tell the FBI to bring a bomb squad. We think the farmhouse doors are booby-trapped." A long silence. "I'd bet a week's pay one of the missing men is Orson Cantree's cousin Roscoe. He grew up in this house."

The sheriff cut the connection and extended his hand to me. "Thank you, Phoenix. You and Annalynn did a great job. I'll make sure everybody knows it."

"I'd appreciate your identifying me only as a Vandiver County deputy."

"If that's the way you want it. The FBI will want to talk to you tomorrow, but I reckon you and Annalynn can go back to your own stakeout now."

Sitting in a cemetery with a paintball gun no longer appealed to me. Annalynn must be hanging on to her composure by a thread. I jogged down the hill to the mayhem on the gravel road. The ambulance crew, portable lights bright, prepared to load the wounded kid onto a gurney. Annalynn stood outside the lights' glow, but I could see big splotches of blood on her uniform. She motioned to me and ran toward our squad car. It blocked the ambulance from driving to the wounded man.

Fearing she was losing it, I forced myself to sprint after her.

She thrust the keys into my hand and went to the passenger door, Achilles at her side. When she slid into the seat, he came in right after her. As I turned on the motor, he put his paws on her shoulders and licked her face. She wrapped her arms around him.

He could help her more now than I could. I made a U-turn to take us back to Vandiver County.

A minute later Annalynn helped Achilles scramble into the back seat and turned the department radio back on to report in.

The dispatcher said calmly, "I got a clear recording of the action from your iPhone. Haven't picked up much since the car hit your tree. We got a call about the vandals about thirty minutes ago. Mark Keller saw a light in Oak Grove Cemetery and fired his shotgun in the air. A vehicle drove off."

Annalynn said nothing for a moment. "We'll go by to check the damage before we come in."

Bad idea. We were both physically and emotionally spent. I searched for a tactful way to say that.

Annalynn turned on the flashing exterior lights that identified our vehicle as a squad car. "You know the way to Oak Grove Church, Phoenix?"

"Yes." No use suggesting she send one of her overworked staff out tomorrow.

We drove in silence on the empty blacktop roads. A few minutes later I pulled into a bumpy gravel parking lot by a little white church. My headlights shone on rows of low tombstones interspersed with an occasional obelisk. I couldn't see anyone or any damage. I swept the car's searchlight over the cemetery and saw nothing amiss. The emergency over, I allowed exhaustion and a deep ache in my bullet wound to bind me to my seat.

"He scared them off. I better check to see if they did any damage," Annalynn said. She got out of the car with Achilles, turned on her flashlight, and walked with him on a dirt track that ran along the far side of the cemetery.

I sat numb, idly watching the beam leave the track and move

down a row of tombstones. Then the light fell and Achilles howled.

Bolting from the car, I drew my gun and raced toward a glimmer of light on the ground between the graves.

Chapter Three

The light went out, but the sound of suppressed sobs led me straight to Annalynn. She sat on the ground by a fresh baby-sized grave with her head on her knees. In the three months since her husband's death, she'd never allowed herself to cry like this. She said that if she started, she'd never stop.

Achilles stood with his snout on her shoulder. He relinquished his place to me, but I didn't know any more than he did how to ease her pain. I knelt beside her and put my arm around her shoulder. "Let it out. You deserve a real cry." Wrong approach. Pity hurt her pride. "You'll never get your uniform clean."

She raised her head to look at me. Then she began to laugh. Hysterically. I don't know how long we sat there as she laughed and cried and Achilles circled around us.

Finally she wiped her eyes and face with tissues and stood up. "I don't know how I would have survived if you hadn't come back to Laycock right after Boom died." She gave me a quick hug. "I'm glad I was able to relieve your boredom with a shootout tonight. Would you mind bringing a small evidence bag? No stones are down, but I saw a gardening glove somewhere over there."

"You're going to try to get DNA from it?"

"No, we can't afford the cost or the time of a DNA test, but when we catch these kids, they won't know that." She smiled. "You've taught me to be sneaky."

★ ★ ★ ★ ★

On the way back to Laycock, I told Annalynn about finding the booby traps at the house. She broke the news that Willetta had taken the rifle and Annalynn's service revolver and insisted our phones remain under the wrecked car.

When I pulled into the drive of Annalynn's ancestral limestone home—and my temporary one—a little after four o'clock, she said, "I have to go to the office tomorrow morning to do the paperwork. Could you please pick up Connie?"

Damn! "Of course." I'd have to leave by ten for the Kansas City airport. Worse, I'd be trapped in the car for two hours while Connie bragged about her darling grandkids. Still worse, she'd tell me how it felt to sing at her ex-husband's wedding. I sighed at the thought.

Annalynn opened the back door to wake up Achilles. "What's that sigh about? You and Connie got on so well during your business trip to New York."

So we had. Connie had shopped for my desperately needed business clothes while I went to meetings. She'd also enlivened our evenings out with my all-male business associates. "She'll talk my ears off. I won't enjoy that drive back."

"Unlike our Saturday-night entertainment," Annalynn said, leading the way to her front door. She unlocked it, switched on the hall light, and punched in the alarm code. "I'll call you from the office to make sure you're up. About nine thirty?"

"That's good. Thanks." My entire body ached. I dreaded walking up the stairs leading from the wide central hall to my bedroom. At least it felt like mine now. I'd slept there since returning to Laycock in May to recuperate and recast my future.

Annalynn reached over, pulled a leaf out of my short black hair, and ruffled it into place. "Are you okay, Phoenix? Maybe someone else can give Connie a ride home."

"I'm fine." Annalynn didn't look great either. She had a two-inch scratch over her right eye, smudges of blood on her right cheek, bruises on her forearms, and loose strands of brown hair flying from her French roll. "We're both going to need a lot of makeup tomorrow. Let's hit the showers."

Pounding on the front door woke me. I looked at the antique grandfather's clock. Nine fifteen. I forced myself up, lurched into the hall, and yelled, "Who is it?"

"FBI, Ms. Smith," a man called back. "I need to talk to you immediately."

What a way to start a Sunday. I shared the usual CIA aversion to the self-righteous FBI. "Have a seat on the porch while I get dressed." I took a couple minutes to apply subtle makeup to play down my fifty-five years. Then I put on white Bermuda shorts and a white tank top to expose my scratches and bruises.

When I opened the front door, a well-groomed blond man around thirty rose from one of the wrought-iron chairs and pocketed a cell phone. "Good morning. I'm Lester Wharton, FBI." He flashed his identification and cast an appraising look. "Could I speak to Phoenix Smith, please?"

Who in hell did he think I was? "I'm Phoenix Smith." I reached for the ID and studied it. Needlessly. Even though he'd had the sense to remove his jacket and wore a short-sleeved shirt, I could have picked out him, and nine out of ten other agents, in a crowded stadium. Like Mormon missionaries, they had an unmistakable look.

He smiled with even white teeth as his eyes swept up my bruised legs and lingered a nanosecond on my breasts. I must look better than I thought. Had he looked up my age and expected to see Whistler's mother? I stood back to let him in.

"Sheriff Towson credits you with saving his life last night."

"My dog gets the credit," I said with a modesty that would have made Connie laugh in disbelief. "We can talk while I eat breakfast. I have to leave for the Kansas City airport in half an hour."

"I'm afraid this interview requires much more time than that, Dr. Smith."

So he'd done a background check on me, though it wouldn't take much of one to learn I had a doctorate in economics. I motioned him to come into the dining room.

Achilles growled low in his throat.

"It's okay, boy," I said, realizing he reflected my hostility. I walked toward the kitchen weighing my options. Better to play nice and get rid of the FBI now. Any hesitation to talk to them would pique their interest. "Have a seat and I'll get us some coffee. What do you take in yours?"

"Black is fine, thank you."

I poured two full mugs, fixed myself a bowl of cold cereal, and took everything on a tray to the table. He was scanning the papers I'd left there the day before. I took the chair across from him.

He turned on a tape recorder. "Full name, address, and phone number, please."

"Phoenix D—initial only—Smith. I don't have a permanent address at the moment." My apartment in Vienna didn't count. "I'm staying with Annalynn while I sell my late parents' home next door. I lost my cell phone last night. I'll give you her address and land line." I recited them.

He gave what he obviously considered an ingratiating smile. "You're far too young to retire, Dr. Smith. Where do you work?"

"I'm a consultant on Eastern European investment for my former employer, an international venture capital firm." I pointed to the papers. "As you can see, I'm also establishing a foundation to assist the families of crime victims."

"Commendable." He sipped his coffee and scribbled a note.

Stalling. I wasn't what he'd expected. Typical FBI arrogance.

He looked up. "Where did an economist learn to put three bullets in a man's chest in the dark?"

Tactical error, buddy. Save your ace. Calculating that he'd buy eager cooperation, I smiled and leaned forward. "In the backyard next door. My father was a Marine sniper in the Second World War. He taught my brothers and me to shoot."

Wharton didn't hide his skepticism. "And did he teach you to identify plastic explosives?"

I chuckled. "No, of course not." I sobered. "He told us about losing buddies to booby traps. My dog smelled the explosives." To save time, I took over the interrogation. "Here's what happened last night." Between bites of cereal I gave a concise but detailed report of what I'd done from the time Annalynn got the emergency call.

Wharton didn't interrupt. He didn't make any notes either. "That's very impressive. Clear. Thorough. I couldn't have written a better report myself."

Pompous ass. I smiled to acknowledge his supposed compliment and finished my last two bites of cereal.

"I'd like for you to go through that again. I want to clarify some points."

I checked my watch. If I didn't leave in five minutes, I'd be late. On the plus side, I had a great excuse for not picking up Connie. But I couldn't leave her stranded. "Please excuse me for a minute. I have to arrange for a rental car at the KC airport." Something flashy to raise her spirits and compensate for not having a friendly ear on the drive home.

I brought the cordless phone from the kitchen to the table so he could hear exactly what I was doing, turned off his recorder, and dialed the Avis 800 number. Wharton jotted notes as I told the Avis clerk I wanted a red sports car and someone to meet Connie's flight and take her to it. The agent looked up as I recited a credit card number from memory to reserve a Chevy Corvette.

"You have an excellent memory, Dr. Smith," he said when I hung up. "I'm sure you can remember more details about last night."

None that meant anything. I added such irrelevant garbage as the crumbling chimney. He asked a few questions about Achilles' skills, but he bore down on what happened between the car hitting the tree trunk and Sheriff Towson coming down to where we were.

The agent frowned after my third account. "And what was inside the car?"

"I never looked into the car," I said for the third time.

He stroked his tie and stared into space. "Did the trunk come open on impact?"

I shut my eyes to visualize the car. "I don't know. The car landed on its roof."

He handed me a card. "Please call me if you think of anything else."

"Of course." I took him to the door and bade him a friendly good day, cooperative to the end.

Then it hit me. They had torn apart the house and the car and everything between looking for the bank loot and hadn't found it. They suspected everyone who had been at the farmhouse last night of taking it. And I'd been the only one who didn't wear a badge.

Chapter Four

Achilles brought me his leash as soon as the FBI agent went out the front door.

The temperature was pushing eighty-five. I didn't feel up to our usual morning jog—two miles for me and about six for him. "Let's play fetch. Bring me your ball."

I poured a thermal cup half full of lemonade and let him out the back door. He sped off to drive away any cat lurking by the hummingbird feeder. I put my cup on the patio table and waited for him to complete his patrol of the fruit trees in the back lot.

Did I need to worry about the FBI probing my past? No. Sheriff Towson and the Volckers' accounts would verify that Annalynn and I didn't have time to hide anything. Wharton was competent but not creative. He would Google me again, check two or three of my articles in professional journals and the *Financial Times,* and dismiss me as a suspect. The CIA would continue to conceal my years as a covert operative. Still, I'd better take care in how I accessed money from my offshore accounts to fund the foundation.

I tossed the ball for Achilles again and again. The sun soothed my sore muscles, but my vague uneasiness didn't go away. I knew better than to disregard my subconscious. Achilles finally dropped the ball by the hummingbird feeder and stretched out to watch his avian friends. I went to my room and sat cross-legged on the high four-poster bed with my laptop to check my high-priority e-mail accounts and the news.

Stuart, who usually called on weekends, had sent me an e-mail: "I wanted to talk to you about this but can't reach you by phone tonight. I'm bringing my kids to Laycock next weekend. I want them to meet you. Can you join us for dinner at my mother's Saturday? I leave on a special assignment at eight a.m. I'll call Monday evening. Love you, Stuart."

That "Love you" always gave me pause. I never signed off with it. He never mentioned that I didn't. He'd never *said* that he loved me, and I certainly hadn't expected him to. When Stuart and I worked together in May, he'd confessed to a huge boyhood crush on me, his frequent babysitter. He'd turned into a tall, broad-shouldered man saved from being handsome by a Roman nose. More important, he'd not asked questions when he stumbled on the truth about my "gall bladder" surgery. I thought we just had a sweet little fling while we were investigating Annalynn's husband's death, but Stuart had pursued the flirtation after he returned to his desk in the Drug Enforcement Administration office in St. Louis. He'd come back to Laycock several weekends to visit his mother, my former math teacher and mentor. Stuart and I enjoyed each other's company. I liked and respected him.

A week ago, he'd said his teenage daughter and son would spend Labor Day weekend with his ex-wife. Would I go away for the weekend, then three weeks away, with him? I'd consented the next day. I hesitated to meet his kids. That marked a crucial turning point in a relationship, a time when you had to end it or move ahead. I didn't want to do either.

I had until tomorrow evening to decide whether to back out of the weekend or agree to meet the offspring.

The shootout and its aftermath needed attention right now. I went to the Web to check coverage. The local, St. Louis, and Kansas City Sunday newspapers had gone to press before the news broke. Their websites carried only short releases from the

FBI saying a gun battle in rural Missouri resulted in the death of one alleged bank robber and the arrest of another man. Just like the FBI not to give local police credit. A Cleveland newspaper's website reported that the FBI had named Orson Cantree a person of interest late Saturday afternoon. Its Saturday edition carried three major articles on Friday's bank robbery. Reporters had interviewed the bank's vice president, five customers, and a wounded teller's father.

I skimmed the articles and formed a picture of the robbery. A mustachioed man with thick glasses requested access to a safe deposit box he'd opened a week earlier. A bank manager went into the secure area with him. A couple minutes later patrons heard four distinct noises. Later police found the bank manager dead with a single bullet in his head. I concluded the robber had used three explosions to open doors and safety deposit boxes. Had to be an inside job. Banks make it difficult to reach those boxes. The mustachioed man had known where something valuable was and how to get to it. The explosions fit with booby-trapping the doors at the farmhouse.

When the noises drew staff and patrons' attention, a bearded man wearing overalls and a black Amish hat threw a withdrawal slip on the floor, pulled an assault rifle—doubtless an AR-15 we had faced last night—from a duffle bag, and ordered everyone to stay where they were. A goateed young man in a baseball cap—the kid we'd wounded?—took another AR-15 from a guitar case and screamed at tellers to fill the case with money. They gave him what they had, but he shot one.

Why rob the tellers of a few thousand dollars when the major target obviously was something worth much more in the safety deposit boxes? And why shoot the teller?

The robbers were a cold-blooded lot, and they were confident they would escape. Unexpectedly, relief coursed through me. We'd shot vicious killers.

A fourth person drove the getaway car. Surveillance cameras caught the license number of one of two cars stolen from a nearby parking garage. The police found the getaway car in a grocery store parking lot. The second stolen car turned up in short-term parking at an airport. Right where police would find it and waste time checking air passengers.

Hmmm. The robbers had planned well. Yet Orson Cantree blew it by leaving his fingerprints on a discarded deposit slip. The FBI should figure out who his associates were and track them down in days. Case closed.

I left word for Annalynn that I'd arranged for a rental car for Connie and stretched out on my bed. A disturbing thought kept me awake a full minute. The sheriff said Orson Cantree—the man I'd killed—had sworn revenge years ago. He surely didn't expect a camera to place him at the house, but he'd booby-trapped those doors to kill someone.

The grandfather clock's chiming three woke me up. As soon as I stirred, Achilles leapt up from his old green blanket, barked once, and trotted down the stairs. He barked twice from the kitchen in case I hadn't gotten the message that he was hungry.

"Coming," I called. I glanced in Annalynn's open bedroom door. Not a wrinkle in the cobalt-blue spread on her king bed. She'd be exhausted when she got home, and exhaustion was probably what she wanted. She wouldn't shake off the shootout as I had.

In the kitchen, Achilles nudged first his water bowl and then his food dish toward me. I filled both before pouring myself a big glass of lemonade and making a western omelet and a tossed salad. As I took my last bite, someone pulled into the driveway.

Achilles trotted to the dining room window to look, yawned, and turned his head toward me for instructions.

I peeked out. Sheriff Tiny Towson in blue jeans and a loose

Cardinals jersey long enough to cover his holster. He carried a small paper sack. I beat him to the door and stepped outside as a hint to keep the visit short.

His eyes looked like he hadn't slept. "Good afternoon, Phoenix. Enjoying a quiet Sunday?" He handed me the bag. His glance indicated he was a leg man. "I had an errand in Laycock so I brought your cell phones. Annalynn had left the office. They gave me this address."

"Thanks. It's kind of you to go to so much trouble." I opened the bag. Both cells appeared undamaged. I didn't care about mine, one I used only for local calls, but Annalynn loved her iPhone. It always held the latest photos of her three photogenic little grandkids. "Annalynn's not home yet."

He rubbed the cardinal on his shirt. "Maybe it's just as well if I talk to you."

He'd piqued my curiosity. I motioned him to the wrought-iron table with three chairs. "Have a seat. Would you care for a glass of lemonade? Or coffee?"

"Lemonade sounds great."

Leaving him under Achilles' watchful gaze, I put ice in two glasses and brought them out with the pitcher. I filled the glasses and handed one to him.

He took a long drink. "The real stuff. Hits the spot."

I took his measure: late forties, a trim six foot three or four, weathered skin, brown hair with gray in his old-fashioned sideburns, and brown eyes, now bloodshot. No wedding ring. "Any sign of the two missing gang members?"

"If there is, the FBI isn't telling me. They made it clear this is their case." He shifted in his chair, crossed and uncrossed his legs, and stared at a pot of pink geraniums on the porch's stone wall. "You saved my life last night. Orson and Roscoe Cantree put those explosives there to kill me." He swiveled in the chair to face me. "The FBI doesn't believe that, but you were there.

What do you think?"

He'd overestimated me, a rare occurrence. "I'm an economist, not a criminologist. I have no idea."

"I don't believe that. Willetta, my extremely competent deputy, got mad when a trooper said you 'gals' had been lucky again. She just wrote a paper for a criminal justice course on the two homicide cases you've closed. She says you're a brilliant team."

"Thank you, and her." Flattery comes before a request for a favor. "I hope you don't expect me to deny our brilliance."

Annalynn pulled into the driveway in her oversized SUV and sat there a moment before she got out and walked toward us. No makeup could cover the deep circles under her eyes, but she walked with the same grace that had made her the star of local charity fashion shows since she turned fifteen.

I went into the house to get her a glass and some ice.

When I came out, she said to her counterpart, "I spent the morning dealing with the FBI and the afternoon fending off the media. I referred everyone to your statement and to the FBI's press officer."

He smiled. "You mean you refused a dozen interviews. You'll get more requests. An hour ago Willetta sent out a release quoting a doctor who said you kept the Cantree boy from bleeding to death."

Annalynn rubbed her temple with the back of her hand. "Orson Cantree, Jr. He's only seventeen." She faced me. "He's the son of the man—uhh—"

"You can say 'the man you killed.' I have no regrets."

"Nor I," she said a bit too quickly. She turned back to Tiny. "I assume this is not a social call."

He straightened like a soldier going on duty. "Here's the problem: I'm not the only one the Cantrees have threatened. The FBI agents don't want to hear about our 'hillbilly feuds.'

They're focused on the federal crime, the bank robbery. The Highway Patrol wants to leave the whole thing to the feds. I'm on my own. I need your help."

"Sorry," Annalynn said, not waiting for my reaction. "My staff is already stretched past the limit. We can't spare anyone."

"I hear you." He pointed his finger at me. "But Phoenix is a volunteer, not a staff member. Think about this: Orson Cantree tried to blow me up for arresting him twenty years ago. You and Annalynn killed one, maybe two, Cantrees last night. You moved to the top of the family's hit list."

Bloody hell! Was he right? Or was he gaming me?

Annalynn frowned. "Phoenix will do as she pleases. She always does. I can guarantee you, though, that she'll do nothing in her capacity as a reserve officer."

Like I cared about that. "I don't see what I could do. Still, for safety's sake, I'd like to know what we're up against. What can you tell us about the Cantree family?"

"Not much right now." He ducked his head. "Willetta's gathering info on Orson and his cousin Roscoe's criminal histories and checking for any arrests of other family members. Wolf's talking to anyone here who knew them. I took some flak for hiring an interracial couple, but they're both top-notch officers." He swiveled to stare at the geranium again. "I can't figure out how the Cantrees knew I'd come to that house." He turned back to us, his eyebrows arched. "Any ideas?"

Annalynn stared into space, distancing herself from the conversation.

Surely he didn't expect us to know anything about the Cantrees. "I've no idea. What happened before we showed up at the farmhouse?"

"A motion sensor turned on a camera I'd set up in case somebody turned the place into a meth lab. It picked up four people moving near the back of the house with nothing but a small flashlight. That meant trouble. The only face visible was Orson's, and we could see he had some kind of rifle. He hadn't been around here in years, but I recognized him. I sent out an inquiry to see if he was wanted and headed out there with the Volckers." He held out his hand apologetically. "I've assigned Willetta to office duty, but she knew we needed her and insisted on coming along. We parked the squad car out of sight—where you met Willetta—and Wolf and I walked up to the house and saw a light. That was maybe quarter to eleven. The light went out a couple minutes later. We heard two voices. We didn't hear anybody moving. We reconnoitered to check for the other two people. We thought they might be sleeping in an escape vehicle. Then Willetta sent word Orson was wanted for a bank robbery in Ohio. We pulled back and called for the cavalry."

That was where Annalynn and I came in. "We parked at the gravel road a little before midnight." I ran through the possibilities. "If they'd spotted your camera, surely they all would have left immediately. Maybe they had a second car and two of them went after food or gasoline, saw your squad car, and called with a warning."

Annalynn frowned. "Or they heard people moving around in the brush and took that opportunity to sneak out of the house. Or they left because they didn't like sleeping with mice and snakes. You're speculating, Phoenix."

"That's what you do when you don't have facts." I went back to the booby trap. "Did the FBI estimate how long it took to rig the explosives?" If I'd had a close look, I would have known the answer.

"The tech said they did a fast, sloppy job, but it would have worked." He took a long drink of lemonade. "Did you see any vehicles as you came?"

Annalynn sipped her lemonade and made no move to answer.

"No," I said.

"We passed a pickup and a car near there, both with Missouri plates. I discounted them as local—unrelated." He glanced at Annalynn's unrevealing face. "Have you read the press reports on the robbery, Phoenix?"

"Yes. Sounded like an inside job using hired guns."

He raised his hand in the air and marked a score for me. "That's the FBI's read. They're looking for the inside man."

"And the one who has the missing loot?"

His whistled. "How did you know about that?"

"Wharton kept asking me what was in the car."

He nodded. "Me and my deputies, too, but I saw an agent take a plastic bag with bills in it from the spare tire." He finished his lemonade and focused on the geranium again. "I don't care about the FBI suspecting us. They'll soon get over it. What worries me is that Roscoe may think one of us has the money."

Annalynn's jaw clenched. She said nothing.

Missing loot provided a much stronger motivation than revenge for the Cantrees to target us. Still, the threat seemed farfetched. Did Tiny have his own agenda? Give him some rope. "The Cantrees sound pretty dangerous."

He directed his reply to Annalynn: "You must have heard what a mean bunch they are. We practically declared a county holiday when the last one moved away about ten years ago. Twenty years ago I brought Orson in for hitting his pregnant wife. She refused to file charges, but I made sure he served some time. When he got out, he and his wife and baby moved to Ohio."

Rather than coming after Tiny. Why target him now? That booby trap could have been for anyone. "Maybe the old family home was only a convenient stopover. The missing two must be a thousand miles from here by now."

Tiny absentmindedly patted the gun under his shirt. "Don't count on it. You both should be damned careful until they're caught. I will be." He stood up. "One more thing, Annalynn. I heard your thirteen-week appointment ends Friday. I'd be glad to call a couple of people to recommend extending it until the November election."

Annalynn finally met his eyes. "No, thank you. I appreciate your offer. I know very well it would cost you. Most local and state law officers have insisted a professional replace me as soon as possible. I agree with them."

He stared at her, one eyebrow arched. "I don't. The only other likely candidates are incompetent jackasses."

I grinned. Those were the exact words used by Vernon Kann, the retired newspaper publisher who was pushing Annalynn to run for an open seat in the House of Representatives.

Tiny handed me his card. "Call my cell if anything comes up." He started down the steps and stopped. "A nice quiet street. If I were you, I wouldn't sit out on the porch." He strode to his car.

I surveyed the street and then looked at Achilles stretched out between Annalynn and me. His supersensitive nose didn't smell trouble.

When Annalynn and I were kids, our fathers had spent countless quiet evenings on the Carr castle porch while we played on the lawn. I'd regarded my hometown as irredeemably dull and serenely safe. Not anymore. I'd faced almost as many close calls in my three months in Laycock as I had in Eastern Europe since the Berlin Wall fell.

"Please stay out of this, Phoenix." Annalynn held up a hand to hush my protest. "He's trying to draw us into his mess."

I thought back over the conversation. "Could be. The odds are heavily against the Cantree gang sticking around to come gunning for us." My gaze swept the street again. "Still, only a fool bets his life on good odds. We have to be vigilant."

"Vigilant, yes. Nosy, no."

I shrugged that off and moved on to another issue: "What made you decide not to extend your time as sheriff?"

She smiled. "All my uniforms are dirty." She reached down to stroke Achilles. "I wanted the job because it was the only way to find out what really happened to Boom. We did that. The county needs a qualified person."

"Vandiver County won't find anyone qualified willing to take a short-term appointment."

"You think I should accept it?"

I felt ambivalent. It was a tough job, but doing it had helped her cope with grief, and given her badly needed income. "I'm not saying that. Do what you *want* to do."

She sighed. "You're too rational. We're meeting Connie for dinner tomorrow night. I'll talk to her about it."

"No one has ever accused Connie of being rational."

A half block away a car turned onto our street.

"Inside," I ordered. Better safe than sorry became a trite saying because it's true.

Chapter Five

The next morning the fugitives remained at large. Annalynn didn't object when I said I'd follow her to the office and insisted she park in the secure underground garage rather than the parking lot. She told me to go home and stay there.

I didn't, but I took Achilles to a neighborhood on the other side of town for our morning run rather than follow one of our regular routes. When we got back to the Carr castle, the limestone mansion that had housed Annalynn's family since the 1800s, her phone was ringing.

"That Corvette is spectacular," Connie trilled. "I forgive you for not meeting me at the airport. How's Annalynn doing?"

I described her breakdown at the cemetery. Still unsure how seriously to take Tiny's warning about the vengeful Cantrees, I didn't mention it. Nevertheless, I introduced a scheme I'd come up with overnight: "Annalynn needs to get away a week or two. Maybe go with me to visit my brothers in California."

Silence.

Naturally Connie would disapprove of anything that left her out. "All three of us," I said. She didn't have a cent to spare. "My treat."

"I can't leave. I'm directing *Oklahoma!* for Laycock Community College. I start auditioning students this afternoon."

"Good luck with finding the talent." I'd forgotten she'd taken the job to supplement her subsistence income from giving voice and piano lessons, directing the First Methodist choir, and singing at weddings and funerals.

"You'd be surprised how many good singers we have around here, but I'm calling about something else. You know what a busybody Trudy is. She's heard about a possible abuse case and wants me to ask Annalynn to check it out. You know, unofficially."

I'd never gotten past my childhood dislike of Connie's nosy older cousin, our occasional babysitter. "Annalynn doesn't have time to satisfy Trudy's curiosity."

"You're absolutely right. That's why I said you and I would check out the rumor. Oh, damn. I have to take another call. Meet me at eight ten North Walnut Street at nine thirty. Bring your broom." She hung up.

My broom? Was that one of her witch jokes? Surely she didn't expect me to clean someone's house. Oh, well. Better this diversion than trying to decipher the forms for setting up our tax-free foundation. The Foundation Center in D.C. promised to refer me to a lawyer but hadn't yet.

I went to Annalynn's computer and Googled the address Connie had given me. It was the residence of T. Tesopolis. It took me a moment to match the name and a face. Mr. Tesopolis had run Laycock's only shoe store when I was a kid. He had such a pronounced Greek accent that he was hard to understand, but he never let anyone walk out of the store with a pair of shoes that didn't fit. If you went in on your birthday, he gave you a piece of baklava. The store had closed years ago. The man must be close to a hundred.

I slipped out of my tank top and put on a blue-and-white checked cotton blouse that came down over my holster. Achilles followed with his leash in his mouth as I carried a broom to my garage and put it in the trunk of my three-year-old white Camry. It was a short drive, but I turned on the air conditioning to counter the heat.

The red Corvette, hogging a maple tree's shade, led me to the right house, a fifties brick rambler. Connie got out as I parked behind her. She wore a turquoise skirt, a white sleeveless blouse with turquoise swirls, dangling turquoise earrings, and white sandals. A turquoise band held her curly blond hair off her forehead. Not housecleaning clothes.

Achilles barked a pleased greeting. He'd been worried when we'd gone to water Connie's flowers and she wasn't home. I reached across to open his door a crack. He pushed it open and trotted to her, sitting down in front of her to offer his paw. I stayed in the car. I wasn't getting out until I knew what she was up to.

"Hi, Achilles," Connie said, fussing over him. "Hi, Phoenix. Thanks for coming on the church's first home visit with Mrs. Tesopolis."

She'd used her stage voice. Half the block could hear her. Unfortunately, I didn't have the script she was following. I raised an eyebrow.

She said softly, "That's our cover story to get into the house."

I'd gone undercover once with Connie and she'd loved it. Life in Laycock was usually boring, and she missed being on stage. "What's your plan?"

"We church ladies come to visit. She must be lonely. We clean so we can look for evidence. I brought dust cloths." Her cheeks flushed with excitement. "We need signals."

She'd spent too much time in plot-impaired musical comedies. "Let's just improvise verbal cues."

She pouted. "You're not taking this seriously."

Not as seriously as a shootout against two AR-15s. "I'm here, aren't I? Let's do it." I'd hated that outthrust lower lip even when she was young enough for some people to think it was cute.

Irritation turned into unease as the three of us walked up a sunken brick walkway toward the front door. Giant oaks on each side of the rambler shaded much of what had been a well-landscaped front lawn. Now brown grass thirsted for water. The flowers in the long beds beside the door had given up and handed over their space to weeds. I held back, not wanting to see what was inside.

Only the bottom hinge kept the storm door from falling on Connie as she eased it open to knock. No one answered. She waited a minute and knocked again. And again.

"Who there?" The high-pitched question came from close to the door.

"Connie Diamante. I'm with the First Methodist Church's Visit Your Neighbor Program."

"I not Methodist," the woman said.

"But you are our neighbor," Connie said.

"Not my neighbor."

Smart woman. She wasn't going to let us in. I couldn't resist the challenge. "Mrs. Tesopolis, I'm Phoenix Smith, Jack and Mary Smith's daughter. I remember the wonderful baklava you made for your husband to give to customers on our birthdays."

A key sounded in the lock, and the door opened a crack. "You liked my baklava?"

Had her hooked. "I've never had any better, not even in Athens."

The door opened wider, and a face as wrinkled as a dried-apple doll appeared. Wild strands flew from a mat of white hair. She stared at me through thick spectacles. "You are Greek?"

My dark coloring, a throwback to Cherokee and Italian ancestors, had prompted the mistake. I hedged. "No, but perhaps some of my ancestors were."

She studied me for several seconds and then spoke in Greek.

Thanks to a mission in Corfu, I recognized the words for welcome and house. I came up with the word for thank you.

"*Efharisto.* We are honored to enter your home."

She responded with a torrent of Greek.

I held up my hands. "Sorry, uhh—*Signomi.* I know only a few words—*kalimera, parakalo, twaleta, ouzo.*"

"*Ouzo.*" She smiled at the mention of Greece's distinctive liqueur, a potent liquid licorice. "You bring me *ouzo*?"

I pretended to pour the drink into a glass. "On my next visit."

Her head disappeared. A moment later the door swung open and a blast of hot, dead air slapped us in the face. "Please come in," she said from the dark interior.

Achilles whirled and trotted over to sniff around an oak tree.

"You first, Antigone," Connie whispered.

I gladly let her contend with closing the storm door and stepped into the house. Coming out of the bright sun, I saw nothing for a moment. Then I spotted a small figure in a peach-colored negligee pushing a wheeled walker through an archway.

"Come to my kitchen," she said. "Cooler."

I let my eyes adjust a moment and glanced to my left into a large living room. A ceiling fan hung motionless over a marble-topped coffee table that sat in front of a faded gold-and-white striped sofa. The room on my right had cardboard boxes stacked in the middle and a stepladder under another motionless fan.

I followed Mrs. Tesopolis through the archway into a hall lined with paintings of Greece. The only room visible was a dust-laden dining room with a lovely cherry table, chairs, and china cabinet. Evidently she had once entertained a lot.

The spacious kitchen, located behind the dining room, was spotless. A glass mug and a matching plate holding a slice of barely buttered toast sat on a small white table. A television satellite dish on a metal pole propped open the storm door. So she had no air conditioning or television.

In what had been a lovely backyard, an oval fishpond with a dolphin fountain stood empty in front of an overgrown grape arbor. An untrimmed hedge bordered the back.

Was the problem lack of care or poverty? Neglect or abuse? Whatever the cause, I had to do something. "I see the glass on your storm door hasn't been pulled up to let the breeze through the screen. Would you like for me to do that for you?"

The old woman angled herself from the walker to drop into her chair. "Please. My hands not so strong. Arthritis."

Connie had dawdled behind us. Now she came into the kitchen. "We could raise all your storm windows, if you like."

Mrs. Tesopolis reached out for her glass cup. A tea bag floated in it, but the water was almost clear. Finally she said, "No screens in front. Raise here and in my bedroom, please."

I moved the prop, raised the glass in the door, and closed it.

Mrs. Tesopolis watched, her face anxious. "Monday is laundry day. My Kiki comes." She pulled open a small drawer in the table and took out a blue-covered checkbook. "She brings groceries. I give her a check."

I could barely restrain myself from reaching for that checkbook and the story it would tell. The bedroom would tell stories, too. "I'll strip your bed for your daughter when I open your bedroom windows."

Not waiting for an answer, I hurried through the nearest door, leaving Connie to occupy the old woman. The bedroom's two windows were open, but I held my breath until I could raise the glass in the storm windows and let in fresh air. I turned on the ceiling fan, but two of the four blades were gone, rendering it useless. I pulled back a dark blue chenille bedspread to reveal light blue flannel sheets. In August. Not just neglect. Anger raised my temperature. I jerked the sheets off the bed and opened a steamer trunk at the end of the bed expecting to find summer sheets. It contained blankets and an eiderdown comforter.

I opened the louvered closet doors. Most of the clothes were old, but they included designer names. She didn't buy those in Laycock. The two missing fan blades, with the nuts and screws still in them, protruded from a shelf. I retrieved them. The cotton sheets rested on the top shelf out of reach. Nothing in the room to stand on. Moving quietly, I brought the stepladder from the front room, took down a set of sheets, and made the bed. Then I fastened the blades in the fan. I could hear Connie talking about how to make her mother's lemon cake. I did a quick search for financial records. Nothing. No tax forms. No monthly bills. They could be somewhere else in the house, but I guessed that the daughter had them.

The front door slammed and quick steps came down the hall. A woman's voice shouted in Greek. I bundled the sheets into a hamper with dirty clothes and carried them into the kitchen.

A small, slightly plump middle-aged woman with dark, wavy hair halfway down her back stood by the table glaring alternately at a hostile Connie and a cowed Mrs. Tesopolis. The new arrival held a plastic bag of groceries in one hand.

"Good morning," I said warmly. "You must be Kiki. I'm Phoenix Smith, an old friend. I recently came back to Laycock, so I stopped by to see your mother."

Mrs. Tesopolis raised her head. "Jack and Mary Smith's girl. Mary made yum-yum peach pie." She pointed to Connie. "Her mother made lemon cake."

Kiki dropped the groceries on the table and grabbed the hamper. "What are you doing with this?"

I smiled sweetly. "Your mother told us you do her laundry on Mondays, so I offered to lend a hand. Where's the washing machine?"

"I do the laundry at home." Kiki's eyes darted between her mother and me. "Thank you for coming. You can leave now."

Not so fast. "It's a little warm in here."

Kiki licked her lips. "Mama likes it warm. Anyway, the air conditioning doesn't work." The faint sound of "Never on Sunday" came from her purse. She pulled out a cell phone. "It's Derek." She stepped out the back door.

I heard him shout, "Where in hell are you?" before she moved out of range. Her side of the conversation consisted of nothing but "But," "Yes," "No," and a final "I'll be right there."

A frown deepening the lines in her forehead, she stepped back into the kitchen and held out one hand to her mother. "I have to go. I need the check for the groceries."

Mrs. Tesopolis signed a check but didn't fill in the amount. Kiki ripped it from the checkbook without recording it.

Too upset or too dumb to hide guilt. Yet she was smart enough to subtly torture her mother.

Connie smiled as usual, but her blue eyes had darkened. "I'll be glad to put away the groceries."

Kiki flushed. "Mama likes to do it herself so she knows where things are." She bent over and whispered something in Greek in her mother's ear.

I didn't know the words, but I recognized the tone. Determined to match threat with threat but in private, I picked up the hamper. "I'll carry the laundry to your car."

Head down, Kiki scurried toward the front door. She whacked the broken storm door open and almost ran toward an old black pickup.

Achilles intercepted her before she could open the door. She yelped in fear.

I stepped between them and thrust the hamper at her. "That house is dangerously hot. I'm going to get the air conditioning and the fans repaired, and they better be working the next time I come by. I'll expect to see nourishing food, too."

Her body sagged against the pickup. "You're making it worse, not better. If she's comfortable, she won't sell the house and go to a nursing home."

So she was trying to force her mother to move. I could understand that, but not using what could well be lethal tactics. The motive must be money, not her mother's welfare. But Kiki's distress was real. I changed my approach. I patted her on the shoulder and softened my voice. "Obviously you're worried about her living here alone. It must be a financial hardship for you, too."

She nodded and eyed me warily. Her upper lip trembled. "I love Mama."

"I can see that." And I see what you're doing to her. I sighed. "I worried a lot about my mother. A neighbor and good friend looked in on her every day so she could stay in her own home." Kiki had relaxed. I zinged her: "Maybe you know my friend, Annalynn Carr Keyser, the *sheriff.*"

Kiki's eyes widened. She'd received the message.

I opened the pickup door for her and softened my tone. "It's wonderful that you're willing to help your mother pay for a nursing home. She'll run through all the money she receives for this fixer-upper fast."

"Oh, no, Derek—my husband—says Medicaid will pay all the bills."

"Only after she's spent every cent she has. They check to see she didn't fake poverty by transferring the deed to the house or her savings to you." Kiki and Derek undoubtedly were already robbing the poor woman. No time to be subtle. "I'm an expert in money management. I'll be happy to look into your mother's finances."

Color drained from the daughter's face. She stepped up into the pickup, turned on the motor, and pulled away with squealing tires.

For a few seconds I felt triumphant. Then I realized that she didn't fear me. She feared her husband. Would what I'd done to help one woman end up hurting another?

Chapter Six

Connie stepped out the front door and called, "Phoenix, do you know anything about air conditioning?"

We'd cast our die. Might as well wade deeper into the Rubicon. "I'll take a look at it." I lowered my voice as I entered the house. "And call a repair company."

"Did you see that cute little cell phone Kiki gave her mother?"

What did that mean? "It's good to carry a phone at all times."

"Especially since she doesn't have a land line anymore," Connie said pointedly.

I remembered ads for cell plans for seniors allowing only an hour or so a month. I suspected Kiki had given her mother one to limit her outgoing calls and virtually cut off calls from friends. The phone book wouldn't list the new cell phone number. We needed to restore the phone and the air conditioning fast—before Kiki's low-life husband showed up to run us off. Without a court order, we had no legal rights here.

While Connie washed and brushed Mrs. T's hair, I "fixed" the air conditioning by turning the thermostat down to seventy-eight and called to reinstate phone and cable service. I also dusted, vacuumed, and searched the two front rooms. I found no financial records, a suspicious sign in itself.

A little before noon Connie and I said good-bye to Mrs. T and walked to our steaming cars. We opened the passenger doors, rolled down all the windows, and turned on our air conditioners. Then we stood in the maple's shade waiting for

Achilles to deem my car cool enough to enter. I was sweaty and dirty. Connie was clean but glowing.

She took out her phone. "What should I tell Trudy?"

The town herald would spread anything Connie told her all over Laycock before sunset. "If you tell Trudy how bad it was, Kiki will say it proves her mother needs to go to a nursing home."

Connie frowned. "We can't let this go."

"We won't. Just say the house was hot and needed a good cleaning. We took care of both. I'll come by tomorrow to make sure Kiki hasn't undone all we did. The church ladies will have to show up regularly for a while."

Connie shook her head. "That's not enough. I peeked at the checkbook. Lots of checks torn out, but the only dollar amounts recorded are the Social Security deposits at Dickie's bank. I'm sure Kiki and Derek are stealing from her."

"Yes, but we need proof." Financial wrongdoing was my area. "I'll ask Elena Cordero to check Mrs. T's and her daughter's accounts. Do you know Kiki's last name?"

"Gribble." Connie's cell rang. She checked the display. "My accompanist for the auditions. Got to take it."

I stepped away and called Elena. She'd helped me before, and I'd been able to return the favor. When she answered, I told what we'd seen and asked her to review accounts for suspicious activity.

"I understand your concern," she said formally. "I'll get back to you with the information when time permits. Good-bye." But she didn't hang up. "Good morning, Mr. Gribble." Her voice was faint but clear. A man said something in a whiny voice. Elena answered, "I'm afraid Mrs. Tesopolis doesn't have enough in her checking account to cover that check." The man's voice again. Then Elena: "I'm sorry. We can't transfer money from her savings account without her signature." She hung up.

I pumped my fist. "Elena is on it."

Connie heaved an enormous sigh. "At least one of us has good news."

Knowing it was a mistake, I gave the intended reply: "What's wrong?"

"The music prof can't play piano for the auditions this afternoon."

Connie had already suckered me once today. "Too bad. Time to go, Achilles."

Connie planted her hands on her hips. "Come on, Phoenix. The kids will be singing songs you can play in your sleep."

"So can you." I followed Achilles into the car.

"I need to sit back in the auditorium to hear how they project, and I have to take notes. We start at three, and we'll be done in a couple of hours." She reached through my car window and grabbed the steering wheel. "Please, Phoenix, I'm desperate. I can't hold grades over these kids. If I'm going to get their co-operation, I have to come across as a professional director, not an accompanist." She let go of the steering wheel. "I'll make it up to you."

Connie cheerful often tried my patience. Connie depressed would be unbearable. I opted to negotiate. "Listening to kids try out would be torture."

Her habitual smile returned as she realized I'd relented. "I know, I know. You spent almost thirty years in Vienna listening to the world's greatest singers. What's your price?"

Hmmm. "Two things. One: You work as long cleaning Annalynn's house, including the bathrooms, as I spend enduring auditions. Two: If I think Annalynn needs to get out of town, you'll suggest we visit my brothers in California."

"Geez, smartass. You don't take no for an answer, do you? Done." She grinned and skipped to the Corvette, calling over her shoulder. "I'll see you at quarter to three in the Arts auditorium. Wear business casual."

Had she ever had an accompanist lined up? I had to stop underestimating Connie.

Achilles listened quietly when I played Mozart and Scott Joplin on the piano but howled along when anyone sang. I dropped him off at Annalynn's office on my way to the auditions. I'd never been on the campus of Laycock Community College, but Mrs. Roper, Stuart's mother, had started my love affair with math in the old brick junior high that now served as LCC's administration building. I drove past it and the abandoned shoe factory, now the sports center, and parked beside the Corvette. It served as a nice prop for Connie, musical comedy director. I groaned at the boxy architecture of the new three-story brick Arts building. A low budget didn't excuse ugliness.

The empty auditorium appeared ho-hum, but when I played an arpeggio on the grand piano placed downstage left on the surprisingly deep stage, the acoustics nearly equaled those of the Musikverein. What I wouldn't give to hear a good concert. I opened the *Oklahoma!* score on the piano and ran through "Oh, What a Beautiful Mornin'."

Connie came from backstage and sang as I played. She had a perfect musical-comedy soprano. Bad luck, bad timing, and living in the wrong places while she raised her two daughters had limited her career to community theater and summer stock.

She handed me a list of students' names. "Twenty-five signed up to try out for ten speaking parts."

I groaned. "At least three hours. I should have brought ear plugs."

"We'll take a break about four thirty." She pointed to my gun. "I can see that. Can't you put it in your purse? You're not supposed to bring guns on campus."

The smells of the Istanbul spice bazaar invaded my brain. I

shook my head to clear it. "No. I have to be able to get to it instantly." I'd worn a long, loose orange-red silk blouse to cover the holster. "Anyone in the auditorium will see only my left profile. When I get up, I'll carry my purse on my right side."

She gripped my shoulder. "My God! You expect trouble. Is it that shootout?"

I saw two young women come into the auditorium. "Just a precaution." I picked up my purse and retreated to a front-row seat.

By three o'clock at least sixty people were scattered around the auditorium in small clusters. The tryouts apparently were the most exciting event in Laycock.

Connie ran up the steps to the stage. "Welcome to the auditions for *Oklahoma!*, one of our greatest musicals. I'm delighted to have an audience to support the performers, but I must ask you not to comment or applaud." She waited for two girls to stop talking. "I'll call up the singers in the order in which they signed up. If you don't have your own accompaniment, Dr. Phoenix Smith"—she pointed to me—"will accompany you on the piano." She came down the steps. "The first singer is Brandon Cort."

A skinny blond kid in jeans and a Hard Rock Café T-shirt ran down the center aisle. He stopped in front of me, his long, freckled face shy and eager. "I'd appreciate your playing 'Oh, What a Beautiful Mornin' for me, ma'am."

Butterflies flitted through my stomach the way they had before my student recitals. I'd thought of this as a chore, but to these kids auditioning was a major life event. I could mess it up. I smiled reassuringly and went to the piano. I checked the key and tempo and showed him some unobtrusive hand signals to use to slow me down or speed me up. Finally I gave him the pitch and played the opening bars.

To my relief, it went well. The skinny teenager had a surprisingly rich voice quite suited to cowboy Curly, the male lead. And I had a pattern to follow in accompanying the others.

We listened to ten more aspirants, some of them no longer kids, before a stocky young Hispanic displayed the voice and acting ability for the other major male role, the villainous Jud. A petite, gray-haired woman nailed Aunt Eller.

By the time Connie called for a fifteen-minute break, we'd gone through fifteen people. No one had demonstrated enough voice or stage presence for the two leading female roles. I took my turn at the water fountain and went outside to check my cell for a message from Elena. Nothing yet.

A gawky young woman with short, spiky black hair and a plain black T-shirt and jeans sidled up to me. "I don't know any *Oklahoma!* songs."

"What a relief," I said, smiling into eyes as blue as Connie's. "I'm really getting tired of them. What would you like to sing?"

She thrust her hands deep into her pockets. "Can you play 'Ave Maria'?"

I'd first played that for Connie to sing at our high school graduation. Incredibly long ago, but I retained notes and numbers. "Enough to fake it. What key?"

She stared at the toes protruding from her cheap sandals. "Whatever."

An odd selection for someone who didn't know the key. "What's your range?"

She raised her head and squared broad shoulders. "I can sing pretty high."

"We'll work it out." She had a singer's jaw line. We walked down the hall together as the others filed into the auditorium. "What's your name?"

"LaDawna. LaDawna McKnight."

Sounded like either romantic parents' overreach or a young dreamer's stage name. "I don't remember any McKnights. Are you from Laycock?"

"No. I moved here this summer." She lengthened her stride and went to the water fountain.

Connie was talking on the phone when I went into the auditorium. As I climbed the steps to the stage, she called, "Phoenix, Annalynn has a church committee meeting at seven. Is dinner at eight at La Vida Loca okay with you?"

"Fine."

The next few voices were mediocre or bad, but the twenty-first singer's voice and manner fit the feisty Ado Annie.

LaDawna was the last woman to audition. I gave her the pitch and played the opening notes. She nodded, clasped her hands together, and took a deep breath.

She didn't breathe properly, she flattened her vowels, and she sang magnificently. She'd be a high-risk high-gain Laurey, the female lead.

"Brava," I said as the last note died away, neglecting my duty to be neutral.

She blinked as though coming out of a trance. "What?"

I smiled. "You have a beautiful voice."

She nodded, apparently accepting the praise as a factual statement.

"The last singer: Fargo," Connie called.

A short, slender kid in a Stetson hat, faded jeans, a rhinestone-laden western shirt, and cowboy boots swaggered down the center aisle. He raised his right hand to touch his hat as he went by Connie. He wore a pistol low on his right hip in Wild West style.

When he mounted the steps to the stage, I saw the revolver was real.

He pranced to center stage. "Oh, What a Beautiful Mornin'."

I gave him the pitch and a few introductory bars just as I had the eight others who'd sung the song.

He started flat. He fell a full note low on the first high note. He stopped and glared at me. "You're playing in the wrong key. Start again."

No one else had asked me to change keys. I wasn't going to do it for this no-talent asshole. I played the opening notes again.

He repeated his mistakes, but this time his voice cracked. He whirled and crouched like a gunslinger. "I said to play in a lower key." He whipped out the six-shooter with his right hand and cocked it with his left.

Ducking down and to my right behind the grand, I drew and racked my gun. I took two quick steps and bobbed up ready to fire.

He stood with his mouth open, staring at where I had been.

"Put the gun on the floor, fool," I said.

He went white but obeyed. "It's just a prop. It's not loaded."

Connie walked briskly toward the stage. "Everyone stay seated. Dr. Smith is also Deputy Smith of the Vandiver County Sheriff's Department."

I didn't take my eyes from the kid. "Hands on your head. Knees on the floor."

He almost fell as he knelt.

I walked slowly to the revolver and picked it up with my left hand. I backed to the piano, put down my Glock, and checked the six-shooter's chambers. Two bullets. My heart pounded. Was the kid a Cantree cousin planning to shoot me "by accident"? My eyes on him, I removed the bullets.

Gasps and little screams came from around the auditorium.

"I didn't know. I swear I didn't know," the kid said, his voice shaking. "It's part of my dad's gun collection. It's an antique."

Sounded like the truth. Didn't make me feel safer. "You could have killed me."

Tears came to his eyes. "I was acting the part!"

"No, you were acting like—" I remembered the audience and

described him under my breath in low German. Now what? Had he broken a law in this gun-friendly state? I punted. "You report to the sheriff tomorrow morning at nine o'clock. With your parents. Get out of here."

He sprang to his feet and held his hand out for the revolver.

"Get out before I lose my temper," I hissed.

He leapt from the stage and ran.

Scanning the quiet auditorium, I jammed the revolver in my purse and picked up my Glock. The kids looked shaken. Two girls whispered to each other. A boy snickered. Three kids held camera phones. I hoped they'd missed the main action. In the front row Aunt Eller comforted LaDawna McKnight, who leaned far forward with her hands covering her face. Tears dropped between her fingers. I saw no threat. I holstered my Glock. "Back to you, Ms. Diamante."

"Thank you, Deputy Smith."

Connie ran up the steps to the stage. She faced the students with an amused smile. "Well, one cowboy and law woman won't be friends." She waited as a few people chuckled at her reference to a lyric from the show. "We've heard some fine voices today. Everyone except Fargo will be on stage when the show opens. I want to hear fourteen of you read lines before I assign speaking parts."

Tiny's warning about the Cantrees sounded in my brain. I grasped my Glock and studied the young faces while Connie perched on the edge of the stage and arranged times for students to read for her. Finally, only Aunt Eller, LaDawna/Laurey, and Brandon/Curly remained.

Brandon came up the steps to me. "Thanks for playing for us. Fargo's a real asshole. Nobody else at LCC would act so stupid, at least not in front of the 'unnamed deputy.' "

Bloody hell! Everyone knew I'd shot the Cantrees. I managed a smile. "You'll learn a lot from Connie. She's played both Laurey and Ado Annie in summer stock."

He nodded earnestly. "I saw her production of *Annie Get Your Gun* last year. She's a real pro. I was afraid she'd move away before I got a chance to work with her." He saw the others leaving. "So long." He loped out of the auditorium.

I couldn't wait to get out of the place myself. I hurried off the stage.

Connie came right behind me. "Annalynn said killing that man Saturday night didn't bother you. I think she's wrong, for once."

I let her assumption of remorse stand rather than explaining I'd reacted to a possible threat from the malevolent Cantrees. She had no need to know, at least not yet.

When we walked out of the building, students huddled in the shade of two trees near the parking lot. They quieted as we walked by.

As a covert operative I'd excelled at being inconspicuous. Today I'd displayed my quickness with a gun on stage. Trudy probably had already heard about it. What could I do about it now? Divert their attention. Give them something to remember besides my holding a gun.

"We need a dramatic exit," Connie whispered as we approached our cars.

For one awful moment I thought she'd read my thoughts. I relaxed. No, she'd read our audience.

"You won the bet, Phoenix," she said just loud enough the nearest group of kids could hear. "I guessed twenty-two would audition and you said twenty-four. We had twenty-five." She dangled the keys to the Corvette in front of me. "Are you really going to hold me to it?"

I laughed. "I certainly am. You know I've been dying to try it." I held out my car keys and she grudgingly gave me the keys to the Corvette.

I got in, turned on the ignition, gave it some extra gas to make sure everyone was watching, zipped out of the parking place, and pushed the accelerator to the floorboard. The tires squealed as I turned into the street and exited stage right.

Chapter Seven

I rambled on country roads testing the powerful motor and trying to figure out whether I'd overreacted to the six-shooter or averted a catastrophe. Habit and unease prompted me to keep watch in my rearview mirror. I found myself at the Oak Grove Church and pulled into the small parking lot by the century-old building. Truth time. I hadn't really gone for a drive. I'd run away. Not from fear of Fargo or the Cantrees and not from dread of what I might have set in motion at the Tesopolis house. I'd run from my own uncertainties. I got out to walk up and down the rows of tombstones and think about how my life—how I—had changed since a person unknown had interrupted my post-retirement courier mission with bullets.

Half conscious in a hospital, I'd dreamed of peaceful, friendly, caring Laycock. Fully conscious, I'd remembered that my hometown could be as petty and bigoted and willfully ignorant as any other place. I'd come back because the CIA wanted me out of Vienna and I didn't know where else to go. And because Annalynn, my oldest and dearest friend, embodied goodness, loyalty, devotion. After years of dealing with human slime, I needed to reassure myself that those qualities still existed.

Annalynn had not disappointed me.

I'd recovered—almost—from my wound and accepted—almost—the loss of my old double life. I hadn't regained the self-confidence and daring that had enabled me to succeed as a covert operative and as an executive of a venture capital firm. A few months ago I couldn't have imagined that I would spend my days groping for ways to support Annalynn. Today I'd ignored the foundation, the one project I'd initiated, to help Connie with a college musical. Time to pull myself together.

I walked past the small grave where Annalynn had broken down and checked around it for anything we'd missed that night. I had the uneasy sense I was being watched. My hand hovering over my holster, I knelt as though to read an old tombstone. I listened for a full minute and heard only a whisper of wind blowing through the corn growing on two sides of the cemetery. Nothing moved among the dense plants. I stood up and strolled among the taller tombstones. I heard something behind me and turned with gun raised. A squirrel leapt from the top of one tombstone to another across the cemetery before he hit the ground and ran to an oak tree behind the church. His mate popped up on a branch and chattered at him, or at me.

I holstered my Glock. "Phoenix, you're out of your element. In every way." Well, not completely. I relished scheming to get Annalynn nominated next summer to run for an open seat in Congress. I'd enjoyed helping Mrs. T and watching those kids sing for their dreams. I'd certainly gotten a rush from the two successful homicide investigations, and even from the Saturday night shootout.

Yet none of these things moved me toward a goal. For the first time in my life, I didn't have one. I was drifting. Professionally and personally. Stuart would call me tonight to ask whether I would meet his kids Saturday. I groaned. What would I say?

Clouds moved in and erased the tombstones' long shadows. Almost eight o'clock. Annalynn would be worried. I jogged to the Corvette and raced back to Laycock.

★ ★ ★ ★ ★

The only space in La Vida Loca's little parking lot was in front next to my Camry. I backed into the spot, got out, and paused a moment to admire the pink flowers covering the Rose of Sharon hedges bordering the sides of the lot.

A couple came out the door. Elena Cordero greeted me: "*Hola,* Phoenix." She smiled at her fiancé. "Would you bring the car, honey?"

He exchanged polite nods with me and walked toward the corner of the lot.

"What do you recommend?" I lowered my voice. "Find anything?"

"The chicken enchiladas are excellent." She whispered, "Gribble's moving business barely pays their bills. He's desperate for money to put a new engine in his truck. I'm sure he's been siphoning off Mrs. T's money, but I saw no proof."

"Thanks. Talk to you soon." I walked in the glass door and paused under a pink burro piñata. On my left, strangers occupied the row of booths against the front windows and the dozen Formica-topped tables in the main dining area. No one sat in the two booths to my right. Connie waved to me from a side booth looking out on the Rose of Sharon.

She and Annalynn sat side by side, doubtless the better to talk without being overheard. When I walked back, I noted the mural on the wall separating the kitchen from the booths now featured neon-green cactus and a pale-blue sky. The scene had changed at least three times since the place had been our teenage hangout. Annalynn probably suggested the place out of nostalgia.

"You're late. We finally ordered," Connie scolded. "I was afraid you'd wrecked the Corvette."

I scooted into the booth. The vinyl seats wouldn't let me slide so I stayed on the outer edge of the bench. "Driving it is great fun."

Annalynn watched me, her worry line showing. "You had two calls. Stuart wants to talk to you about this weekend. A lawyer who does *pro bono* work for the Foundation Center will contact you for an appointment tomorrow."

"Good." I had little faith in lawyers who worked for nothing. Or ones who charged ridiculous fees. A waitress who couldn't have been more than twelve appeared at my elbow. I took Elena's advice: "Chicken enchiladas, *por favor, senorita.*"

"Okay." She hurried to the kitchen's swinging doors a few feet in front of me.

Annalynn smiled. "Connie told me Mrs. T is convinced you're Greek." The smile vanished. "She also said you made an appointment for me at nine tomorrow."

Connie pushed the salsa and chips toward me. "Plenty of time to explain that later. I've waited a whole day to tell you both about the wedding." She went into a monologue about her ex-husband pleading with her to sing at the wedding to show their daughters that their parents remained friends. The bride-to-be added her entreaties, but Connie knew the woman didn't mean them. The food's arrival interrupted Connie.

Annalynn took the opportunity to say, "He had a lot of nerve to ask you to sing. He didn't think about your feelings or hers." She turned to me. "Would you ever ask a favor of Russ?"

"No, but Russ and I were married less than two years, not twenty-five, and I divorced him because I caught him cheating, not because we'd drifted apart."

Out of the corner of my eye I saw a movement in the Rose of Sharon. "Down!" I grabbed Annalynn's arm to pull her to safety as the first of three shots came through the window.

Chapter Eight

"Down! Everyone down!" I crouched on the floor with my gun ready. Broken glass glistened on the bench where I'd been sitting.

Annalynn knelt beside me. "Is anyone hurt?"

Connie, now flat on the bench, shook her head.

If anyone said yes, we couldn't hear it over the screams and scraping chairs.

"Everyone stay down and keep quiet," I yelled. I glanced at three bullet holes in the wall. A message from the infamous Cantrees?

A Hispanic man stuck his head out of the kitchen door.

"Turn off the lights," I called over the din.

A moment later our only light came from a nearby streetlight. Keeping low, I crept to the empty booth behind ours.

No sound of running feet outside. No motor. No squealing tires.

I slid into the booth head first on my elbows with every intention of raising my head to look out the window. I couldn't do it. I'd already faced guns twice in the last two days. I doubted the third time would be a charm.

Annalynn slid into the other side of the booth. "I don't have a deputy nearby. I called the LPD for back-up." She lifted her head and moved closer to the window.

"Stay down!" I forced my head up until I could see the hedge. Nothing moved. Sprinkles splashed on the window. I strained my eyes and ears for a full minute. "I think he's gone." And the longer we waited, the farther away he would be. "I'll go out the back door and circle around to come up behind the hedge."

"I'll go out the front door in exactly one minute."

Nothing would stop her from going outside if I did. I wormed my way out of the booth. "Make it two minutes. Then dart behind my Camry."

Connie blocked my way. "I can cover you from here with the pistol in your purse."

A firearm in Connie's hands really scared me. Then I remembered: "It's not loaded." Bent low I ran into the kitchen. A man ducked behind a counter as I opened the door. "I'm going after the gunman. What's out back?"

The girl who'd taken my order answered from under a table: "The Dumpster and then nothing until you get to a big tree by the alley."

Damn! I'd have a couple of seconds with no cover. I couldn't visualize the area. "What's behind the hedge?"

"Another alley," the child said. "Are you the deputy?"

"Yes." For the moment. I crept to the back door, opened it an inch, and listened. Nothing but rain. I spotted the tree—big enough to hide behind—about twenty feet away. Annalynn would be bursting out the front door in about a minute. I dashed to the tree. No bullets whined past me. Nothing moved. The Rose of Sharon hedge ran up to the edge of the back alley. I sprinted down the alley and pressed my body into the hedge.

A police siren sounded two or three blocks away.

I leaned forward and peered through the leaves to where the shooter had been. And now wasn't. The intersecting alleys ran behind and between old business buildings—an auto parts store, a used-furniture place, a shoe repair shop. All closed. I stayed put, straining eyes and ears until the police car slid into the parking lot.

Annalynn called, "Jim's here."

Good. He was the most competent officer on Laycock's police force, and an old friend. I debated a moment about giving away my position before answering: "Jim, light the alley behind the hedge."

The tires squealed. Seconds later his headlights illuminated an empty alley and a slight indention where the shooter had stood. I stepped out.

Jim saluted me and turned right with his spotlight, searching the back doors of the businesses and the yards that bordered the alley.

The rain came down steadily now.

"Come inside, Phoenix," Annalynn called. "We have to talk to everyone here."

I raced to the back door. Annalynn took the people in booths while I questioned those at the tables. Connie collected their contact information at the door. No one had seen anyone go into the alley.

Jim had returned to the alley by the time Annalynn announced the diners could leave whenever they wanted. Fighting fatigue, I went back to our booth. Shattered glass littered the table and bench. I perched on the end of the bench and tried to remember my exact position the moment before the first shot was fired. I imitated it as best I could and looked at the bullet holes. They formed a triangle several inches above my head. Consistent shooting—an experienced marksman.

I needed a dummy to take my place so I could see how accurate the shots had been. "Connie, could you help me for a moment?"

She came from chatting with a piano student's family. "Good Lord, Phoenix. You're almost as gray as you were when you came in May. Are you hurt?"

"No, just tired." I longed for a scotch, but my regenerating liver wasn't ready for alcohol yet. "Maybe something sweet would perk me up."

The child waitress appeared at my elbow. "Would you like a peach milkshake?"

"Wonderful idea. Milkshakes for everyone, please." I smiled at the solemn face with the lively brown eyes. "You kept cool tonight. Great job. What's your name?"

"Mariela." She smiled back, pleased but not bowled over by my compliment. "I know who you are—Tucson Smith, the unnamed deputy."

Brandon had used that term, too. So much for anonymity. "Not Tucson, Phoenix."

I resumed the position I'd been in when the bullets came. "Connie, could you please sit like this so I can check the line of fire?"

She stared out the window a moment. "I suppose so."

We changed places. Connie was five-two to my five-six. I estimated the bullets had been a foot high but in a direct line with my head. If I'd missed a target like that, I would have missed on purpose. The shots were meant to warn or frighten, not to kill.

Police Chief Jim Falstaff came in to report finding no suspects. The skinny athlete who'd been my younger brother's best buddy had gained a paunch and a twice-a-day shaving habit. He pulled a paper napkin from a dispenser and wiped rain from his whiskers. "You want to handle this one, Annalynn?"

"No, Laycock's your jurisdiction," she said. "I'll help however I can, of course." She motioned us to a table with no window view. "Did you find anything?"

"Nope. From the holes, I'd guess the shots came from a .22 pistol. We'll see when we dig the bullets out." He focused on me. "You musta made somebody awful mad."

Connie gasped. "I had no idea he would do anything like that." She opened her purse and put Fargo's revolver on the table. "Did the bullets come from a gun like this?"

Jim leaned over to look at it. "Nope. Is that the one the kid in the YouTube video called a prop?"

I swore beneath my breath. The last thing I wanted going all over the world was a video of me drawing on Fargo. "Were we identified?"

Jim grinned. "As the Frog and the Unnamed Deputy. I doubt it was him. I took him home to his folks a couple years ago for shooting rats at the dump, but he's never been in any real trouble."

Connie gripped my wrist. "Maybe it was Mrs. T's son-in-law."

Jim threw up his hands. "For God sake, Phoenix, how many people did you piss off today?"

Everyone shut up as Mariela delivered a round of milkshakes and coffee.

Connie began a dramatic account of our morning at Mrs. T's house. I cut her off and gave the salient facts, omitting my call to Elena.

When I finished, Annalynn stared at me several seconds and then turned to the weak link: "Anything essential Phoenix neglected to tell us, Connie?"

I held my breath, afraid she'd mention my illegal request to Elena.

Connie shook her head. "That's the short of it."

Jim slurped up the last of his milkshake. "My wife and I used to bowl in the same league as the Gribbles." He pushed the glass away. "Derek's no saint. He flirts like a teenager and keeps Kiki running to do things for him. He's a hard worker, though. When the Chair-Mart closed, they gave him the old delivery truck as severance pay and he started his own moving business.

He's never been violent."

Or never been caught at it. "Kiki's afraid of him."

Connie pushed her untouched milkshake across the table to Jim. "Phoenix is right. Mrs. T told me her late husband was a wonderful man. She hinted that Kiki's husband isn't."

Jim scratched his beard. "I can believe he wants to get his hands on Mrs. T's money, but I don't see how shooting Phoenix gets him anything except trouble. Besides, how would he know you were here?"

I'd thought about that. "He could have driven by on his way to the bowling alley and noticed that red Corvette. His wife probably mentioned the fancy car to him."

Jim chuckled. "Or he saw you peel away in it on YouTube."

Bloody hell! Privacy had gone the way of the dinosaurs.

Jim sobered. "I don't buy it. I've learned to look for the obvious. Too many coincidences for it to be Derek. Who else knew you'd be here?"

Connie clapped her hands to her cheeks. "Fargo knew. We talked about it right in front of him during the auditions."

Her voice had carried throughout the auditorium. "In front of Fargo and about fifty other people."

Jim scribbled in his small notebook. "Could be one of them, but my money is on the Cantrees. So far as I know, neither Fargo nor Derek Gribble is related to them. All the Cantree men have a real distinctive look."

Connie frowned. "I thought you shot them Saturday night."

"Two got away," Annalynn said. "I agree. We can't discount the Cantrees."

"They couldn't know I'd be here unless someone in the auditorium told them. After all, they wouldn't recognize our cars. Or me," I pointed out. "Besides, the shooting pattern indicates the gunman wanted to scare me, not kill me. That doesn't sound like a Cantree."

"Oh, hell. Anybody coulda done it." Jim stood up. "Annalynn, I'd appreciate it if you would follow up with Tiny on the Cantrees. I'll go check Fargo and Derek's alibis."

Tired and on edge as I was, I was disappointed not to question the two myself. I gave Jim a lead: "Fargo said the six-shooter is part of his father's gun collection. See if it includes a .22 pistol."

Achilles greeted me at the door, licking my hand and sniffing the take-out meals I carried. Neither Annalynn nor I had any appetite, so I stuck the enchiladas in the refrigerator.

The phone rang twice, signaling a call from the sheriff's department. Annalynn picked up the hall phone. Her side of the conversation told me nothing.

I went into the former ladies' parlor, the back of which now served as Annalynn's home office, and turned on her computer. I was watching the Frog audition on YouTube when Annalynn came up behind me.

"Fargo sings flat," she said. "You probably *wanted* to shoot him."

I turned off the sound. "Did Jim find out anything?"

"Fargo swears he didn't do it but his alibi doesn't hold up. He claims he was rehearsing with his band until nine. He said a friend would vouch for him, but the boy said Fargo left about eight. Jim said it's not enough to arrest him."

"And the gun collection?"

"The father refused to let Jim see it without a warrant. He called a lawyer." She patted me on the shoulder. "You look exhausted, Phoenix. Please go on to bed. If I hear anything vital, I'll wake you."

I went upstairs and watched the videos on my laptop. To my relief, neither had a close-up of my face. I soaked in the tub to ease my tense muscles and think about the day's events. When I came out, Achilles and Annalynn were still downstairs. To relax, I picked up *The Economist* and propped myself up with pillows to read.

Annalynn tapped on my door and leaned against the frame. "Did you call Stuart?"

"It's too late tonight." And too early for me to give him an answer. "I'll call him tomorrow. Has Jim talked to Derek Gribble?"

"Not yet. Kiki claimed her husband was at the bowling alley. A teammate says he got a call and left there at seven fifteen. Jim is checking his other hangouts now." She rubbed the back of her neck. "Gribble has a concealed carry permit."

So did tens of thousands of other Missourians. It's a gun-loving state. "We can't eliminate him, but Fargo seems a better bet. If he shoots rats, he's likely to be a good shot—good enough to miss me." I dredged up a smile. "I don't know why Connie thinks Laycock is boring."

Achilles trotted past Annalynn to my bed. He carried his tennis ball.

"Bedtime, boy. We'll play fetch tomorrow."

Annalynn straightened and cleared her throat. "No, you won't. I made two decisions tonight. One, I'm going to accept the extended appointment. I can't leave this mess to someone new. Two, I'm kicking you out. Tomorrow you and Achilles go to visit Quintin and Ulysses."

She'd stolen my plan to get her to safety. Well, it wouldn't work. "You know damned well I'm not going anywhere until"—until what?—"I've set up the foundation. Besides, Laycock is getting interesting." Much too interesting for Annalynn to handle alone. "Good night." I yawned, closed my magazine, and turned out the light.

She didn't move. "I mean it, Phoenix. I want you out of the danger zone."

I considered retreat an acceptable option, but I wouldn't leave her behind. "I'll get out of Dodge if you do. If you stay, I stay."

"You know I can't leave." She stood silent in my doorway, her silhouette visible in the light coming through the hall window. "Phoenix, that person in the hedge shot at you tonight, not me. You're the target. Please. Leave."

CHAPTER NINE

Neither Annalynn's nor the shooter's warnings convinced me to leave. They did, however, seep into my subconscious. I dreamed that I was walking through a shadow-filled graveyard wearing a white T-shirt with a red glow-in-the-dark target stamped on the front and back. A squirrel atop a tombstone morphed into a shrouded figure carrying an AR-15. I shot him with the green water pistol I'd carried everywhere the summer I was eight. The figure turned back into a squirrel.

I woke to a cloudy morning and a sunny attitude. Figuring out who'd shot at me would be far more engrossing than setting up a foundation. Besides, the aroma of good French breakfast coffee wafted up the stairs. So did two voices. Connie was here. She'd back me up if Annalynn still insisted I skip Laycock without her.

I slipped into brown shorts and a lime-green tank top and went down to the dining room. Connie, dressed to be noticed in a red sundress, and Annalynn, in white slacks and a blue blouse, were eating one of my favorite breakfasts, blueberry pancakes with bacon.

"I put your plate in the oven," Annalynn said, cutting off my greeting.

I interpreted the pancakes as a peace offering. Inhaling the aroma, I hurried into the kitchen. "Thanks."

Connie watched me. "You look much healthier and happier this morning than you did last night." She turned back to Annalynn. "What did Derek Gribble say?"

Annalynn didn't answer immediately.

"Come on," Connie pleaded. "You know you can trust me."

Annalynn relented. "Of course I trust you, but you're as bad as Phoenix about running right into the middle of a mess." Tension tightened her voice.

Now what? She was holding back something that would annoy me. "So tell us *both* what Jim found out."

"Not much." Annalynn leaned back in her chair and folded her arms. "He finally found Gribble at Harry's Hideaway a little before midnight. He said he spent the evening with 'a special friend,' one whose name he was too much of a gentleman to give."

"So we definitely need to check him out." The calendar caught my eye. Thirty-two years ago today I'd walked into my husband's office and found him and his paralegal on the couch with no briefs. The sight had sickened me. I'd never managed to erase that image of Russ. I shook it off.

"I'll ask the gossip queen about Gribble," Connie said. "Trudy can find out faster than any cop if he has someone on the side. Annalynn, have you talked to Sheriff Towson about the missing Cantrees?"

"He's checking with the FBI. He'll get back to me this morning."

I discounted the Cantree theory. "The odds of them sneaking into Laycock and finding me at that restaurant are statistically insignificant."

Connie poked the air between us with her fork. "Not if Fargo or Derek is a Cantree."

"They're not," Annalynn said. "I checked."

Connie's eyes widened. "Then we need to find out if anyone related to the Cantrees came to the auditions."

"Worth a try," I said. "Can you compile a list of everyone

there and access their student records? We may find a Cantree among their mothers' maiden names."

"No, she can't do that. That would be illegal." Annalynn glared at me. "Don't you dare pull her into this."

"Broken glass in my refried beans pulled me in." Connie reached down and brought up a folder. "I have the names of everyone who auditioned but not of the people who came to watch. I'll get those today during the readings." She tapped the folder on the table and winked at me. "I'll need proof they're all enrolled."

"Of course," I said. Annalynn acted out of a sense of duty. Connie wanted excitement. I had another thought: "Kids put personal information online these days. We'll split up the names and see what we can find on them tonight."

Annalynn pressed the fingers of both hands against her temples. "Why won't either of you listen to me? You're both far too reckless."

A car pulled into the drive, and Achilles trotted to the dining room window.

I got up to check. "It's Tiny Towson. He's wearing his uniform today."

Connie stood up. "Damn, and I have to get to the college." She went with me to the front door and slipped out as Tiny came up the porch steps. She nodded and smiled.

He swiveled to watch her bounce down the steps.

I said, "I hope you've come to tell us the FBI caught the rest of the gang."

He turned back to me reluctantly. " 'Fraid not."

"Come in, Tiny," Annalynn called. "Would you like a cup of coffee? Toast?"

"No, thanks. I'm due in my own county in half an hour. Did the Laycock police come up with anything solid on your two local suspects?"

Annalynn shook her head. "No alibis for either one, no evidence for us."

Tiny handed her a folder. "You and your people need to be able to recognize Roscoe Cantree. I had a breakfast meeting over here, so I photocopied my pre-computer mug shots of him and Orson to bring by. They looked a lot alike."

She opened the folder as he pulled out the chair next to me. "They don't look familiar." She handed the folder to me.

They had jutting chins, eyebrows that resembled black wooly worms, and small ears clinging to close-cropped skulls. "What color is their hair?"

Tiny rubbed his chin. "Light brown, sandy. They wore it short. If it grew out, it got real curly. They considered that unmanly."

I tried to visualize the men older. "They used wigs and fake facial hair during the robbery. They probably have other disguises, but they may not think to cover those distinctive ears." I closed the folder. "Any more information on the two who got away?"

"No, but then the FBI doesn't share everything." He squirmed in his chair before he went on. "Here's what I've heard from—various sources. The FBI found signs of at least one other vehicle but no clear tire tracks or fingerprints. They've tapped Roscoe as the gang leader, the one who killed the bank employee."

I had my doubts. "Does he know anything about how banks operate?"

Tiny snorted. "No. My source says the planner is a former banker, an embezzler, Roscoe met in prison. He always liked to play with firecrackers and go fishing with dynamite. And he liked to steal cars. He was in prison for running a chop shop."

I guessed that these disclosures were the real reason for Tiny's visit. He didn't want to discuss his unofficial findings through official communications.

Annalynn sighed. "I can't understand why Orson Cantree would involve his teenage son in a major crime. Have you heard how the boy is?"

"Touch and go. He's in a coma in a Kansas City ICU. The FBI won't be able to question him for days, maybe weeks. Maybe never."

I knew the boy's survival, not his ability to answer questions, concerned Annalynn. I took the conversation in another direction: "Did the gang get whatever they went after in the safety deposit boxes?"

"Oh, yeah." He pressed his lips together, apparently debating whether to go on. "Not to leave this room: They got three hundred or so South African gold coins."

"Krugerrands. Gold bullion." I'd collected them in Vienna before owning them became legal in the United States. "A good choice. You can sell them all over the world, and they appreciate nicely if you hold on to them."

He sat up straighter. "You know about the market for these—uh—coins?"

"It's international. In legal transactions, one is worth about fifteen hundred dollars, depending on the price of gold. In many countries, even hot coins sell for that. You can always melt them down."

"Is there a market for them in this country?"

"Certainly, but you stand less chance of being caught in Africa or the Middle East. Cleveland isn't far from Canada. Why not sneak over the border by boat and smuggle the coins out to—I don't know the best place right now."

Tiny pulled a pad and pen from his pocket. "Three hundred coins would weigh—"

"About nine kilos, roughly nineteen pounds." I spoke my thoughts. "Easy for one person to carry, hard to conceal from an airport X-ray. But with a half million or so in your carry-on, you could charter a small plane and avoid customs."

Annalynn touched my hand. "But Phoenix, four people took part in the robbery, and four people came here. I doubt that there's enough honor among thieves for them to entrust those coins to someone else to carry overseas."

"I agree with you on that." Tiny stood up. "I've got to go." He took a step toward the door. "Is the woman who was here another one of your reserve officers?"

Annalynn rose to show him out. "No, she's an old friend."

"She looks familiar." He waited a few seconds. "Where would I know her from?"

I hoped he was more subtle when he interrogated criminals. "You may have heard her sing at some event. Her name is Connie Diamante. She's divorced, loves to dance, enjoys good food and wine, and likes considerate men with a good sense of humor."

Annalynn shot me an angry look and said, "Connie's awfully busy right now. She's directing *Oklahoma!* at the college."

He beamed. "I played Curly. Back then I was." He brushed a hand over his receding hairline and went out whistling "Oh, What a Beautiful Mornin'."

He'd barely left the porch when Annalynn exploded. "You sounded like you were setting up teenagers. What were you thinking?"

I gathered up my empty dishes. "Connie's always complaining that she can't find anybody to date. He's not wearing a wedding ring. He's attractive." What had I missed? "You don't trust him. Why?"

"I'm not sure." She closed her eyes a moment in thought. "It was odd that he came by yesterday when he obviously was exhausted. He had even less reason to come today. He could have faxed those photos and called from a personal cell phone with that information."

I weighed what she'd said. "He said we're all under suspicion. He definitely wants allies. Whether it's against the FBI or the Cantrees, I'm not sure."

"Maybe both. We'll see. Anyway, he's not Connie's type." She picked up our dishes and hurried into the kitchen.

I'd heard that before—in high school. "That's for Connie to decide."

"Then don't play matchmaker." She said nothing for a moment. "Dick's wedding was harder on Connie than she's let on. A call from a reasonably attractive man may give her ego a boost." She came back to the dining room and motioned for me to sit down. She took a deep breath. "Before I go meet Fargo and his parents, we have to talk about *your* love life."

No we didn't. Before I could say that, the phone rang.

Annalynn picked up the hall phone and listened a moment. "Hold on, Tiny. I'm going to put this on speaker so Phoenix can hear. Start again."

I joined her in the hall.

Tiny said, "When I came to your house, a man was sitting in a rental car in front of the second house to your right. He was looking at a map. He's still there. I don't like it."

Neither did I. I hurried to the window to look up the street beyond my parents'—my—house. The neighbor's lilac bush hid all but a corner of the car's trunk. I returned to the phone. "Where are you?"

"Around the corner a block to your right."

I mapped out the neighborhood in my head. "Go through three backyards until you reach a house with a brick wall about waist high. Get him in your sights and call me. I'll walk up the sidewalk toward him."

"I'll be in place with my rifle ready in two or three minutes."

"Hold on, you two," Annalynn ordered. "You're prepared to

shoot a man for parking on the street. He could be completely innocent."

We couldn't chance it. "It's already too hot to sit in a car."

Tiny said, "We won't shoot unless he displays a weapon."

Annalynn bit her lower lip. "For God's sake, be sure what you're doing." She took a deep breath. "I'm coming with you. Tiny, call my cell when you're ready. We'll keep the connection open as we go toward the car." She gave him the number.

I raced upstairs to get my Glock. I wanted it in my hand, but I needed to hide it. I grabbed a big-brimmed straw hat Annalynn insisted I wear when I tended my yard.

Achilles waited at the foot of the stairs, his tail still and his posture anxious.

Annalynn came down the stairs. A long blouse covered her holster.

I had an idea. "Keep Achilles with you. When we approach the car, tell him to bark. That will draw the driver's attention and let me sneak up to get the drop on him."

"Okay. Don't shoot unless you have to." She hesitated on the bottom step. "I need to tell you about the Foundation Center's message yesterday."

Her cell rang.

I opened the door. "That can wait. We have to get out there before the guy spots Tiny."

She answered the phone. "Tiny, I'm going to use Achilles to distract the driver while Phoenix sneaks up on him." She opened the door. "Heel, Achilles. Come with me."

She stayed at my right side, sheltering me, as we strolled down her front walk to the sidewalk. She moved ahead of me as we turned right to move toward the car.

Placing my faith in my Glock and Tiny's rifle, I dropped a step behind and moved to her left. The guy in the car had a clear shot at me if he planned to take one.

We passed my house. His head moved to watch us in his rearview mirror.

Annalynn said. softly, "Tiny says his right hand is on the steering wheel. His left arm is on the door. He's harmless."

Why couldn't she see the risk? "Be ready on a count of five."

The moment Achilles barked I dropped the hat, ducked down behind the trunk, and raced to the passenger door. I put the barrel of the gun against the neck between a blue starched collar and gray-flecked brown hair. "Don't move."

"Good morning, Phoenix. You're still a beautiful woman. That shade of green always suited you."

The voice of the man who had vowed to love, honor, and cherish me.

Stunned, I lowered my gun and walked away.

Chapter Ten

I couldn't believe Russ had come to Laycock. I hadn't seen him since we signed the divorce papers. Halfway to the castle, I looked over my shoulder to make sure I wasn't dreaming.

Annalynn stood by the driver's window.

Bile rose in my throat. When she said we needed to talk about my love life, she'd meant about my ex-husband, not my would-be lover. She'd known Russ was coming. She suspected he was the man in the car. No wonder she told Tiny and me to be careful.

Achilles trotted toward me, glancing back at her, obviously confused as to where his duty lay.

Fuming, I marched across her yard and stomped up the porch steps. Out of the corner of my eye, I saw the car door open. I went inside, leaving Achilles on the porch. I couldn't resist peeking through the dining room window. Russ held a cane—a shillelagh—in his left hand and carried a large black briefcase in his right. Once drop-dead handsome, he'd aged well, but without his squared shoulders and cocky stride, he appeared almost frail. He hadn't lost that beautiful baritone voice—the kind made for radio and foreplay.

Anger at Annalynn's betrayal swept through me like a fire through straw. I doused it, but it left me light-headed. Unleashed anger leads to foolish mistakes. Better go through the underground passage between our houses and take off.

Reason reasserted itself. Why should I run? He meant nothing to me anymore. I'd spent less than two years married to him, and that was more than half a lifetime ago. I'd loved and left and led a satisfying life.

They approached the porch. She took his briefcase in her right hand and his elbow in her left hand to help him up the steps.

I dashed up the stairs to my bedroom and closed the door. And opened it to strain my ears to overhear their conversation. They went into the dining room. I could hear nothing but the murmur of their voices.

Achilles trotted into my room with his ball. He dropped it to lick my hand.

I stroked his head to reassure him all was well. That calmed us both. Annalynn's steps sounded in the downstairs hall. I rushed to stretch out on my bed, resolved to control my anger and keep my mouth shut until she explained the inexplicable.

She came into my room, closed the door, and leaned against it. "You're furious with me."

"How perceptive." I waited, staring at the ceiling.

"I'm sorry to surprise you this way. The Foundation Center's message said he'd call before he came. I didn't expect him to be sitting in that car."

The Foundation Center? I made the connection. "He's the *pro bono* lawyer." That didn't explain his coming here, and it didn't excuse Annalynn's behavior. I continued to stare at the ceiling.

"He didn't call because he was afraid you would refuse to see him. He's been sitting in the car twenty minutes trying to work up the courage to ring the doorbell."

"At least *he* had some concept of my feelings." I turned onto my side, putting my back to her.

"Please, Phoenix, look at me. I'm so sorry to have—umm—ambushed you. I started to tell you last night, but those shots interrupted. I was trying to tell you when Tiny called." She waited for an answer I didn't give her. "I Googled him after the call. He had bypass surgery last December. He's recovering from knee replacement surgery. He wants to—to take care of unfinished business."

I sat up to face her. "And his wishes are more important to you than mine?"

She stepped toward me, her hands outstretched. "No, of course not. Phoenix, I think *you* need to talk to him."

I couldn't hold back any longer. I leapt to my feet to reinforce my words. "*You* think! This isn't like your convincing my mother to buy me the white rather than the green prom dress, Annalynn. I've made my own decisions for many years and been quite happy with them. I chose to erase Russ from my love life more than thirty years ago."

She didn't blink. "Really? Then you have no reason not to go downstairs and accept his help."

Good point. I had no apt answer. But she'd always had the knack of maneuvering people to do what she thought was best. I'd learned to stand my ground as a toddler. Surely she didn't expect to manipulate me now. Emotionally spent, I sank down on the bed and tried a different tack. "How did he find out I'm here? Did you contact him?"

"No, of course not! The Foundation Center assigned him our request for legal advice because of the Missouri connection. He didn't come from Washington to see you. He's visiting family in Columbia and Kansas City."

An excuse, not a reason. "He didn't drive a couple of hours out of his way to do a little paperwork. What's he really after?"

She bit her lower lip and ducked her head. "Maybe he's realized he's not immortal."

That shut me up. She had connected my ex's health problems with the death of her husband. Grief made people irrational. I considered what she'd said. Russ had begged me to forgive him from the time I caught him cheating until I signed the divorce papers. I couldn't. I had loved, admired, and trusted him. For me he'd gone from Dr. Jekyll to Mr. Hyde.

Achilles whined and nuzzled my hand.

I scratched him behind the ear a bullet had almost torn off. "Why would Russ want to see me now? More important to me, why do you care?"

She stepped forward and kissed me on the forehead. "Because I care about you. Because you once told me he's the only man you ever really loved. Because you've carried a distrust of men into every relationship you've had since then. When you start to love them, you find a reason to push them away. Just the way you're doing with Stuart right now." She sat down on the bed beside me and took my hand in hers. "I don't care about Russ. I want you to forgive him—really forgive him, not just say the words—so you can *forget* him."

For a nanosecond I wondered if she was right. No way. "As Mom would say, hogwash. I forgot him years ago."

She squeezed my hand. "Then go downstairs and accept his help. You know we need it to complete those forms."

Suckered. "I'll be down as soon as I brush my hair."

She walked to the door and paused, her back to me, her shoulders rigid. "Do you mind if I go on to the office? I'm already late."

"Go ahead." If I cussed him out, I'd prefer to do it in private. "Tell him I'll be down in a couple of minutes."

I brushed my hair and applied subtle makeup. Might as well look good. By the time I went downstairs, curiosity had conquered dread.

Russ rose from his chair on the far side of the table and tucked his thumb into his belt, a sign of nervousness. He looked almost exactly as his father had at our wedding. Bifocals didn't hide the sky-blue eyes gazing at me with the same appreciative intensity that had made my heart hammer at twenty.

My heart held steady. I extended my hand. "Hello, Russ. Sorry about the gun. We're cautious now that Annalynn's sheriff. I wasn't expecting you."

He grasped my hand and didn't let go. His smile hinted at our past.

"Let me get you some coffee." I extracted my hand.

"No, thanks. Annalynn gave me some lemonade."

He used to drink coffee by the gallon. I poured myself a cup and added lots of milk. I sat down across from him, the papers I'd puzzled over between us. I waited, but he watched me with a half smile and said nothing.

His attention both flattered and annoyed me. I broke the silence: "You're working for the Foundation Center?"

"Only an occasional *pro bono* assignment. When I left the Hill, I joined a political consulting company." He leaned his elbows on the table. "I couldn't believe you'd come back to Laycock after living in Vienna so many years."

He'd kept track of me. An alarm bell dinged. Had he used his contacts on the Hill to learn I'd been an undercover operative? Surely not. I gave him my cover story: "I came back to sell my parents' house."

He nodded. "And stayed to help Annalynn. Is that why you're establishing this foundation? Setting up Annalynn to run for the House?"

How in hell did he know she planned to run? Maybe this visit concerned the present rather than the past. "Cut to the chase, Russ. Why are you here?"

He raised a restraining hand. "Don't take offense. That's not a criticism. The foundation is an inspired ploy. I wouldn't have recognized it as such if a savvy political observer like Vernon Kann hadn't talked to one of our clients about initiating Annalynn's primary campaign." He leaned forward. "Phoenix, she's months behind. She's received wonderful press because of the way she's taken over as sheriff, but a wide-open race like this comes along about once a decade. Everyone is jumping in. She faces huge odds."

My stomach knotted. He knew what he was talking about. "You came to warn us off? To tell *me* that Annalynn shouldn't run?"

"No, no. I came to help." He took a deep breath and stretched his right hand across the table to within an inch of my left. "And to see you, to tell you once more that I'm sorry. I was an arrogant, self-indulgent fool. It took me years to get over losing you, and I've never stopped kicking myself for the way I hurt you."

I thought of the life we would have led. His path would have been the same. I would have been the supportive spouse. Bored stiff. His cheating had given me the push to do what I was meant to do. Forget past wounds. Consider Annalynn's future. I said what he wanted to hear: "You hurt me deeply, Russ, but I got over it a long time ago." Now be humble. "I appreciate your concern, and I welcome your legal and political advice."

He cocked his head and grinned. "You look like Phoenix. You don't sound like Phoenix. I expected you to spit fire." He put his briefcase on the table and took out a black folder. "This information will tell you how to finish filing the papers. I made some notes on the political ramifications, too."

I forced myself not to reach for the folder. He was a Washington insider, every bit as cynical as I was and just as likely to have a secret agenda. I decided to throw him off balance by telling the truth: "If this foundation gives Annalynn's campaign traction, great. Our main purpose is to provide financial counseling and assistance to crime victims—primarily women—and their families." And to give Annalynn a desperately needed salary.

He straightened his shoulders and put on his lawyer face. "Phoenix, you've laid out a worthwhile but very ambitious plan. Are you aware what carrying it out will cost?"

His condescension irritated me. "Of course I am. Why do you think I want to be sure the money I donate will be tax deductible?"

"Ahhh. I see. Now that you're back in the States, you face tax problems." He fiddled with the folder. "To protect your assets, I need to know what they are."

Apparently he'd forgotten I wasn't an idiot. I kept my face and voice neutral. "I'm an expert on Eastern European investments. Part of my income comes from those." Say something to imply I trusted him. "I do most of my banking overseas."

He smiled wryly. "Of course. I'm on my way to visit my brother in Kansas City. He's a tax lawyer who knows much more about this than I do. I'll review the tax implications with him before I give you my final recommendations. I'll stop by on my way back to Columbia next Sunday afternoon to answer any questions. I'd also like to meet with Vernon and Annalynn an hour or so to talk about their campaign plans."

"I'm sure they'll be delighted to meet with you." He definitely was up to something. He knew Annalynn couldn't raise the money for big-time consultants.

"Excellent." He handed me a sheet from the folder. "We need to go over these points."

We worked together for an hour—lawyer and client, no visible emotion on either side. He answered my questions and pointed out problems I hadn't identified.

When we finished, he said, "One thing you should tackle immediately: finding some prestigious nonpolitical backers for this foundation. Annalynn knows the local ones. A grant from a big national foundation would add credibility, too. If you provide all the money, the opposition will say the foundation is a political organization."

Annalynn and I had already figured those things out. "Thanks for the advice." I'd seen the advantages of letting men underestimate me. I added, "I'm out of my depth when it comes to politics."

He raised a skeptical eyebrow.

I smiled guilelessly, confident of my ability to deceive.

He picked up a notepad and opened his briefcase. A four-by-six photo fell out.

Russ pretended not to notice. Playing along, I picked it up. For a moment I thought I was looking at a teenaged Russ, but the clothes were contemporary. I handed the photo to him. "Your son?"

"Yes. We call him R. J." He ran the tips of his fingers across the photo before placing it in the briefcase. "He's a great kid. He and I flew to Columbia to get him settled at the university. He's going to study journalism."

My ex-husband was pointing out the son I'd never had, the child I'd wanted to have with him. He waited for a comment. I wouldn't say R. J. was handsome—like his father. I followed a hunch to zing back: "Are you two close?"

Russ focused on closing the briefcase. "I've worked on that since—since I left the Hill." He brushed his left hand over his heart. "I hoped he would go to Georgetown or the University of Virginia. He wanted to get away."

That confirmed Russ had neglected his son until a health crisis changed priorities. Not my worry. "I'll walk you to your car." I'd left my gun upstairs. "Back in a sec."

I dashed upstairs, strapped on my Glock, and slipped on a white blouse to cover it.

Russ watched me coming down the stairs. "You went to get that gun. What's going on here, Phoenix? Why are you acting like Laycock is Deadwood?"

I went to the dining room window and checked the street. No one in sight. "Right now, that's exactly what it is."

We walked to the car like casual acquaintances. He gave me a business card with his personal cell phone number scribbled on it. I thanked him for his help. He drove away.

I didn't buy that advising us on the foundation required a personal meeting or that his brush with death had compelled him to apologize, again, in person. He could be trolling for clients, but no one spent big money on campaigns in this district. One thing for sure, Russ came to Laycock because he wanted something.

Chapter Eleven

As Russ pulled away, Achilles nudged my hand to remind me we hadn't taken our morning run. The heat and my reluctance to be a target convinced me to substitute a game of indoor fetch. We played in Annalynn's basement and the tunnel built between the Carr and Smith houses as a bomb shelter. While he chased the ricocheting ball, I remembered how thrilled I'd been when Russ, the sexy law student, flirted with me, a nerdy undergraduate.

I sent Achilles out back to visit the hummingbirds while I called Vernon Kann. He'd tipped us off that the U.S. House of Representatives incumbent would retire and encouraged Annalynn to run. He'd know whether Annalynn needed Russ. The veteran newspaperman also would be able to fill me in on Fargo, Derek Gribble, and possibly the Cantrees.

I despised the prying press in general, but I respected Vernon.

He picked up on the first ring. "Phoenix, just the person I want to talk to. I'm about to post an update on last night's shooting. How about a quote from the target?"

How did he know I was the target? He didn't. He was fishing. He certainly knew he wouldn't get a quote from me. I ignored the question. "I have other news for you. Russ Torrint just left here."

"Torrint, Torrint . . . Oh, yes, the political consultant's husband. She e-mailed me this morning that he's in Missouri and might come by."

"Russ didn't mention he worked for his wife. He and I talked mostly about the foundation. He's coming back through Sunday to finish up and to meet with you and Annalynn." I didn't look forward to that. "Do you need him?"

"Yes and no. We can't afford to hire Janet Rockney's firm, but if they put a good word in the right party ears, Annalynn could get national support."

Bloody hell! I had to be nice to Russ *and* his wife. "Vernon, this could get complicated. I was married to Russ in my misguided youth."

"Oh. I didn't know that. Was it an amicable divorce?"

"Not on my side." Enough about my personal life. "That's not my immediate concern. I need to pick your brain for some information related to last night's shooting, but what we discuss has to be strictly off the record."

"Damn it, Phoenix. That's not fair." An exaggerated sigh. "I'll agree to deep background—no indication of source."

I wanted to be sure we were on the same page: "No direct use of any information I give you. You use it only as a guide to other lines of inquiry."

"Will you confirm or deny what we find?"

"Only off the record." We'd worked this way before. We'd both benefited. "Let's start with Fargo."

"Thought you'd never ask. I called Paul, my grandson, after I saw the YouTube video. He went to school with Fargo, aka Frank Klimton and Spiderman. In grade school he loved to put insects in the girls' desks. The peer review: He's an overachiever desperate to be popular. He plays keyboard and put together a decent high school band. Paul says he's impulsive and careless, the kind of idiot who might pull a gun without making sure it wasn't loaded."

More info than I'd expected. Vernon was good. "Do you know his family?"

"Not well. His father is dean of students at the college. He strikes me as a decent sort. Mrs. Klimton works in the insurance department at the hospital. They have an older son at Truman State, which shows he's a far better student than Fargo. That could be part of the boy's problem."

I knew what he meant. My younger brother groused that I made his life miserable by raising teachers' expectations. "Any arrests? Drugs? Cruelty to animals? Shoplifting?"

"Not that we've heard about. From the research I've done for the follow-up on the shootout Saturday, I'd say the Cantrees are more likely suspects. I'll e-mail my article and my notes to you and Annalynn this afternoon."

"Thanks. They aren't the only other suspects." Distrust of the press almost stopped me, but I needed Vernon's input. "What do you know about Derek Gribble?"

He whistled. "I wasn't expecting that name. What connects him to the shooting at La Vida Loca?"

I told him what Connie and I had observed at Mrs. T's house and Kiki's reaction to finding us there.

"I'd say that makes Gribble a better suspect than the boy. Jim or Annalynn must have questioned both by now. What did they say?"

"Both denied it. Jim has nothing conclusive one way or the other."

"I'll check out Gribble." Silence. "I'll also interview our local and state government people for an article on elder abuse—how to spot it, where to report it, what to do about it, possible consequences."

"Good idea. A community service." Why didn't the press do more of this? "Besides, the article may scare the Gribbles straight. What can you tell me about them right now?"

"Let me think." Keys clicked in the background. "I used to see Dorkas Tesopolis eating out with friends. She was a handsome woman in her day, vivacious, friendly. Quite a bit younger than her husband. She worked on a couple of charities with my late wife. I wouldn't have thought Dorkas the type to be bullied."

"She's dependent on her daughter now, an easy victim."

"True, but they were well off. Dorkas should be able to afford to have help come in, even hire a caregiver." He sighed. "Most people insist they can take care of themselves, and they certainly don't want to bring in a stranger. They expect a child, particularly a daughter, to give them any help they need. They're too proud to complain to an outsider if the child takes advantage of them. This article is a damned good idea."

Yes, but not my immediate concern. "Know anything about Gribble?"

"The name's familiar. I'm looking him up in our online archives." A faint clicking. "He lost his job when a furniture company closed. I did a follow-up story a few months ago on what happened to employees when local businesses went under. He refused to talk to me. Harry of Harry's Hideaway told me Gribble spends a lot of time there. He fancies himself a pool hustler and a ladies' man."

That fit with what I'd heard. "Anything about hunting or target shooting?"

"I'll find out if he shoots at that new target range outside of town."

"I'd appreciate that." I needed to give Vernon something. "A tip for you: Sheriff Towson is supporting the extension of Annalynn's appointment."

"Thanks. I'll call him for a quote. Tiny's a good sheriff. That will carry weight."

"What do you think about him as a person?"

"I've never heard anything negative, but we don't cover his county. Like many officers, he's divorced. They deal with trash all day and take the stench home with them."

I knew that stench all too well from my CIA work. I thanked Vernon and hung up.

Now what? I itched to get out of the house and find out more about Derek Gribble myself. I'd told Kiki I would check on her mother today. A visit would tell me whether the Gribbles had taken my warning seriously. With a few offhand questions to Mrs. T, maybe I could get a better read on her son-in-law.

A little after eleven I parked in the shade of her maple tree. I let Achilles out and pulled on my long-tailed white blouse to cover my holster. Giving him a new chew toy, I walked him to the backyard and told him to stay. The back door was closed. I went back around to the front, eased open the broken storm door, and knocked.

"Who there?"

"It's Phoenix Smith, Mrs. Tesopolis."

"Coming to door."

It took her almost a minute to open it.

She smiled up at me. "You bring my *ouzo,* Greek girl?"

"Not today, but I will." Cool air flowed out the door. She still had air conditioning. Did she have groceries? "Shall I make us a cup of tea instead?"

She backed her walker away from the door. She wore a pretty lime-green housecoat with lots of white embroidery. "Tea is not so good as *ouzo,* but tea is good." She pointed at the television playing a game show in her living room. "My price is never right. Everything so expensive."

"Yes, it is." I helped her settle into her chair and went into the neat kitchen. I filled the kettle on her electric stove and took a tea bag from a box on the counter. I needed an excuse to open the refrigerator. "Do you like tea with milk or lemon?

"Just a teaspoon of sugar, please. Kiki bring me sugar this morning."

The threats had worked, at least temporarily. Good news for Mrs. T, but it didn't tell me whether Gribble was scared or mad enough to take a shot at me. I took the lid off the sugar bowl on the table. Empty. I opened cupboard doors until I found a small bag of sugar and some delicate white china cups and saucers with gold trim. Someone, probably Kiki, had scattered cans of soup, vegetables, tuna, and fruit on the shelves, most likely in an attempt to make them seem well stocked. I filled the sugar bowl and opened the refrigerator. Milk, eggs, margarine, and other basics. Not a wide selection, but more than Connie had seen yesterday. Relieved, I prepared the tea and took it into the living room.

Mrs. T turned off the television with her remote control. "Tell me how you like my Athens."

An easy subject for both of us. After a few minutes of listening to my impressions of Athens and Greek food, she told me what she remembered of her childhood before her family fled to the States to escape the hard times after World War II. I got up to look at the family photos on the piano. One was Kiki's wedding photo. The groom had brown hair and eyes, a square jaw, broad shoulders, and a long body over short legs.

When I commented on the wedding photo, her face clouded. I pointed to an amateurish but striking oil painting of the Acropolis hanging over the piano. "This is lovely. Did you paint it?"

She smiled. "My Kiki painted long ago. She has much talent." She grimaced. "Now she paints walls." Mrs. T moved her right hand up and down as though wielding a big paintbrush. She struggled to her feet. "I show you her painting." Leaning on the walker, she led the way to a room I hadn't entered the day before.

Paintings covered the walls above the furniture—a dresser cluttered with brushes and sketchpads, a single bed submerged under pillows with Greek scenes, a glass cabinet holding trophies and treasures. Near the window stood an empty easel and a card table with neatly arranged tubes of paint. Dust covered everything.

"Wow!" I began my walk around the gallery with the crayon drawings on my right and, commenting as I went, proceeded around the room to increasingly sophisticated work. Kiki's talent resembled LaDawna's—deep but undisciplined. LaDawna had time to develop her voice. Kiki would remain a hobbyist. I paused before a sketch of a statue of Socrates in a park. The "r" on the label was reversed. Kiki must be dyslexic.

"Many talents, my Kiki," Mrs. T said, pride in her voice, tears in her eyes. "Many awards."

I peered into the cabinet at ribbons, medals, and assorted trophies. I forced my eyes to flit by a familiar one—first in the junior division turkey shoot. My matching trophy was in a box in my parents' basement. If Kiki had continued to practice, she could easily have made that pattern above my head last night. Add one more suspect to the list.

I commented on a baton wrapped in ribbons from twirling competitions and eased Mrs. T back to her chair in the living room.

"Kiki is certainly talented." I wondered why this only child hadn't pursued a brighter future, and why she'd stayed with a man like Derek. "What kind of work does her husband do?"

"He drives truck." Mrs. T spoke brusquely, discouraging further questions.

Distressing her was the last thing I intended. "Do you have any other relatives in Laycock?"

She shook her head. "My brothers and sisters died. My nieces and nephews live in California and Texas."

No one near enough to be of any help. Her body sagged. She picked up some amber worry beads and fingered them. How could I cheer her up? "I hope you taught them all how to make baklava."

She straightened. "I will teach you, Greek girl."

"I'd love that." It would give me an excuse to check on her. I glanced at my watch. Noon. I stood up. "But not today. I have to go. When you have time, please list the ingredients for me to buy. One day we'll make baklava."

She reached for her walker. "When you come again?"

I motioned for her to stay seated. "I don't dare come again until I find you some *ouzo.*" How would I get out of drinking the awful stuff? I picked up the cups. Kiki could have spotted my car and be waiting to take another shot. "I left my dog in your backyard, so I'll take the cups to the kitchen and go out the back door."

The moment I opened the door, Achilles jumped up and trotted toward the car.

"Sorry if you were bored." I drew my Glock and walked along the edge of the yard next to an undisciplined hedge. Achilles loped back to my side, nose in the air and eyes perplexed. He didn't know someone had shot at me last night.

Next time I intended to shoot first.

Chapter Twelve

No one lurked outside Mrs. T's house. No one followed me as I drove toward the castle, the most likely place for a shooter to plan an ambush. I drove around the block twice before parking in my garage and quick-stepping into the castle. I checked the four motion-sensitive cameras I'd set up: two in Annalynn's backyard, one in mine, and one on her front porch. Her backyard was the most likely entry point because the orchard behind it provided cover for anyone coming from the street. If the alarm went off, I could watch the cameras' transmissions on my laptop or the television.

My cell phone rang. Stuart. Berating myself for being both cowardly and rude, I didn't answer. He didn't leave a message.

The house phone rang. Stuart? I checked the caller ID. JRC with a McLean, Virginia, number. A CIA handler calling from a shell company? I picked up. "Keyser residence."

"Mrs. Keyser?" An unfamiliar woman's voice, low and pleasant but brisk.

"She's at work. May I take a message?"

"Actually I'm trying to reach Russell Torrint. Is he there?"

JRC—Janet Rockney Consulting. "He left for Kansas City about two hours ago."

"This is Russ's wife. To whom am I speaking?"

Well, well. I smiled to warm my voice. "This is Phoenix Smith."

The silence told me she'd recognized my name and hadn't

expected to hear it. Curious, I waited.

She finally said, "I'm a little worried. His cell keeps going to voice mail."

I heard concern, not suspicion. "He's probably in a no-service area for his provider. Coverage is spotty out here."

"Yes, of course. That must be it. Thanks." She hung up.

I'd taken two steps when the phone rang twice. The sheriff's department. My anger at Annalynn surged as I answered.

She got right to business: "The FBI has finished at the farmhouse. Tiny wants us to bring Achilles out about three to look around. Are you free?"

What could he possibly expect Achilles to find? "I can be."

"Since we're going out that way, I'd like to set up cameras at those two cemeteries." She spoke in her sheriff voice. "How long would it take us to do that?"

I matched her tone: "If the equipment is in order, I can rig one up in a quarter of an hour."

"Good. I'll be home in a few minutes."

"Have an officer follow you," I cautioned before hanging up. I smiled as I walked to the kitchen. Annalynn would be trapped in the car with me for more than an hour. She'd have plenty of time to explain that crack about Russ's cheating affecting my relationship with Stuart.

Hold on. Her emotional fragility had brought on a breakdown in the cemetery. Going back there would be hard for her. So would returning to the scene of the shootout.

Concern and anger wrestled as I put the untouched meals we'd brought from La Vida Loca onto plates and squeezed lemons for lemonade. Neither emotion won. I had to be sensitive to her feelings but make it clear I wouldn't tolerate her interference. Burying my anger would hurt both of us, as individuals and as a team.

When I heard her car pull into the driveway, I put our meals in the microwave and tried to think of an opening line. I stayed quiet as she came in the front door, stood in the hall for several seconds, and then walked slowly toward the kitchen.

At the doorway, she licked her lips and planted her feet as though to withstand a physical attack.

Scheisse! She was more upset than I was. I picked up the pitcher. "I made fresh lemonade. We should take some with us this afternoon."

She blinked and put one hand on the doorframe as though for support. "Oh, Phoenix. You were so angry this morning. I was afraid . . ."

Her vulnerability alarmed me. I chose my words carefully: "I'm still angry. We're still friends." The microwave dinged. I busied myself taking out our meals. It would be condescending to treat her like anything but a strong woman. I glared at her. "I can't imagine why you thought you had the right to bring that man in this house."

The phone rang twice.

Annalynn fled to the hall to answer it. A few seconds later, she said, "Phoenix, I have to deal with something. Go ahead and eat. I'll have a snack as we drive out."

She was still on the phone in her home office when I finished eating. I went upstairs to change into green cotton slacks and a matching blouse that would blend into vegetation. When I came downstairs, a blue Kevlar vest was draped over the banister. I ignored it.

Annalynn emerged from her office and handed me a manila folder. "These are Vern's notes on the Cantrees. I'm going up to put on civvies. I don't want someone to drive by the cemetery and see the sheriff there."

Before I could open the folder, Achilles demanded my attention. I gave him fresh water and a couple of biscuits. Then I made a turkey sandwich for Annalynn.

She came down the stairs in cream slacks and a long-tailed navy blouse that hid her holster and her Kevlar vest from casual glances. She tossed the other vest to me. "We're running late. Put this on under your blouse."

"It's hot and it doesn't fit," I protested. "More important, these don't stop bullets coming out of anything bigger than a handgun, and then only if the shooter is nice enough to aim at the vest."

"Don't be difficult. The department requires all officers to wear vests while on duty. You're on duty. Put it on. Please."

Achilles whined and looked at me and then at Annalynn and then at me. Tension between us upset him.

I gave up. "We're just discussing, Achilles. It's okay." I took off my blouse and put on the vest while Annalynn fussed over him. "He's quite right," I said. "We have to be on high alert, not discuss . . . issues."

"Good, but . . . was it awful for you to talk to Russ?"

I thought about it as I retrieved her sandwich, the thermos of lemonade, and the folder. "Not really. He's still the jerk I divorced, but he knows his stuff. By the way, he wants to meet with you and Vernon Sunday afternoon."

She opened the front door. "Why? Vern has no formal role with the foundation."

My cynical self was relieved that she didn't know Russ had become a political consultant. "He works for Janet Rockney's firm." I checked the street.

"Vern mentioned her. He said she's very good."

So Annalynn didn't know my ex was the consultant's current. I'd save that little surprise for later.

Annalynn locked the door behind us. "Do people recognize my SUV?"

Her personal vehicle was rigged to serve as her official one, but it had no markings. "I doubt it. This is SUV territory. I'll drive." And keep a sharp eye out for anyone following us.

She nibbled on the sandwich and went through papers in the folder as we left Laycock. "Here's an obituary for Orson. Divorced. Parents deceased. His survivors include two children, Orson, Jr., seventeen, of Cleveland, and Madonna, nineteen, of Dayton. An older sister lives in Tucson. Roscoe might go there, I suppose. Orson's brother, Norval, lives in Boonville. No cousins listed. Tiny will give us their names."

"The kids' mother may have siblings living around here. They're more likely to talk to police than the Cantrees are. What else?"

"Articles on arrests or convictions. The newest one is seven years old. Roscoe Cantree, visiting from Detroit, beat up a man outside a bar after a high-stakes poker game. Roscoe is the cousin Tiny suspects. Here's one from twenty years ago about Roscoe crashing into a police car. Tiny was the arresting officer."

She flipped through several pages. "No more about Roscoe. Various Cantrees, various small crimes—shoplifting, joyriding, DUI. All at least fifteen years old. Apparently the Cantrees either left the area or reformed after that." She read silently for a couple of minutes. "Orson received two years for assaulting his eighteen-year-old pregnant wife, Shirley Sue. It doesn't give her maiden name. That was twenty years ago." She went to the next page. "Here's a coincidence for you: Roscoe and two juveniles were arrested for vandalizing rural cemeteries, one of them Oak Grove."

"When?"

"Almost thirty years ago." She held up the last page. "Vern sent me the link to Janet Rockney's website. He says he found her photo intriguing."

We'd reached Oak Grove Church. No one was in sight behind or ahead of us. I turned in and drove down the dirt road beyond the parking lot to conceal the SUV in the high grass behind the church. Three old oak trees provided dense shade.

Achilles sniffed the air and ran off to explore. Annalynn carried a box with a camera, portable battery, and transmitter to the first row of gravestones. "The corn is so thick anyone could disappear between the stalks in a few feet and we'd never find them. Where shall we put the camera?"

I scanned the area. "On one of those old fence posts still standing in that far corner by the sumac."

Avoiding the new grave where Annalynn had collapsed, I led the way across the graveyard and found a post sturdy enough to hold the camera. I had to break off a couple of twigs to give the lens a clear view, but it would be fairly well hidden.

Achilles trotted up and stared into the cornfield to my left. I motioned to Annalynn to get down and sprinted for a six-foot obelisk. Achilles barked once and trotted toward the corn.

"Hello," a man called. "Who's in the cemetery?"

Didn't sound threatening. "Who's in the corn?"

"Mark Keller." An older man in a big straw hat and baggy overalls emerged from the tall, dense stalks. He held a shotgun across his body.

I came from behind the obelisk but kept my gun in my hand. "I'm Phoenix Smith. You have a permit for that gun?"

"Don't need one. I'm on my own land." He grinned. "You must be that unnamed lady deputy." He raised his trigger hand in greeting to Annalynn. "Glad to see you out here tendin' to business, Sheriff Keyser."

"Hi, Mark. How did you know we were here?"

"Your dog came trottin' through the corn into my yard a little bit ago."

Annalynn pointed to the camera. "We're setting up a night-vision camera with a motion sensor. It will transmit photos to my office if the vandals come again."

He cocked his head. "Think you could get here in time to catch 'em?"

"It depends on where our closest squad car is. Even if we don't, the camera will help us identify them. I appreciated your nine-one-one call Saturday night. Please don't go after them by yourself."

"Heck, no." He patted his shotgun. "I scared them off with a shot in the air."

I could barely see the roof of a house beyond the tall corn. "How did you know someone was here Saturday night?"

"I woke up and looked out my upstairs window. A light over here was a lot bigger than any lightning bug. I reckon they set one of them battery lanterns on a tombstone. I watched it for a minute and then called nine-one-one. They said it would take a while for anyone to get here, so I fired my shotgun."

"You did exactly the right thing," Annalynn said. "Could you see how many people were here?"

"Nope. Just the light. After I fired, I heard a car start. I saw you come by about an hour after I called. I was pretty mad about you taking so long to get here—till I heard you'd fought a battle with the Cantree boys. I thought we'd run those ornery cusses off years ago."

Hmm. Maybe he could tie the loose ends together for us. "I understand Roscoe still has friends around here."

He grinned, displaying yellowed teeth. "I doubt it. I don't think he ever had any friends. He ran around some with Orson even though he was younger. Before their voices changed, they got drunk as skunks and raced around in an old jeep. I caught them trying to steal my tractor one night and called the sheriff. He let them go. I told them if I saw them here again"—he patted his shotgun—"I'd shoot, not talk."

Annalynn shifted uneasily. "I'd appreciate it if you don't

mention the camera to anyone. The vandals probably live nearby."

"Sure," he extended his hand. "You're doing a fine job. You run for anything, you got my vote. My sympathies for the loss of your husband."

Annalynn donned her public face as she shook his hand.

He walked back into the corn and disappeared.

Russ had been wrong about Annalynn getting a late start on her campaign to run for the House. Without my realizing it, the campaign had begun. Every action she took as sheriff would win or lose her votes.

Chapter Thirteen

I felt like a lobster in the pot by the time we finished setting up both cameras, but Annalynn threw a fit when I suggested shedding the Kevlar vest. We pulled into the grassy dirt drive leading to the abandoned farmhouse at five after three and backed into the weeds on the other side of an unmarked beige Ford 150 pickup. Tiny Towson stepped out of a tree's dark shadow, a rifle in his hands.

Did he really fear a Cantree might lurk nearby, or was he making a point? No sign of a backup. He'd come in a personal vehicle, but then so had Annalynn.

Achilles had been fine at the cemeteries, but he whined and held back when I opened the car door here.

"He remembers this is a bad place," Annalynn said. She walked toward Tiny.

I pulled my Glock and stayed by the car until Achilles jumped out and trotted after Annalynn. Holding my gun at my side, I followed slowly. "Achilles doesn't like this place. We better do whatever you want him to do fast."

Achilles sneezed three times.

Tiny pointed at him. "He's the one thing that differentiates you from everyone else here Saturday night. He could be the reason you were the target at the restaurant."

I doubted Tiny's theory. "What could anyone possibly think he would sniff out? He can find drugs and explosives. He can't smell Krugerrands."

Annalynn inhaled sharply. "He can smell people. Could the other two be hiding in a cave or tunnel?"

Tiny shook his head. "The FBI brought in dogs and combed every inch for at least a mile." He ground his teeth. "Damn it! There's got to be something here."

He was grasping at straws. I knelt by Achilles. He'd calmed down enough to watch squirrels playing in a hickory tree, but he remained uneasy. "We have to retrace our steps, boy."

He sneaked in two licks on my cheek and grinned at me.

I stood up. "We'll do it in reverse, starting at the front door."

Achilles refused to let me approach either doorway—the doors were gone—but didn't object when we looked in the windows. The place was bare. When we gathered around where the Cantrees had crawled out from under the house, Achilles' attention wandered to a blue jay flitting from branch to branch in a tree.

Tiny swore under his breath. "One of them has gotta be Roscoe. The bastard grew up in this house. I played basketball with him in high school. He was the dirtiest player I ever saw." He checked himself when his phone rang. He handed me his rifle and stepped away to answer it.

Uneasy in the open, I moved into the brush where the deputy and I'd taken cover.

Tiny put away his phone and joined us. "They got the getaway driver. He drove the Cantrees to a parking lot near the bank. Then he switched to the second stolen car and drove to the airport short-term parking lot. The driver couldn't have been the fourth person here."

Annalynn frowned. "You're sure four people came to the farmhouse?"

"The camera picked up only a blurry shoulder, but I'm pretty sure there was a fourth person." He wiped sweat from his forehead. "The FBI isn't ready to announce it, but Roscoe's a person of interest. He's a known gambler. A casino near here deposited five hundreds from the robbery in a bank this morning. I'd bet he's still in the area."

Annalynn and I exchanged glances. Orson Cantree's brother lived in Boonville, home to a casino.

Tiny reclaimed his rifle. "I've notified all the banks, gas stations, convenience stores, and bars in the county to let me know immediately if anyone gives them a hundred. I'll ask the neighboring counties to do the same." He frowned. "Too bad most of the bills they took were tens and twenties. They're practically impossible to spot."

Achilles raced into the brush after a zigzagging rabbit. We all jumped.

"Achilles! Come!" He obviously didn't sense anything amiss. "I think we're wasting our time, but let's finish up."

Tiny pointed to the rickety barn. "Let's take him to where they stashed the cars."

The place threatened to collapse. I stopped outside an opening wide enough for a loaded hay wagon, or two cars, to pull through. I saw no tread tracks. "Any clue what the second vehicle was?"

Tiny grimaced. "No, just that it had old tires. Orson bought the car he was driving about a month ago. The dealer wouldn't take his beat-up 2002 red Mustang as a trade-in. The mechanic who checked it told the FBI the body was in good shape but the engine would have blown before they got out of Ohio. He offered to buy the car for a couple hundred. He figured he could rebuild the engine and sell the car."

I thought about it. "The Mustang would have been too unreliable and too conspicuous for anyone making a getaway."

Achilles trotted into the barn and sniffed at a clod of mud.

The remains of a big mud-dauber nest. A wasp flew from another mud house on a rafter. "Achilles, come." I remembered my grandmother putting mud on a painful sting when I was a kid. I wheeled to follow the grassy track that curved down the small hill.

Tiny's phone rang again. He fell behind as Annalynn and I—eyes scanning the landscape—strolled toward the tree trunk that had protected us. Achilles trotted ahead until we approached the spot where Orson Cantree had died. Achilles came back and walked between us. By common consent we swerved around the spot. A chill went through me at the sight of the shredded leaves and broken twigs above and on both ends of our tree trunk. I braced for a flashback from the Istanbul bazaar. It didn't come.

Annalynn reached down to stroke Achilles. "I don't feel guilty for shooting them anymore. They did their best to kill us."

Traffic and rain hadn't erased the car's skid marks. Annalynn and I followed them to the tree trunk. Achilles held back.

"I count five bullet holes," Annalynn said as Tiny came up behind us.

He pointed to a hole two feet to the left of where Annalynn had crouched. "That one went through." He surveyed the fields behind us like a soldier on patrol. "I just got a summary of the autopsy report. Phoenix, you put three bullets in Orson's chest. Fine shooting." He took a deep breath and exhaled. "They found something else that I hope you can make sense of. I sure can't."

Bloody hell! I hated surprises. "What is it?"

"Orson had terminal lung cancer. He had maybe two months left. Why rob a bank? You can't take it with you."

Annalynn rubbed her temples. "Perhaps he wanted to provide for his family."

Tiny shook his head. "Don't think so. You can't count on the FBI to tell you anything, so Willetta—Lieutenant Volcker—has been digging for us. Orson's parole officer said he'd lived alone for three years. Court records show he didn't ask for visitation rights during the divorce, and he refused to take custody of his son and daughter when their mother died. As far as we can tell, the boy hadn't even visited him since the divorce—ten years ago—until this summer. Orson senior's landlord says Junior showed up in early July. Nobody knows where the daughter is. She ran away from a foster home and dropped out of sight at seventeen. She's probably on the streets or a Jane Doe in a morgue." He looked at me. "Any ideas?"

"Not a one." The whole damned day had been questions without answers. Why had Russ come? Was Annalynn right that I'd let my experience with him affect my relationships with men? What should I tell Stuart about meeting his children?

Annalynn touched my shoulder. "Ready to go?"

"Yes." The place gave me the willies. "We can't find any answers here."

Chapter Fourteen

As we walked back to our vehicles, Tiny confirmed that the only Cantree living in Missouri was Orson's younger brother, Norval.

When I asked for Orson's abused wife's maiden name, Tiny hesitated a long time before answering. "She was a Glasgow, the baby in her family. They tried to talk her out of marrying Orson. When he went to jail for assaulting her, her parents took her in. I heard that her father gave her an ultimatum when Orson was released: Divorce him or get out. She got out. With Orson and their baby girl."

Tiny had known these people better than he wanted to let on. "Could Orson have come back to settle the score with her father?"

"No. Her parents both died a few years ago. Her brother left right out of high school, like most kids did. And do. You won't find a single Glasgow on the voter list anymore." He opened his pickup door wide and stood back to let the hot air flow out. "You worked with a DEA friend of mine, Stuart Roper, last spring. Have you talked to him about this?"

Annalynn raised an eyebrow at me.

"No. Why do you ask?" I opened the SUV's front and rear doors.

"He knows several of the FBI agents, including Lester Wharton." Tiny placed his rifle in the built-in carrier. "Stuart called him early this afternoon and asked if the FBI was investigating the shooting at the restaurant."

Damn! I'd have to call Stuart. I smiled as if his call to the FBI didn't surprise me. Then it hit me: It shouldn't have. "I'll call Stuart this evening and fill him in."

Annalynn turned away, smoothed back her hair, and went to stand in the shade with Achilles. He clearly had no intention of getting into the SUV until I'd cooled it with the air conditioning. I'd made the mistake of humoring him—and myself—in June. Now he demanded a cooled car.

Tiny left, but Achilles and Annalynn stayed in the shade.

She patted her forehead with a handkerchief. "Do you think Roscoe will go to the casino again?"

"He's probably too smart to go back to any place where he's laundered money." I rethought that. "Maybe not. He was stupid to go there in the first place."

"He's a gambling addict." Annalynn came to the car. "Willetta told me the FBI found only a third of the stolen twenty thousand in Orson's car, so the four had already divided the cash take. Tiny thinks Orson hid his share of the coins somewhere around here and Roscoe won't leave until he can get to them."

"So that's why Tiny wanted us to meet him here. He's getting desperate. Even the FBI would have found them if they were here." I called to Achilles, "Come. It's cool."

He trotted over and hopped in.

Relieved to get out of the soggy air, I got behind the wheel. "Still, sticking around to recover missing loot makes sense. It also explains why the FBI suspects one of us of grabbing it." I thought about it as I pulled back onto the road. "Maybe Roscoe suspects us, too, and fired those shots at me during dinner." Didn't hold water. "He and his accomplice would have to assume that I—not any of the other people here—found the Krugerrands and somehow tracked me down last night."

"Doesn't seem likely. Besides, shooting you wouldn't give

them the coins."

"But the shooter aimed high. The shots might be a warning." A second thought: "But a warning requires a follow-up, like a call from a throwaway cell phone threatening to kill me if I don't hand over the coins. Nothing has happened."

Annalynn chewed on her lower lip. "Are you sure? You don't answer the phone if you don't want to talk to—people."

Connie must have complained. No, not Connie. "You mean Stuart. I didn't think he would hear about last night."

"Of course he heard. His mother called him the moment the news broke."

Wait a minute! With the road clear ahead and behind us, I pulled over to the edge and stopped. "How do you know she called him?"

Annalynn shifted to face me. "She was filling up at the gas station in the lane next to mine when he called. He was upset because you weren't answering either phone. Phoenix, why on earth were you so thoughtless?"

She sounded like my mother. "I had a few things on my mind—like my ex-husband suddenly appearing. It didn't occur to me that Stuart would be worried."

She reached over and shifted the SUV into park. "Why else would he be calling you? He always uses e-mail during a workday."

"I thought he was calling about something else."

She averted her eyes.

Bloody hell! She knew exactly why I had been avoiding his calls. Anger bubbled up and burst out. "You have no right to talk to Mrs. Roper about Stuart and me!"

Achilles stuck his head and shoulders between the seats and barked at me.

Scolded by my own dog. Unfairly. "You're taking her side."

He frowned and barked again.

Annalynn stroked him. "I'm always on your side, Phoenix." Her voice shook.

"I know." Guilt assailed me. Then I remembered her attempts to guide my and Connie's dating in high school. "I don't always trust your judgment when it comes to men."

She drew back in surprise. "Exactly what I was thinking about you."

Low blow. I'd not exactly applauded her choice of a good-ol'-boy jock either.

A tractor came around the corner behind us with a wide piece of equipment. I released the parking brake and took off to avoid getting stuck behind it. "Are you denying Mrs. Roper told you that Stuart wants me to meet his kids Saturday night?"

"Yes. Well, no. She asked me whether you prefer barbecued chicken or steak. She said Stuart's kids like both." She waited several seconds. "He told her you're spending Labor Day weekend with him. I never mentioned it."

I shuddered that my math teacher—she'd always be that to me—knew I was planning an intimate interlude with her son. "She told you that at the gas pump?"

Annalynn smoothed back her hair, still neatly tucked into a French roll. "No, when I ran into her in the grocery store. She's thrilled that you and Stuart are—let me remember how she put it—that you two are getting along so well."

I had an insight: "She expected you to tell me. She wanted me to know I have her approval to move to the next level with her son. Why didn't you say something?"

Annalynn pointed to the entry into a field ahead of us. "You better pull over."

Dreading whatever she felt compelled to tell me, I put on my poker face, stopped the SUV, and shifted to Park. "Okay. Let's have it."

She unfastened her seat belt.

"Bloody hell! Are you getting ready to jump out and run?"

"Don't be silly." She faced me and put her left hand on my right arm. "Promise you'll hear me through without exploding."

She'd scared me. I took a calming breath. "I promise. Go ahead."

"When Stuart came to Laycock in May, you two connected. You had physical chemistry. You worked well together. You claimed it was only a flirtation, but he clearly wanted more than that. I thought you did too when you agreed to spend Labor Day weekend with him. Then you started not answering his calls." She closed her eyes a moment and took a deep breath. "That's why I encouraged Russ to come inside and help you with the foundation papers."

My mouth dropped open. *"Encouraged?"*

"You promised to listen."

Achilles barked at me again.

I counted to ten in four languages before I dared answer. "Okay. Talk."

"Since you caught Russ cheating on you, you've dated at least a dozen men and had two or three serious relationships. You never moved on to a commitment."

For good reasons. How dare she? I clamped my mouth shut, afraid I'd say what I was thinking.

"Russ made you distrust men. I thought if you would realize that he was a young, arrogant fool, an aberration, you would—well, stop viewing Stuart as another potential Russ." She waited. "Well?"

Her assurance in being right offended me even more than her amateur psychology. I hadn't been so angry with her since . . . when? The last time she'd gently but persistently pushed me to do something for my own good. We'd had some terrific fights as kids over her playing Annalynn knows best. She didn't have the emotional stamina for one of those now. Did I? My experience as an operative took over. We were in a tough situation. Personal tension unleashed could be disastrous. "I'll give your theory some thought, Frau Doktor Freud. Meanwhile, butt out." I pulled back out onto the road. "Did you test your theory on Connie?"

Annalynn fastened her seat belt. "I mentioned you seemed to be following a pattern by backpedaling with Stuart."

I could vent by having it out with Connie. "And what did she say?"

Annalynn grimaced. "That you're old enough to know your own heart and I should butt out."

"You should have listened to Connie." I never thought I'd say those words.

Connie's yellow VW Bug was parked in the castle's driveway. When we opened the front door, I smelled a roast cooking.

Achilles raced to the kitchen to drool.

Connie came out of the ladies' parlor. "Hi. I got the names of forty people who were at the audition. I've already looked up a dozen on Facebook."

"Good work." I felt ashamed that she looked surprised to hear praise from me. "I'll give you a hand right after I call Stuart. The roast smells wonderful." I hurried upstairs, eager to say what I'd come up with during the silent ride home.

He answered on the first ring: "Phoenix, finally. What's going on? Who's shooting at you?"

"I don't know. Maybe the Cantrees, maybe a local guy. Sorry I didn't call you sooner." I pictured his lanky, well-muscled frame and open, pleasant face. "Annalynn and I just came back from a meeting with Tiny Towson at the farmhouse where the Cantrees camped out." I gave Stuart the whole story, a welcome catharsis. An office-bound DEA agent who'd spent time undercover, he asked all the right questions. He didn't have any new answers. I didn't tell him I knew he'd called the FBI agent.

He said, "Come stay with me while the FBI runs down the missing bank robbers."

"I can't leave Annalynn alone."

"I was afraid you'd say that. At least be careful."

"I will." This was my chance to say what I'd called to tell him: "Unless we find the shooter, we can't risk my coming to your mother's Saturday."

He said nothing for a moment. "That's very logical. It's also an excuse. Am I moving too fast for you?"

He had a knack for listening to what I said and cutting through the crap to what I meant. I owed him an honest answer. "I like you, Stuart, a lot, but I'm still adjusting to leaving my life in Vienna. I'm not sure I'm ready to meet your kids."

"I love you, Phoenix."

I caught my breath. He'd never said *that* before. I couldn't say it back.

He waited a moment and then went on: "I fantasized about you from puberty to long after I attended your wedding in a brand-new suit. It made me look like a grown-up, not the kid you remembered. It killed me when you didn't notice. I'm willing to let you set the pace. I'm not going to give up this time." He hung up.

For a moment I thought I'd have to breathe into a bag. I hadn't even considered marriage or even a long-term relationship for almost ten years, not since I found another woman's heavily perfumed scarf in Mario's suitcase when he returned from singing a role in Milan. Stuart was a wonderful companion and probably a good lover. I wouldn't lead him on. "Stay open a little while," I advised myself. "Meanwhile, don't get killed."

Picking up my laptop, I went downstairs. Annalynn and Connie were engrossed in something on the monitor. I looked over their shoulders at a photo of a woman with shoulder-length black hair and brown eyes. She looked eerily familiar.

"Uncanny," Connie said. "Change the hairstyle and you have her."

I drew a blank. "Who is that?"

They jumped and exchanged glances.

Annalynn said, "Doesn't she remind you of anyone?"

I leaned in to read the text. Janet Rockney. Then it hit me. She looked a helluva lot like me. "Oh." I remembered her reaction on the phone. "I wonder if she knows."

Connie closed the page and typed something into Google. "That style really isn't ideal for her. I'll bet she never wears her hair as short as yours for a reason."

Earlier in the day I might have dwelled on this. Now I didn't care. "He's her problem, not mine. Have you found a Cantree among the students yet?"

"No." Annalynn stared at the screen. "You were on the phone a long time."

"B.O."

Connie whirled around. "Does that still mean butt out? Are you two fighting?"

"B.O.," Annalynn and I chorused.

Connie grinned and opened a genealogical site. "If the Cantree lineage is online, we can find the daughters' married names and match them to my list."

We spent twenty minutes going through Cantree genealogies, but none appeared linked to Orson's branch of the family.

"Try the Gribbles," I suggested.

Nothing.

"Fargo's last name is Klimton," Connie said. "I'll try that."

We found the Klimtons, but none had married Cantrees.

"Try Glasgow. That was Orson's wife's maiden name." I still thought the abused wife's family could be a prime source. Why hadn't Tiny pursued that?

"Bingo," Connie said.

I focused on the Glasgow pedigree. In the late 1800s two of five Glasgow brothers had moved from Maryland to Missouri. The five produced numerous descendants, some of whom remained in both states. We found two names of men who could have been Shirley Sue Glasgow Cantree's late father. I insisted we stop there and go have supper. I had the lead I needed to begin my hunt for Roscoe Cantree.

Chapter Fifteen

With no intention of divulging my plans to search for the missing gang members, I guided the dinner conversation to Connie's progress in casting the show.

"I gave Laurey to the girl who sang 'Ave Maria.' Phoenix, that girl has a fantastic upper range. With proper training, LaDawna McKnight could be an opera singer. And she can act. She read really well."

Annalynn had been preoccupied. She roused herself to say, "I don't know of any McKnights around here. Where's she from, Connie?"

"Some Chicago suburb. Relatives in Moberly told her LCC has a good music department. They loved my *Annie Get Your Gun* production."

That stirred a memory. "So did Brandon Cort. You've earned a reputation."

Connie stared at me suspiciously a moment. Then she brightened. "He's Curly. I'm a little worried that her voice will overpower his in the duets." She glanced at Annalynn, who'd spaced out again. "The only one I'm not worried about is Aunt Eller. Nancy Alderton is a pro."

Annalynn snapped to. "She's not a student. She teaches comparative religion at LCC. The selection committee chose her as our new minister last night.

"Really?" Connie laughed. "That's one person we can take off the suspect list."

The telephone rang twice, and Annalynn excused herself to take the call.

Connie leaned forward and spoke barely above a whisper: "I don't blame you for going ballistic about her letting Russ come in, but she meant well."

"I know. I'll stay cool." I heard Annalynn coming back and raised my voice. "Mrs. T is doing fine. Our visit worked."

Annalynn paused to pick up her plate. "Jim hasn't found out anything definitive about Gribble or Fargo." She went into the kitchen to give Achilles the rest of her roast beef. "I have to go back to the office for a couple of hours."

Connie's eyes lit up. "I'll hang out with Phoenix. Talk over the cast."

Annalynn was too lost in her own thoughts to challenge this obvious lie. I dreaded hearing what Connie really had in mind.

I waited until we were alone in her yellow VW following Annalynn to the office to find out. I didn't bother to be subtle. "What mischief have you cooked up?"

"Going undercover to check out Derek Gribble."

In May, too physically weak to go undercover on my own, I'd taken Connie with me. She yearned to do it again. "Before I ask why, Connie, tell me where."

"The bowling alley. Bars. The places he hangs out. Why? To observe him in his natural habitat."

Not a terrible idea. "Okay. Jim couldn't find him last night. Let's make some calls before we start running all over town." I was carrying my purse with my Glock, my local cell phone, and a throwaway that transmitted no ID. I turned the radio on low to hide the sound of the car and called the bowling alley.

I needn't have bothered with the radio. I had to shout to be heard over the balls, music, and chatter. "Is Derek Gribble there? I have a job for him tomorrow."

"He's not here, but his wife is. Hold on." The man didn't

come back for a couple of minutes. "He'll be at Harry's Hideaway for a half hour or so, until she calls him to pick her up. If you miss him, you can reach him at home after nine in the morning."

A late riser. "Thanks. Mighty nice of you. Bye." I put away my phone. "Gribble's at Harry's."

"Harry and some of his regulars know us. We'll need full disguises."

"We don't have time." I pictured the bar as I watched Annalynn drive into the secure underground garage. "Gribble's a pool player, and the pool tables are the only places well lit. We'll watch him from a dark spot."

"Okay." Connie didn't say anything for a block. "Why aren't you scared of him?"

Being scared hadn't occurred to me. "We'll be in a public place. I have my gun. Besides, anyone who treats his wife and his mother-in-law that way is a bully. Most bullies are cowards." Careful. A scared coward is dangerous.

"Annalynn says Stuart scares you more than the shooter. Is that true?"

Nonsense. "Right now Annalynn is the one who scares me."

Connie laughed. She stopped abruptly. "Actually, that's not funny. I think this overwrought anxiety about your love life is part of her grieving for her own loss. She's certainly feeling guilty about your staying here to help her rather than accepting Adderly International's offer to start a New York branch."

"Please convince her I didn't want the job. I'm done with long days at a desk and interminable meetings."

"It's hard to believe you're content to walk away from all that money, all that power. Or from all that man. Really, Phoenix, don't be hasty about brushing off Stuart. I've watched you two together. You have a spark. Enjoy it."

"He told me he loves me." Stunned that those words had

come out of my mouth and gone into Connie's ears, I covered my mouth with my hand.

"In bed? Men say that in bed all the time."

"No, they say it to get you there." The urge to tell overcame caution. "He said it today. On the phone."

"That's huge. I gather you didn't say it back?"

I'd been an idiot to tell her anything. "For God's sake, don't tell Annalynn."

"Okay." She chuckled. "This is a first, my keeping your secret from Annalynn." She turned into Harry's parking lot. "It's awful when one person says it and the other one doesn't. No wonder you're in knots over whether to meet his kids."

I relaxed. She got it. I shifted my focus to what we needed to do. A dozen cars and pickups were parked out front and one big truck over at the side. Probably average for a Tuesday night. "Find a pull-through place between vehicles so we have something to duck behind and can leave fast if we need to."

Connie parked the car. "Should we have a skedaddle signal?"

Not if it went the way I intended. What the heck. Let her have her fun. "I'll brush lint off my right shoulder. You run your hand through your hair."

I considered the layout of the old garage/convenience store that had been converted into a sports bar. A pool table rested on each of the former car lifts. Men congregated at the one to our left, college kids at the middle one, and high school kids on the right. Directly behind them were tables where Harry's patrons ate mesquite-grilled hamburgers and home fries. At the back, the bar boasted a huge selection of beers. A hall led to restrooms and an exit. "We'll cut right, go around the center pool table, and veer left to a table halfway between it and the men's game."

"Why should you be the one who blocks out the scene?"

"Because . . . I'm the one with the gun." Annalynn would

have accepted what I said without question, but Connie didn't know I'd led a double life. As we walked toward the entrance, I checked the vehicles. The only one I recognized was the Gribbles' pickup.

"The place is dead," Connie murmured as we went through the double doors.

Five men watched a man rosin his cue stick on our left. I didn't recognize any faces. Couples and families occupied five tables, two young men watched a baseball game at the bar, and four young women cheered a player at the pool table on our right.

I led the way to a dimly lit table. As I pulled out a chair, I spotted Gribble's distinctive long body and short legs. "He's Mr. Muscles in the light-blue T-shirt."

Connie pulled a paper napkin from the dispenser and wiped off the table. "A *tight* T-shirt. He's a past-prime body builder." She waved at a toddler at a nearby table. "We have to order something. Harry added cheesecake to the menu. Want to split a piece?"

"Sure. You choose it."

As she went to the bar to order, the toddler made a face at me. I replied in kind, and he laughed. Playing with him gave me cover for watching the pool table. Gribble and a man in a green shirt with a logo on the pocket shook hands. Other hands reached for wallets, and one of the men collected bets. I estimated the stakes to be fifty dollars. Probably illegal gambling, but too small an amount to pull anyone in for. Hmm. An old trick might put pressure on Gribble to talk.

Connie brought cherry cheesecake and two forks. "Any action?"

"Gribble's hustling a guy." I pulled out my local cell phone and called Jim's private number. He didn't answer. Damn! I didn't want to have my call register at the LPD. As I debated what to do, Jim called back.

"Hey, Phoenix. What's up?"

"Are you on duty?"

"No, but I can be if it's worth it."

"Say a man at Harry's has a drink and ten minutes later drives to the bowling alley. What are the chances he'll be pulled over in, say, twenty to thirty minutes?"

"Pretty good. What kind of vehicle would he be driving?"

"A black Ford pickup about ten years old."

"Derek Gribble. A DUI could cost him his commercial license. Call me when he leaves Harry's."

"Will do. Bye."

Connie, struggling to swallow laughter, choked on a bite of cheesecake. When she recovered, she whispered, "Absolutely brilliant."

Gribble sipped from a can of Dr Pepper.

An unexpected complication. "Only if we get him to drink alcohol."

"I have a knack for driving big, strong men to drink." She tilted her head and simpered.

Harry's bald head loomed over us. He leaned on our table, his big hands covering much of the space between Connie and me. He glared at me. "Nothing wrong with a little friendly bet. The boys know I won't let the pot go over fifty bucks."

He wasn't fond of me. One of my visits had landed three of his patrons in jail. "You're walking a thin line, Harry." Having established that, I smiled and patted one of his bear paws. "We're here to try your cheesecake, not your patience. In fact, we want to buy the winner of that game a drink."

Connie batted her eyes at Harry. "What does the body builder over there like?"

"I would never have picked him for your type." Harry

straightened up and pulled in his stomach. "Besides, he's married."

I shrugged. "We're looking, not touching."

Harry eyed me and then Connie, obviously suspicious. "He likes Coors, but he never drinks when he's got a sucker."

Connie smiled sweetly. "He will if you tell him it's from a secret admirer."

Harry glared at me. "What are you up to?"

I beckoned to him to bend down. "In about five or ten minutes, he's going to receive a call. As soon as he does, bring him a Coors."

Harry's lip curled.

I added, "Or I can call the sheriff's department to check on gambling laws in Vandiver County." I handed him a twenty. "Deliver it with a smile, please. It's for a good cause."

Five minutes later, Gribble answered his cell phone. He said, "Give me fifteen minutes."

I motioned to Harry.

He came from behind the bar with a tray holding three bottles of Coors. He plunked two down on our table and went on over to Gribble. "A drink from your secret admirers," he said, nodding toward us.

Bloody hell! I held up my beer in salute.

Gribble swelled like a toad and raised the bottle in return. He squinted to see Connie and me in the dim light and smiled a self-satisfied smile.

He hadn't recognized us. He couldn't be the shooter.

He took a long drink before ostentatiously lining up his next shot. He won the game a couple of minutes later and explained loudly that he couldn't give a rematch because he had to go pick up a girlfriend. He saluted me again and swaggered out with the half-empty bottle in his hand.

"That was close," Connie said. "I would have gagged if the

jerk had come over to flex his muscles."

I dialed Jim. "He's not the shooter, but he deserves a good scare for the way he treats his wife and his mother-in-law. He left with an open bottle of Coors in his hand."

"How much did he drink?"

"He's well under the limit."

"I'll let him know big brother is watching. Maybe he'll say somethin'." He hung up.

Connie stood up. "I challenge you to a game of pool."

We'd played billiards at the castle as kids. I'd always won. I shook my head no.

"Come on. It would look weird if we walk out now. You can break."

She'd improved her game. I hadn't. All the men gathered around to watch her win two out of three. Harry invited her back.

Jim called as we walked to her car. "He was nervous but he didn't volunteer anything. He has no idea you set him up. Any other errands before I go home?"

"Thanks, Jim. I'd appreciate whoever is on duty escorting Annalynn home."

"Will do, and I won't mention to her what we just did. Goodnight."

The LPD escorting Annalynn home gave me a little more time to prepare for tomorrow. I set up my first move: "I'll pick up the Corvette first thing in the morning, Connie. I'm going to turn it in for a car no one will recognize."

"Good. You'll be safer that way."

If she only knew what I planned to do.

Chapter Sixteen

Back at Annalynn's house, I mixed my special powder for graying my hair. Early in my undercover days, I'd perfected instant aging. Older women move around unseen. I could add two decades in two or three minutes by brushing gray into my black hair and eyebrows, accenting my lifelines, and adjusting my posture and movements. I could transform again just as fast.

I tucked the next day's supply into my purse and brought my laptop downstairs to the ladies' parlor so I could use Annalynn's printer. First I searched for Norval Cantree's home and employer. A quick find. He ran a new and used tire business at his home on the edge of Boonville. Then came my big job, using the online Glasgow genealogy to construct a cover story and locate a relative of Shirley Sue Glasgow Cantree. Genealogy websites yielded all the information I needed except one key piece—a relative living close by. I printed off the genealogy and tucked it into my purse. Online directories showed no Glasgows in Vandiver or neighboring counties. Finally I visited the high school sites in Tiny's county and looked for class reunions. The contact for a thirtieth reunion was Lily Lou Glasgow Stringer, almost certainly Shirley Sue's sister. Lily Lou lived on a farm two miles southwest of the abandoned farmhouse and taught band and chorus at her alma mater. Not the occupation I would have expected for anyone linked to the Cantrees.

Annalynn came in the door, and Achilles ran to greet her.

"Hi," I called. "Anything new?" I went to the Avis website,

found the directions to its office in Columbia, and printed them off.

Annalynn stopped in the door, her face drawn with fatigue. "Nothing new. What are you working on?"

"Locating the closest Avis office. I'm going to Columbia tomorrow to turn in the Corvette for a less conspicuous car and do some shopping. Want anything?"

"No." She rubbed her eyes. "I have the familiar feeling that you're not telling me everything."

I turned it back on her: "I can think of a thing or two you haven't told me lately."

"Then don't make my mistake." She sat down on the loveseat and pointed to the laptop resting on my knees. "You shouldn't work like that, or on your bed, or at the dining room table. And it will get worse when you have consulting assignments and applications to the foundation. You need a comfortable, fully equipped office."

She'd brought this up before. I'd avoided setting up an office because that would make my stay appear permanent. "I don't have time to look for office space right now."

"I know a place that's spacious, convenient, and available."

I smelled a trap. "Where is this perfect place?"

"Your house." She held her hand up palm out to silence me. "Just listen a moment. The bedrooms could be offices and the front rooms the reception and conference area. You could leave your piano there and play whenever you like." She pointed to Achilles, who sat watching us with a concerned look. "He wouldn't get separation anxiety if you're working there."

I put on my thinking face. She'd tried to persuade me not to sell my childhood home from the moment I arrived. She wanted to anchor me to Laycock. Recovering from my wounds, I'd weighed that anchor for months, but soon I had to sail. So did she. Was either of us ready? I studied her. She wore her calm public face. Both hands were clenched. I hedged. "An interesting idea, but surely turning my house into foundation headquarters would violate zoning laws."

"No, I checked." She leaned back as though relaxed, but her left hand opened and closed. "Think about it, Phoenix. You've updated everything in the house except the kitchen. You could buy all the office furniture and equipment you need in Columbia tomorrow. For a few hundred tax-deductible dollars and a few hours of work you could set up a functional workspace. It's a simple, logical solution, at least for the time being."

True. I felt cornered. "Let me sleep on it." Did the obvious convenience outweigh the danger of letting Annalynn maneuver me into doing this?

"Of course." She stood up, her hands now relaxed. "I'm going to bed. See you tomorrow."

A simple, logical solution. She'd used those same words when she tried to convince me to let her father pay my way to the college he had chosen for her. Neither I nor my parents would accept the charity. Putting the past behind me, I browsed the Web for information for a cover story, found what I needed, and set up an e-mail account and a brochure website to back up my story. Fighting fatigue, I sent Lily Lou Glasgow Stringer an e-mail saying I was a distant cousin and asking to visit her tomorrow afternoon. Satisfied with my preparations, I allowed myself to go to bed.

The reply inviting me to stop by arrived right before I went down to breakfast and told Annalynn that I'd use my house as the foundation's *temporary* headquarters.

She and Achilles dropped me off at Connie's to pick up the Corvette. After a watchful but uneventful hour-plus drive, I reached the Avis office. Before going in, I surveyed the cars in the small lot so I could request a model that wasn't available. That allowed me to accept a little Aveo to drive to Boonville and then return to exchange it for a six-cylinder vehicle. Many people base first impressions on what you drive.

From there I went to a nearby Office Depot. An hour later I'd bought and arranged delivery for everything we needed except executive desks. I preferred that most of the office furniture have the frugal look befitting a nonprofit, but Annalynn's desk—an antique?—should impress visitors and please photographers. For myself, I wanted an old-fashioned wood desk with space to spread out papers and drawers in which to hide things.

Now my real work began. With the noise of the mall's food court and merry-go-round in the background, I called Annalynn and Stuart to establish where I was and convince them that shopping would take me most of the day. I spent an hour buying the clothing and props I needed for my fact-finding jaunts. After a quick lunch in the food court, I went to a restroom in a nearby city park to age twenty years and change into a white short-sleeved blouse with a blue rose embroidered on the Peter Pan collar, a denim skirt with giant pockets, and a pair of denim slip-ons. The blouse was one size too large, the skirt two inches too long. Then I traveled west on I-70 about twenty miles to the Boonville exit nearest Norval Cantree's home and drove until I saw a tire atop a huge arch. White letters on the tire announced "Tires Old and New." I put on my new cataract sunglasses and drove through the arch and down a gravel driveway past a doublewide trailer. A row of huge tractor tires stood against the outside wall of an old white barn.

Bloody hell! I knew nothing about tractor tires. I decided to stick with the story I'd prepared. I opened the door, planted my sturdy new cane on the ground, and struggled to get out of the car.

A skinny thirty-something brunette in a white T-shirt and short shorts came out of the trailer and walked toward me.

"How're you doin' today?"

"Good. How are you?" I spoke with a trace of a Russian accent. "I am looking for good used tires for a Volkswagen Bug. You have such tires?"

"I don't know, honey. Do you know the size?"

"I am not sure." I pointed to the tractor wheels. "I know they are not so big as those ones. You have a book that says the size?"

"Nope. Norval keeps all that stuff in his head. Did you tell him you were comin'? Most folks call first."

I bit my lip and sank back into the seat. "No. When the accident ruined my front tires, a friend said to come here."

"Don't worry, honey. He'll be back any time. He went to Kansas City this morning to pick up some parts and visit his nephew in the hospital."

So Norval had family loyalty. "I am sorry to hear. They are close?"

"Nah. He hasn't seen the kid since he was nine or ten." Her jaw muscles tightened. "A couple of years before his mother died. Norval wanted to take him and his sister in, but we just couldn't afford to feed two more teenagers."

She was talking to herself rather than to me. I said, "Your Norval sounds like a good man."

"He is, one of a kind in that family of his." She put her hand to her mouth, suddenly aware she'd said too much.

To ease her mind and encourage more revelations, I pretended ignorance of the infamous Cantrees. "In-laws can be a problem. My brother's wife . . ."

"You can say that again!" She relaxed.

"Maybe I should go to the casino for some minutes and come back."

"Sure, honey. Write down what you're looking for and I'll give it to him."

A small truck came down the drive, passed us, and backed

up to a big double door. A brawny man with brown ringlets and tiny ears stepped down from the cab.

Roscoe? I slid my hand into my purse and gripped my gun.

The woman walked toward him. "Sweetie, this lady wants to know if you got two used tires for a VW Bug."

He glanced at me. "The classic Bug or the new model?"

"My car is five years old."

"I got a pair for forty dollars a piece that'll give you at least fifteen thousand miles, if you treat 'em right."

I closed the car door and leaned on my cane. "You have any a little less expensive?"

He wiped sweat from his forehead with the back of his hand. "Only those. You can have both for seventy-five."

I pursed my lips for a moment. "I would like to see them, please."

"Sure." He led the way inside and down a row of tire racks. "These two." He tapped two tires on the top rack. "Want me to take them down for you?"

I fumbled with my dark glasses. "Please."

He lifted the tires down as though they were as light as beach balls and leaned them against the lower rack. "Look 'em over all you want." He strode back toward the front of the barn.

His wife met him at the door. "How's he doin'?"

"He'll live long enough to die in prison," the man said bitterly. He glanced back at me and said something too softly for me to hear.

"I'll not have either of them in my house." She stalked off toward the trailer.

"They're blood," he called after her.

She answered, "I need a car to drive to work in twenty minutes."

Could he have given her car to Roscoe? I bent down and checked the tires carefully. They would make good spares for

Connie's car. I walked slowly back outside and toward the truck. No one there. I limped around it toward the sound of tools. Behind the barn was a shed with open rolling double doors. Inside Norval Cantree worked on the motor of an old Chevy sedan. By the shed stood two more old Chevys, a beat-up Ford pickup on blocks, and a surprisingly neat-looking wood-paneled station wagon. Only the car in the shed carried a current license plate. Roscoe Cantree and the fourth gang member had several vehicles to choose from. Even the FBI would have figured that out.

What could I learn that they hadn't? Probably not much, but I had to try. "Sir, I will buy the tires."

"I'll be with you in the shake of a lamb's tail."

My grandfather had said that. "You raise sheep?"

He barked a laugh. "No, I mean I need a minute to finish this."

"Let the lamb shake his tail," I said, walking slowly toward him. "I have time. You repair cars?"

"More rebuild than repair." He jerked his hand back and swore under his breath.

"My brother in California does such things." Nice to tell the truth. "He likes the Model A. You study this rebuilding in school?"

"Nah. I pretty much learned it on my own." He stuck his tongue out of one corner of his mouth as he loosened a badly corroded battery from its moorings. "My dad always had old cars and tractors. He taught me and my brother to fix 'em."

Opportunity. "You work with your brother now?"

"Nah." He brushed off some of the corrosion. "He's dead. Cancer."

Norval had known Orson was dying. "My sympathy. A sad thing for a young man to die. Did he leave children?"

"Yeah, well, they're teenagers. The girl's been out on her own two or three years." He straightened, stepped over to a worktable, and picked up a filthy towel.

I tsked sympathetically. "Very sad."

He turned his head to hide his face and wiped his hands. He cleared his throat. "She's a good kid. She tried like the dickens to watch out for her little brother." He strode past me toward the barn. "I'll put those tires in your trunk for you."

"Thank you." Norval had to be the white sheep of the Cantree family. I wondered if a black sheep or two had driven off in a rebuilt car.

While Norval loaded the tires into the small trunk, I counted out the money.

"Thanks for your business," he said, closing the trunk.

"Can you tell me about the casino?" I handed him the bills. "I have never seen one. I would like to look but not to lose money."

He barked a laugh. "I never been there. I heard they got lots of machines where you can play for pennies and nickels. If you want to lose your money fast, you can play for bigger stakes."

"Pennies are good," I said. "Thank you." Not a gambler like his cousin Roscoe.

I followed the casino's signs through a pleasant old residential area into a parking lot big enough for every car within twenty miles. Searching for an empty space, I noted that about three-fourths of the cars carried Missouri tags. Most of the rest came from surrounding states. A great place to steal a license plate. No, too many surveillance cameras. The FBI should know from those tapes what kind of car Roscoe and his accomplice drove on their visit. And what I was driving. I should have parked on the street and walked in. Roscoe probably had. Leaving would just make me conspicuous. I waited for four elderly women to get into a Buick and vacate a parking space. With my cane and cataract glasses, I'd fit right in. Taking care to keep my movements consistent, I limped onto the walkway leading to the entrance. Two nondescript young men in spotless maintenance uniforms lingered by a trash can. They held cigarettes. They didn't inhale. FBI rookies assigned to a long-shot but high-risk watch.

When I stepped inside, stale cigarette smoke assailed my nose and eyes. At the entrance to a huge restaurant, a tall, light-skinned black woman with curly, close-cropped black hair wore lightly tinted sunglasses and a blue blazer too warm for the day. She rocked a stroller with a well-covered baby. Another rookie agent. I went to my right toward the noise. To go into the room with the gaming machines, I needed a pass, which required photo ID. No thanks.

I sidled up to a smiling young man directing the patrons. "Could I go in to look for a friend?"

"Sorry, ma'am. I can't let you in, but I can page someone for you."

I thought for a moment. "I think that would embarrass him. He claims he never comes here. Maybe you know him. Norval Cantree."

The young man laughed. "I can guarantee you Norval's not in there. He fought to keep the casino out of Boonville."

"I see. Thank you, young man." So Norval hadn't laundered the money.

Nothing more for me to do here. The Cantree gang members might still be in the area badgering poor Norval to help them, but if they came back to the casino, the FBI would pounce. I'd have to hope Lily had some idea where a Cantree might hide out.

Chapter Seventeen

I visited a restroom in a different park to get rid of the gray and change clothes before exchanging the Aveo for a dark blue V6 Malibu. As myself, I stopped at a Greek restaurant to buy *ouzo* for Mrs. T. Then I assumed my next identity, deepening my age lines and adding gray flecks and a memorable white streak to my hair. To complete the disguise, I donned my upscale outfit: a peach-colored silk sleeveless blouse with a matching short-sleeved jacket, charcoal-gray linen trousers, and low-heeled black leather sandals.

I drove west again on I-70. This time I turned north before Boonville to take the most direct route from Norval's place to Lily Glasgow Stringer's house—and to the abandoned farmhouse where the Cantrees had hidden. The two-lane road wound up and down through fields where cattle grazed, corn reached as high as a giraffe's eye, and unfamiliar crops grew. I watched for empty farm buildings where the gang could hide out until the FBI moved on.

Coming down a long hill, I slowed to study an unpainted house surrounded by grass and weeds. A car pulled out of a side road near it and drove toward me. I reached for my gun, but this was a fairly new car, government issue. I pretended to scratch my nose as I passed Lester Wharton and another agent. Safely down the road, I pounded the steering wheel in frustration. I was duplicating effort and coming up empty. Doubtless the FBI already had questioned Lily.

But she might say more to the long-lost relative whom I had created using the Glasgow genealogy. I'd have to be in top form. She'd be wary of strangers. On the other hand, she'd had time to dredge up memories of the Cantrees, incidents and insights she'd never mention to the law.

Right before five o'clock I came to a big black mailbox with "Stringer" in metal letters on the post. I pulled into a gravel driveway running between a row of yellow roses and a cornfield and ending at a metal shed. I parked in the shade of a small maple tree near the back door of an old but well-kept one-story white farmhouse. A cement walk led to a wooden ramp that angled to the right and then back to the left and onto a small porch, bypassing the three steps. Hmm. Someone with a serious physical disability lived here.

When I opened the car door, the strong fragrance of heritage roses drew me. I left my new beige leather briefcase in the seat, put on my ten-dollar reading glasses, and meandered down the well-tended row inhaling the blessedly unimproved flowers.

The back door opened. "Hello, I'm Lily Glasgow Stringer. You must be Mindy Geitner."

I took one last whiff. "Yes. I simply had to stop to smell the roses. I haven't run across such a marvelous fragrance in years." I picked up my briefcase and walked up the three steps to extend my hand to a tall, slender, middle-aged woman with short, light-brown hair. She wore a blouse and skirt similar to those I'd worn to Norval's place. "Thank you so much for taking the time to see me."

"Certainly. Please come in." Her lips smiled. Her alert hazel eyes didn't. "Would you care for a cold drink?"

"A glass of water, please." She'd be no pushover. I'd have to seem open and, if possible, charming. "I passed my coffee quota before noon and my iced tea limits by the end of lunch. Hotel conference rooms make me thirsty."

She motioned me to a chair at a polished cherry table in the center of the big farm kitchen. "You're attending an accountants' conference in Kansas City?"

Her overly casual tone warned me she had checked out my story. "Actually it's in a hotel near the airport. I have my own small business so I attend one conference a year to keep up with what's happening." I smiled. "And, of course, it's tax deductible."

She put ice in two glasses and poured iced tea for herself and water for me. "Your conference ended at noon today?"

She'd been suspicious enough to check the schedule online. Probably wary of the press. "No, at noon tomorrow. I skipped the last two afternoon sessions to come here, and I have to leave in about an hour to get back for an awards banquet." I opened my briefcase and took out the Glasgow pedigree I'd run off and the form on which I'd recorded my fictional family, a branch of the Maryland Glasgows.

She wriggled her shoulders, apparently releasing tension. "I didn't recognize your name. Was your maiden name Glasgow?"

"No, my grandmother's, Arminda Glasgow Jones." I turned the pedigree sheet around and went through Arminda's connection to the Missouri Glasgows. To account for the fictitious Arminda not appearing in the family records, I concluded with, "Her family disowned her because she married a Catholic." I aimed for an emotional soft spot: "My mother still can't forgive what happened when her mother died during childbirth. No one in the family stepped forward to help Mom take care of her baby sister."

Tears filled Lily's eyes.

I stretched out my hand to cover hers. "Have I said something wrong?"

"No, no." She sprang up and went to a counter for a tissue. She wiped her eyes. "My baby sister and her husband died in a car accident almost five years ago. Right after a tractor rolled over on my husband. He was paralyzed from the neck down. I wanted to bring her son and daughter here, but we just couldn't do it."

True or not, she felt guilty now that the boy would go from a hospital bed to prison. "Of course not. I noticed the ramp outside."

She pulled another tissue from the box and kept her back to me. "He died in November, but I haven't taken it down." She took a deep breath. "I hadn't heard from my sister's son and daughter for more than two years. Last December I tried to find them." She leaned on the counter. "I planned to ask them to come for the holidays as sort of a trial run while my boys were home from college." She fell silent.

The poor woman didn't deserve to be deceived, but I had to play it out. "Did your niece or nephew come?"

"No." Her shoulders shook. She took several deep breaths. "I couldn't find Madonna. Her younger brother knew where she was, but he wouldn't tell me." She turned to face me, her face contorted. "At first he wouldn't even speak to me on the phone. The third time I called, he screamed obscenities at me until I finally hung up."

My heart ached for her, but she'd been lucky the vicious Orson Junior didn't come into her home. "How terrible for you. I'm so sorry."

She collapsed into her chair. "My sister was a gentle, bright, pretty girl with a beautiful soprano voice. We all spoiled her. The man she married was a little wild, even violent. I begged her not to marry him, but she wouldn't listen. I only met her second husband once. He was fine as long as he was sober, but that never lasted long. He got her to drinking with him. Madonna, her daughter, held the household together." She jumped up. "You don't need to hear my troubles. Let's go in the living room and look at some family albums."

Damn! Just when I thought I could segue into the Cantrees. I followed her into a small living room with a worn but comfortable couch and two recliners, a row of bookcases on one wall, and a console piano where most people would have put a television.

"I'll be right back," she said, going into a bedroom.

I went to study the photos on the piano, my hands automatically going to the keys to play an arpeggio. "Nice tone." In the center was a family photo: the parents, Lily at about thirteen, a boy a little younger, and a girl about three. Lily's wedding photo was on one end of the piano, and high school graduation photos of two sandy-haired all-American boys on the other.

She returned with three big photo albums.

Getting back to the Cantrees was going to be a challenge.

She put the albums on a wood coffee table in front of the couch. "Don't worry. I won't make you look at all of them." She opened one bound with string ties. "This was my grandmother's. I thought you might like to see if anyone looks like your family."

We turned through several pages before I considered it safe to declare our families looked nothing alike.

She opened a newer volume. "This was my mother's. She went to her reward eight years ago." She turned the pages until she found photos of her own childhood. She and her younger siblings were towheads. "My brother is career military. He didn't want to farm." She turned the page. "My big problem in high school was whether to be a majorette or a cheerleader."

I dutifully looked at a photo of her in a cheerleader's uniform. She stood between two towering boys in basketball uniforms. The one glowering had Cantree ears. The other one resembled Tiny Towson. "Is one of them your husband?"

"God, no!" She tapped the Cantree photo. "He was one of

our neighbors. I hated him from the first day of school. He pulled my hair so hard he made me cry. He pestered me from then on. I celebrated the day he moved away."

Once again she had avoided saying the name. She didn't want to acknowledge any connection to the Cantrees. I turned the page. "Did he ever come back?"

"To visit, but that was years ago. His family all left or died."

A short-legged kid in jeans among basketball players caught my eye. Surely that was a Gribble. Maybe this visit hadn't been a waste of time after all. "This fellow looks like someone I know. Is his name Thompson?"

"No, that's Derek Gribble. He used to run around with the guy who tormented me, but I think that was because he was scared not to, not because they were friends."

She turned the page. "This is my husband." She closed the book. "Sorry. I can't bear to look."

I put my arm around her shoulder. "I'm sorry to have upset you." To my discomfort, I meant it. "I can't leave you this way." For her sake and because she might have useful information. First, be nice. "Talk to me about what makes you happy."

She nodded and closed her eyes a moment. "My boys make me happy. They're both doing really well at Mizzou." She pressed her lips together. "I miss them terribly."

Great. I'd just reminded her of that. "Do you enjoy teaching?"

"Yes." She forced a smile. "I had some good news yesterday from one of my favorite students. He got the lead in a college production of *Oklahoma!*."

Good grief. Everybody here was connected. "That's wonderful."

"Yes, the woman directing it is a professional. Brandon will learn a tremendous amount from her."

I heard a car slow at the driveway. I glanced out in time to see an old beige Chevy sedan speed up and drive past. A chill went down my spine. It could be Roscoe in one of Norval's rebuilt cars. "Did you recognize the car that just went by?"

"I didn't see it. Why?"

I threw up my hands. "Your house is so *isolated.* I'd be scared to death to live alone out here."

"I couldn't stand living in a building with dozens of other people. Besides, a neighbor lives half a mile down the road."

"I don't find that very reassuring."

She looked down at her hands. She'd cut her nails very short. "Now that my boys have gone back to Mizzou, I keep a loaded revolver in my nightstand."

The hair on my neck rose in fear for her. I wished I could speak as Phoenix Smith, reserve deputy, and urge her to go stay with a friend. I had to try: "I saw something on TV about bank robbers hiding out around here. If I were you, I'd be sleeping on a friend's couch until the police find them."

She replied through closed teeth, "I won't let him drive me out of my home."

She knew the danger but refused to run from her old enemy. Courageous but foolish. "Then you think he's around here. Where could he hide?"

She shrugged. "A vacant house, a hay shed, the middle of a cornfield. I've no idea where he could be."

I believed her. "I admire your courage, but please be careful. At least get a watch dog."

"That's just what Tiny—an old friend—said."

Tiny had held out on us. Why? I'd better get out of here in case he dropped by and caught me questioning his friend. Her description of Mindy wouldn't identify me, but he'd recognize me in person. I looked at my watch. "I need to start back in a few minutes. Could you fill in your and your siblings' information on my chart before I go?"

"Yes, of course." She completed the form.

I glanced at the sheets before putting them in my briefcase. She had listed the last name of Shirley Sue and her children as Johnson, once again omitting Cantree. She hadn't said where the son and daughter lived now. I pretended not to notice. "Your sister died in Dayton, Ohio?"

"Yes. She moved there after she divorced her first husband. She joked that she got married again to change her name so he couldn't find her. It wasn't far from the truth."

Again Lily had taken care not to say Cantree. Was she suspicious of me? Ashamed to be connected to the venomous family? Anxious to avoid questions and maintain privacy? She certainly wasn't protecting Roscoe. I glanced up at the top of the back door. A rifle hung over it, just as it had in my grandparents' farmhouse. Good. "Thank you so much, Lily." I gave her a quick hug. "And, please, don't be too brave to ask for help or to run if you feel threatened." I gave her the strongest motive for self-preservation I could imagine: "Your boys need you."

A little after six I started back to Laycock. Since my route took me by the Oak Grove Cemetery, I decided to test the camera that Annalynn and I had set up there. As I approached, a red pickup turned out of Mark Keller's drive. He raised his hand in greeting as he drove past me. A friendly wave in farm country didn't mean you knew someone, but it reminded me that I still had white flecks and a streak in my hair and lines on my face.

I pulled over, removed ten years from my face and hair in seconds, and writhed my way out of my slacks and silk top and into the cotton top and jeans I'd worn when I left home. I drove on into the church parking lot, stepped out of my car, and rang Annalynn's direct number as I walked into the graveyard.

"I'm at Oak Grove," I said when she answered. "Can you see

me?" I heard a car coming fast and turned my head to watch the old beige Chevy slow as it neared Keller's drive. The way that same car had slowed at Lily's. Now a red splotch showed above a shattered left headlight.

I reached for my Glock. Roscoe had gone after Mark Keller and was headed toward me.

Chapter Eighteen

I ducked behind the closest tombstone, dropped the phone, and prepared the Glock to fire. The driver gunned the motor and rocketed down the road. I sprang up to try to see the license, but I could tell only that it was a Missouri plate.

"Phoenix!" Annalynn's voice came from the phone.

I picked it up and ran for the car. "Call an alert. I think Roscoe Cantree just drove by Oak Grove headed east. He's in an old beige Chevy with the left front fender damaged. He must have hit Mark Keller's pickup."

"Don't follow him! Stay there in case he doubles back." She called for her admin assistant and came back on the line. "We'll cover the county roads and the Highway Patrol will set up watches on the highways."

The beige car had disappeared. He'd be a mile or two away before I could get out of the lot. "I'm worried about Mark Keller. I'm going to drive west to look for him. You better alert an ambulance crew."

"Okay. Stay on the line."

I peeled out. Little more than a minute later I saw the back half of the pickup sticking out of a cornfield. I picked up the phone. "I see the pickup but not the driver." I parked at the side of the road. "Mr. Keller? Mark?"

"In the cab," he answered. "Could use some help."

At least he was conscious. I pushed through the corn to the

driver's door and stepped onto the small running board to peer in.

He was crumpled on the floor with his head at the passenger door.

I jumped down and went to the other door, fighting my way through the dense green stalks. I opened the door far enough to put my hand on his carotid artery. The pulse was strong.

"It's my shoulder," he said. "Hurts like hell. Shoulda had on the damn seatbelt."

I spoke into the phone. "We need an ambulance about a mile west of the Keller farm. Probably a broken shoulder. Vital signs are good." I put away the phone and drew my gun as I heard a car coming. I peered through the corn as an old but well-waxed red Corolla pulled over in front of my car.

A moment later Brandon Cort's flop of blond hair and boy-next-door face looked over the top of the Corolla. "Need some help down there?"

"Yes. Do you have a blanket?"

"Nope. Sorry." He charged through the corn toward the pickup. "Mr. Keller, you all right?"

I holstered my gun. "I've called for an ambulance. I'm not sure yet whether we should move him."

"Dr. Smith! Hi." He plowed through the corn.

"I got a blanket behind the seat," the old man said. "I'd sure like to get off this shoulder, but I can't move."

Working together, Brandon and I got the blanket under Keller and eased him out of the pickup. We propped him up against it. The blood had drained from his face and sweat drenched his shirt.

I pulled the blanket around his shoulders, afraid he'd go into shock before the ambulance arrived.

Brandon took a cell phone off his belt. "What's your daughter's number, Mr. Keller?"

"I'll watch for the ambulance." I walked around to the other side of the pickup and to the left front fender. Sure enough. A major dent with flecks of beige paint on it. Roscoe had forced him off the road. I went on to my car puzzling over how to get Lily out of her house to a safe place. I couldn't call to warn her as Phoenix or Mindy.

Brandon came around the pickup. "Mr. Keller wants to talk to you."

I hurried down to the old man. He was so pale and drawn that I reached for his wrist to check his pulse.

"I'm awful woozy. Tell the sheriff this was no accident. I got a call to come to town to pick up a package. An old Chevy drove out of the field and came right at me. I didn't see the driver very good, but I'm darn sure it was Roscoe Cantree."

Of course. The call lured him away from his shotgun. "I've already reported that. They're setting up roadblocks." I heard an ambulance siren in the distance.

His head dropped. He'd passed out.

I stepped away and dialed Tiny Towson's cell. "Mark Keller just told me that Roscoe Cantree ran him off the road and may be going after Lily Stringer."

"Shit!" Brandon jumped in his car and spun his tires taking off.

From bad to worse. "Brandon Cort just took off for there."

"So did I," Tiny said. He disconnected.

I stepped into the road to direct the ambulance crew. While they loaded Mark Keller into the ambulance, I called Annalynn.

"Come on home," she said. "A farmer just reported finding a damaged Chevy behind some hay bales. We have no idea what Roscoe's driving now."

But he knew what I was driving. He'd seen my rented blue Malibu twice today near intended victims. The second time he'd seen me. I'd spent the day as the hunter only to become the prey.

Chapter Nineteen

I drove slowly, Glock in hand, my eyes searching the fields ahead and behind me for any threat. Why had Roscoe accelerated rather than fire at me at the church? Simplest—and usually the best—answer: He knew I had a better chance of hitting him than he, shooting from a moving vehicle, had of hitting me. That was the only sane thing he'd done. Attacking his old enemy put him in psycholand.

Switching cars had done me no good. I couldn't endanger Connie by leaving this one in her garage. I called Annalynn to arrange to park it in the garage beneath her office and the county jail.

When I arrived, she raised the gate for me and pointed to a reserved space. Achilles loped over to greet me. I made a fuss over him, glad to see a happy, loving, nonjudgmental being.

None of those adjectives applied to Annalynn at the moment. She called from her SUV, "It's almost eight o'clock. Let's go."

I let Achilles hop into the front and sit between my knees. "Any sign of Roscoe?"

"No. Tiny thinks he may be holed up somewhere fairly close to the abandoned farmhouse. He and a deputy, Wolf Volcker, will patrol in unmarked cars from ten until five. Since Roscoe came into Vandiver County, one of my deputies will also patrol out that way. I'll be on call."

That placed me on call, too. My chance of getting a full night's sleep was fifty-fifty at best. I needed sleep badly. Twelve hours of effort and heat had drained me. I had barely completely recovered from my wound. My eyes closed. Alarmed, I roused myself to check the streets.

Annalynn noticed. "I see you've had a full day. I'll warm up the roast and make a salad while you write your report."

"Report? Oh, you mean on Mark Keller's wreck."

"I mean on your *entire* day. You obviously did more than return the Corvette." She pulled into her garage and turned off the motor but didn't move. "Please, Phoenix, don't be so reckless."

Still angry about her foisting Russ on me, I neglected to be reassuring. "I'd rather risk getting shot down as a hawk than as a sitting duck." The stricken look on her face compelled me to add, "I don't intend to be shot down, or even shot at. I know my craft, Annalynn." Yet I'd slipped up in Istanbul. "I'm not taking chances."

Achilles whined and stretched his head over to lick Annalynn's hand.

Stung at his rebuke, I opened my door. "I'll take a quick shower and give you an oral account of my day during din—supper. I'll write a report on the crash before I go to bed." I jumped out of the SUV and zipped into the house and up the stairs to my bathroom before she could ask anything else.

The shower gave me both a chance to remove any powder stuck in my hair and to decide whether to give Annalynn the full story. I concluded that I had to share the information I'd gathered—and emphasize that what I'd done was not reckless. I checked my e-mail. Russ had sent me a short, businesslike message and three attachments to study. Stuart wanted to know what I had been up to. I told him I'd run errands all day and happened across Roscoe's latest victim on my way home. I hesitated. Stuart was too sharp not to realize I was omitting something. I said I would give him details in the morning.

When I went into the dining room, Annalynn was pouring lemonade at three places. Connie put the warmed-up roast on the table.

Now I had to debate whether to tell Connie everything, too. I stalled. "Did anyone tall, not dark, and not quite handsome call you today?"

She blinked. "Not that I know of. Who are you talking about?"

We took our usual places. "Tiny Towson, a former Curly, tricked me into giving him your name and preferences in men this morning."

"He hinted, she told all," Annalynn said. "You don't have to go out with him."

Connie studied her reflection in a spoon. "Is there something wrong with him?"

I hesitated, regretting my matchmaking. "I didn't think so, but I found out today he's been hiding information."

Annalynn stiffened. "What? What's he holding back?"

"That Lily Glasgow Stringer, Orson's late wife's sister, lives near the abandoned farmhouse, and that Norval Cantree, the family's white sheep, rebuilds old cars—like the Chevy that hit Mark Keller."

"You're the one always talking about need to know." Annalynn shook her finger at me. "Phoenix, you overstepped yourself again! What did you really do today?"

Her mother had scolded me that way many times. Despite myself, I drew back a nanosecond before I said in a reasonable tone, "I did not interfere in the investigation. I did nothing risky. I bought Connie some tires in Boonville and visited a woman who has contended with the Cantrees her entire life."

Annalynn inhaled and reached out to grasp my hand. "It drives me crazy that you consider yourself invulnerable." She closed her eyes. "Just this once, forget your prejudices and trust the FBI. The agents requested a list of Norval's cars from the state and have him under surveillance."

Of course. And they had a bug or a camera in that barn, too. Good thing I'd worn the disguise and bought the tires like a real customer. "And learned what? I heard Norval's wife say she didn't want *either* of them in her house. They expected young Orson and one other person. Probably the two who got away Saturday night took the Chevy as a getaway car before the FBI came on the scene."

"Roscoe may be alone," Annalynn rubbed her temple. "Willetta Volcker tells me the FBI found no evidence of a fourth person and thinks what the film shows may be a shadow." She pushed the roast around on her plate but didn't take a bite. "You must tell me what you found out, but I don't want to hear how you did it."

Connie almost knocked her glass over. "Well, I do." She blotted the spill with her napkin. "Ahhh. I see. You need deniability. Phoenix can tell me later."

Can. Won't.

"Naturally," Annalynn said, obviously relishing the idea Connie would hound me. "So you went by Oak Grove after you'd been to see the Glasgow sister. Did you learn anything more significant than her connection to Tiny?"

"I think so. Do either of you know Lily Stringer?"

Connie said, "No, but I've heard that name somewhere."

"She teaches music. She sent Brandon Cort to LCC to perform under a professional director."

Connie smiled. "A woman of great taste and perception."

I summed up my impressions: "She struck me as an honest, caring woman. She lost her husband recently and lives alone. She sleeps with a gun because she's afraid of Roscoe." A chill ran through me. "She's right. The same car that hit Mr. Keller drove by her house. One other thing: She says Derek Gribble was Roscoe's flunky in high school. Gribble could have seen the red Corvette and told Roscoe I was in La Vida Loca."

Annalynn pushed her chair back. "I'll call Jim." She stopped halfway to the hall phone. "Tiny didn't connect Gribble and Roscoe, or at least he didn't tell us."

I'd thought about that a lot on the way home. "We need to find out why without tipping him off that we know."

"Maybe through Willetta, that pregnant deputy. She's been very cooperative." Annalynn went on to the hall phone.

I held my fingers to my lips and said softly to Connie. "I'd like to talk to Brandon about places Roscoe could be hiding out. I need an excuse to do that."

"Give me a sec." A minute later, she tapped her forehead. She said nothing until we heard Annalynn hang up the phone. "Phoenix, I'm worried about my two leads learning to sing together. LaDawna doesn't even know the music. Would you be able to work with them an hour or two tomorrow afternoon?"

I winked. "That will cost you a lemon cake, and I can do it only tomorrow. You'll have to find someone else after that."

The phone rang the double ring, and Annalynn went back to answer it. "Phoenix, Sheriff Towson has a question for you."

She punched in the speakerphone as I joined her in the hall.

That warned me to be careful. "Hi, Tiny. How can I help you?"

"I was wondering how you came to find Mark Keller this afternoon."

An easy one. "I went to test a camera we put in the cemetery and saw him leave in his red pickup. A couple of minutes later a damaged car came by with a streak of red paint on it."

"Did you see the driver?"

"Only a baseball cap pulled low. He had no passenger, as far as I could tell."

"How did you know it was Roscoe?"

I couldn't say I'd seen Norval's cars. "I *assumed* it was

Roscoe. Was I wrong?"

"I *assume* you were right. Norval Cantree owned that car, and Norval was in Boonville when it ran Keller off the road. I'd hoped you had something concrete. Mr. Keller *assumed* rather than saw, too." A pause. "I asked him how come he sent a warning to Lily Stringer. He didn't remember doing that."

Stick to the literal truth. "He was pretty woozy by then. He passed out right before the ambulance got there."

"What, exactly, did he say?"

End of truth time. "Something about Roscoe might go after others." I fished for likely names. "A John or Joe. Her name was the only one I caught. Maybe it will come back to him. Is he badly hurt?"

"A mild concussion, a dislocated shoulder, and a lot of bruises. He's a tough old cuss. He told the doctor he had to go home to protect his place. His daughter put the kibosh on that."

Annalynn said, "We could move our camera from the cemetery to his house."

"No need," Tiny said. "The FBI moved in a couple of agents. They want our departments to keep our units well away from there."

"Gladly," Annalynn said.

No night calls for us. "What about the Stringer woman? Is the FBI guarding her?"

Tiny didn't answer for a moment. "They don't tell me everything."

And he didn't tell us everything. Had he even mentioned her name to the FBI? I tried a gentle probe: "Do you know what Roscoe has against her?"

"She opposed Orson's marriage to her little sister." He cleared his throat. "I'd appreciate it if you don't mention her to the press, or anyone else, for that matter. She's a real nice woman who's had a lot of heartache the last few years. She doesn't want her old quarrels with the Cantrees dragged into the open. The FBI has taken over the public statements just the way they've taken over the case, but we're still getting a lot of calls from reporters looking for 'local color.' That's the last thing she needs."

"Agreed," Annalynn said. "What are you telling reporters?"

Relieved to escape more questions, I went back to the table to finish my meal.

Connie leaned across the table to whisper, "Annalynn's really worried about you. I think that's why she agreed to continue as sheriff." Connie drew invisible patterns on the table with her right forefinger. "I wish I had more time to work with LaDawna. She has so much potential. Nancy—Aunt Eller—and I talked about LaDawna at choir rehearsal tonight. She rents a room in an old house with three other girls, including the girl playing Ado Annie. She hired LaDawna to help her clean offices at night."

"Good for them. They've got drive."

"They've also got rehearsals." Connie drew a checkmark with her finger. "Those girls ride bicycles to save money on gas. I'd give them a few hundred for food and utilities while they're rehearsing, but I don't have it."

"And I do." I didn't mind helping these young women, but I didn't appreciate Connie pushing me to do it. "Working their way through college won't hurt them. I did it. My brothers did it." Connie didn't. What I'd done a generation ago was irrelevant. I took another bite before I eased her mind. "I won't give them money, but I'll pay them well to assemble my new office furniture this weekend and arrange the place."

"Thanks." She leaned forward to whisper. "Quick. Tell me how you found out about the cars and got into Lily Stringer's house."

The only way to shut her up was to tell her, so I did.

"Not bad, but really, Phoenix, the next time you want to play undercover cop, call me. You don't have the experience to handle these operations alone."

At that moment I would have given a million dollars to tell her the truth.

Chapter Twenty

The next morning I went downstairs to feed Achilles and make coffee. I turned on the local radio station and heard that officials warned Roscoe Cantree might still be in the area and must be considered armed and dangerous. I added smart to that. He'd eluded the local, state, and federal cops since early Sunday morning. Today was Thursday. I couldn't sit around waiting for the law to snare him or for him to come after me.

Stuart understood my need to act rather than react much better than Annalynn did. Maybe she was right. Maybe I risked spoiling my relationship with him by anticipating problems. In any case, I needed information I could get only through him. I called him on my cell before the seed of guilt for using him could germinate. I began with the personal: "Assuming the FBI will catch Roscoe Cantree, what can I bring for dinner Saturday?"

"Stuff for s'mores! You make great ones." His voice carried jubilation. "I was beginning to think you're more afraid of me than the bad guys."

Not of him, of his teenage kids. I relaxed, slightly, as I pictured his well-muscled body and his lopsided, laid-back grin. "Please don't make a big deal of the dinner with Kaysi and Zeke. Or with your mother."

He laughed. "Too late. Mom is already making notes about the wedding reception she and Annalynn will throw in the castle."

"Bloody hell!" I found absolutely nothing amusing about that. "Tell her to"—I searched for a mild but clear term—"to stop pushing."

"Don't worry, Phoenix. Mom doesn't rule my life any more than Annalynn does yours."

I was beginning to wonder if either of them knew that. My stomach knotted at this unexpected complication in my life. I jumped to my area of comfort: "Forget their fantasies. I'd like your input on Roscoe Cantree. Surely only a psychopath would risk capture to take revenge on an old man he hasn't seen in about twenty years."

"I managed to pull up Cantree's records. Not a psychopath but definitely a sociopath—mean, angry, arrogant. He linked up with a white supremacist group in prison. He could be getting help from one of its Missouri cells."

Hard to envision those hatemongers among the friendly people of northern Missouri. "Are there cells in Vandiver County?"

"No, but he wouldn't have to go far. Would they risk thumbing their noses at the FBI for a felon they don't know? Hard to say."

"I gather the FBI thinks he's the only gang member still free." I waited for a confirmation. I didn't get it. I didn't get a denial either. "Has the FBI realized Annalynn and I didn't spirit away those Krugerrands?"

"They haven't confided in me."

So we were still under suspicion. "Idiots! They're wasting resources investigating us, not to mention all those rookies staking out that casino in Boonville."

He chuckled. "I'm pretty sure they missed your visit. They found Roscoe on the tapes. Until they picked him out, they thought Tiny was an idiot for saying Roscoe stayed in the area. They'll search from a helicopter today, so stay out of northern

Vandiver County." He paused. "What *are* you doing today?"

"This morning I'm waiting for delivery of a ton of unassembled furniture to set up a temporary foundation office in my house. This afternoon I'm helping two students rehearse their songs from *Oklahoma!* at the college."

"Sounds harmless. What are you really doing?"

I decided to share. "I'm hoping one of the students can give me some leads on where to look for Roscoe and who shot at me. Another thing: Annalynn is running a national check on Derek Gribble, Roscoe's high school buddy and one of our suspects for the restaurant shooting. Gribble needs money desperately. Maybe Roscoe is paying his old pal to hide him." Better that Agent Wharton receive that tip from Stuart than from Annalynn or me.

The boxes of furniture and supplies filled most of my living room and dining room. While Achilles busied himself sniffing them, I relaxed by playing Scott Joplin on my console piano.

Annalynn called to report, "We can't place Fargo near La Vida Loca Monday evening. We're dropping that investigation. We've struck out on Gribble, too. He has no arrest record anywhere. Tiny barely remembers him from high school. He was a year or two behind him. What do you think we should do?"

"Let's keep an eye on Gribble anyway." They had no one to tail him. "We need a tracker on his vehicles in case he takes food or gas to Roscoe."

I heard Jim's voice in the background.

Annalynn came back on. "We don't have enough to persuade the judge to authorize that. Maybe Tiny can suggest it to the FBI."

"Don't bother." I could handle it myself.

"Leave this to the FBI, Phoenix," Annalynn ordered. She hung up.

She and Jim had discounted Fargo. I hadn't. Evil sometimes comes in deceptive packages. Besides, eliminating him as a suspect would help. So how could I do that? The simplest way would be to scare the truth out of him. Did that work with college kids?

My phone rang again. Connie.

She sounded rushed. "I've scheduled you to work with Brandon and LaDawna in practice room B from one until two and with her from three until four. Brandon will bring the music for you. By the way, those practice rooms are chilly. You'll need a sweater."

"Do you know if Fargo will be there this afternoon?"

"Could be. His dance instructor told me the dancers are her call. She won't cut him for 'a foolish mistake.' The dancers meet in the big room down the hall. Please don't go near him while he's on campus. 'Harassing' the dean's son could cost me my job."

Damn. Connie and Annalynn were hemming me in. "Okay. Did you ask Trudy to dig for more dirt on Derek Gribble?"

"She's got the busiest busybodies in town working on who he sees and where he goes and what he spends. I told her it's to protect Mrs. Tesopolis. Trudy's taking Mrs. T some tomatoes this afternoon. I'll get a full report tonight."

I dropped Achilles off at the sheriff's office on my way to the college. I drove around the campus twice to make sure no one was tailing my Camry before parking in a pull-through spot in the half-empty student lot.

As I walked toward the building, LaDawna rode up on an old blue boy's bike and locked it in a stand by the door. Today she wore all white rather than all black. A white stripe ran through the top of her spiked black hair. From her complexion I guessed her hair was blond rather than black.

"Congratulations on winning the Laurey role," I said.

She stepped back as though I'd threatened her and blushed a deep red. "Thanks, Dr. Smith."

"I'm not on the faculty. Call me Phoenix."

She dropped her chin and mumbled, "Okay."

How was anyone so shy going to carry a musical? I reminded myself that Mario panicked if we met strangers at a cocktail party but his nerves steadied the moment he sang the first note before a demanding Viennese audience. I pushed through one of the double doors. "Do you know where our practice room is?"

She blinked several times and hugged herself. "Are you—Ms. Diamante didn't say you were coming."

"She asked me to play the piano for you and Brandon." The girl was afraid of me. Did she think I'd tell Connie she didn't know the music? Surely LaDawna knew she had a great voice. Maybe my gun, clearly visible today, frightened her. She'd become hysterical when I drew on Fargo.

"Hi," Brandon said, running up to us. He tipped his Cardinals' baseball cap to me and smiled at her.

At her age I would have found him irresistible, but she barely nodded at him.

He held up a geometry worksheet. "Did you figure out how to do the third one?"

She shook her head and hurried on down the hall.

Opportunity. "I'll be glad to work on geometry with you after we rehearse."

"Gee, thanks," Brandon said.

LaDawna said nothing.

I checked the practice schedule posted in the hall. Connie had put my name as well as theirs on it. Apparently LaDawna hadn't looked at it.

The practice room was freezing. Brandon took the music and a long-sleeved shirt from his backpack. LaDawna shivered in her sleeveless top. I'd brought both a sweater and a shawl in a tote bag.

I handed her the shawl, put on the sweater, and took my place on the piano bench. Both singers moved nervously. I tried to ease their tension. "You may have to do jumping jacks with the vocal exercises to warm up."

I'd sometimes played exercises for Mario. I began with a simple one. Brandon did fine. LaDawna's throat was tight. Now what? I remembered a breathing exercise Mario used to relax him. I took them through that and went back to the vocal exercises. Gradually she became engrossed in the notes. I ran Brandon through his lower range, skipped to a range comfortable to both, and then quieted him as I took her higher and higher. I couldn't believe the clarity and precision of her upper register.

"LaDawna, you have a truly remarkable voice," I said. "You have a great future."

A smile transformed her face and her shoulders lifted. "Really?"

"Really. Surely your voice teachers have told you that."

She wrinkled her nose. "In seventh grade the music teacher said my voice was freaky and I shouldn't sing so loud."

"What an idiot," Brandon said. "I never heard anything so beautiful."

A good kid. Enthusiasm rather than jealousy for another's talent. I wanted to reward him: "You two are going to make beautiful music together. Let's start on your first duet, 'People Will Say We're in Love.' "

A little later the girl who played Ado Annie opened the door. "Sorry, but your time is up. It's my turn."

"You'll want my sweater. You can just leave it on the piano. LaDawna and I are coming back at three." I handed the sweater to her. "I intended to call you. Connie told me you run a small cleaning business. I need two or three people to help me assemble office furniture and set up an office Saturday at my house. Can you handle that?"

The girl hesitated. "I'll need to find someone free. Okay to let you know tonight?"

"I can work then," LaDawna said.

"Me, too," Brandon said, "if you don't have anybody else."

"You're hired," Ado Annie said.

I extended my hand to her. "Excellent. I'll pay your going rate plus a bonus for working on the weekend. Now let's go conquer geometry in the cafeteria."

The two young singers talked excitedly about the show as we walked to the cafeteria. LaDawna sniffed appreciatively when we went into the giant room.

It hit me that the girl was quite hungry. "Their hamburgers smell great. Would either of you like one?"

She swallowed but said nothing.

Hungry and proud, I reflected. I handed Brandon a twenty. "I know you're hungry. My brothers ate like lions at your age. Get burgers and fries and drinks for you and LaDawna. Coffee with lots of cream for me. LaDawna, what would you like to drink?"

"Milk, please," she said.

I led the way to a table in a quiet corner. "Tell me what you're doing in your class."

The smile vanished. "I wish I could. I've been working the last three years. I didn't realize I'd forgotten so much since high school."

"Don't worry. I got Connie through high school geometry. She hated it." Tutoring her had driven me crazy. I'd persisted only because Annalynn wheedled me into it.

LaDawna and Brandon proved more pliable than Connie. Most of the hour and all of the food was gone before I could question him about hiding places for Roscoe. My chance came when LaDawna went to the restroom.

He watched her go. "This is the happiest she's been all week."

"What's wrong? Is she homesick? Worried about money?"

"I think she misses her boyfriend. I saw her sniffling over some guy's picture in her billfold."

Brandon didn't seem insulted that she'd indicated no romantic interest in him. He probably had other interests. "By the way, was Mrs. Stringer okay when you got there yesterday evening?"

"Yes." He looked out the window. "She's pretty scared, but she says she won't let Roscoe Cantree bully her this time. My brother and I stayed at her house last night."

Bloody hell! Kids versus a killer.

He focused on my face. "Funny thing. She barely knows Mr. Keller. She was surprised he warned her."

I shrugged. "He probably heard from someone that Roscoe had it in for her. Do you know anyone else he might target?"

"Well, he hates Sheriff Towson. Mrs. Stringer thinks Roscoe wanted Mr. Keller in the hospital so Roscoe could hide out in his house."

Quite possible. "I'm amazed Roscoe's managed to stay free so long. Could he be hiding out in a cave somewhere?"

"Nope. Lots of caves in south Missouri, but I've never run across one here. I think he's probably been camping out." He leaned across the table. "I'm afraid he'll hear Mrs. Stringer lives alone now and figure he can move in on her." He sat back. "We watched that video of you I posted on YouTube. She said you look a lot like a distant cousin of hers from Maryland. You got any relatives there?"

I'd been careless, foolishly overconfident, to go in with such a simple disguise. "Possibly. My father's mother grew up near Baltimore."

He stood as LaDawna came toward us. "What time should we come Saturday?"

"Nine o'clock, if that's okay."

They both nodded.

My last chance to mine him for information. "By the way, do either of you know where Fargo spends most of his free time?"

She shook her head. "I'd never seen him before the auditions."

"He claims his band rehearses every night," Brandon said. He picked up the tray. "Time for me to get home. It's my turn to help with the milking. See ya."

Nothing on Roscoe's hiding place. Nothing on his enemies' list. Nothing on Fargo. I'd struck out.

LaDawna tensed up again as we walked back to the practice room. I tried to relax her by talking about the music. "Let's run through your first big number, 'Many a New Day.' It fits your voice."

The corners of her mouth curled slightly. "I really like singing that one."

I tapped on the closed door. No one answered. I opened the door and left it open in hopes the warmer air would penetrate the room.

"This place is so cold," LaDawna said, reaching for the shawl on the piano. She staggered back and screamed a high C sharp. She pointed to the shawl and bolted out the door.

Gun in hand, I scanned the shawl.

A small brown spider with a violin-shaped mark on its back scurried under a fold. Someone had left us a poisonous brown recluse.

Chapter Twenty-One

My mother's repeated warnings about the poisonous spider flashed through my mind. Holstering my gun, I reached for the sheet music on the piano. I slammed it down on the shawl a half dozen times. Taking a piece of fringe between finger and thumb, I pulled the shawl off the piano and shook it. A squished spider fell out. I found a tissue, picked it up, and dropped it into my tote bag. I inspected the front and back of the shawl inch by inch before folding it and draping it over my shoulder. Then I rolled up the music, edged one end under my sweater, and lifted it up. A tiny spider clung to the neck. I shook it off, stepped on it, and dropped the sweater on the bench to give it a thorough beating. Finally I picked the garment up with my music roll and inspected every centimeter.

I heard a cacophony of voices in the hall and walked out to find LaDawna. She leaned her back against the wall and covered her face with her hands. Five young women in leotards and leggings and the waif-like dance teacher stood around her. Fargo, smirking, watched from a door down the hall. Ah, yes, the boy who liked to scare girls with spiders.

He sobered when I stalked toward him.

I grabbed him by the ear and twisted it. "Let's go, Spiderman."

He yelled ouch and then obscenities as I dragged him down the hall, shoved him into the practice room, and slammed the door. "Call security, please," I said to the dance teacher.

"I'm here." An older man in a blue uniform hurried up. "What happened?"

"A student put brown recluse spiders in this practice room. Lock him in, please." Seeing him hesitate, I touched my holster. "Or would you prefer I handle it?"

He locked the door and hurried down the hall holding a cell phone.

I pushed my way through to LaDawna, now sitting on the floor with her head buried on her knees. "Did it bite you?"

She raised her head. "No, just scared me." She struggled to her feet. "I'm allergic to insect bites. I got stung Saturday night and spent hours in the emergency room."

The Reverend Nancy Alderton, aka Aunt Eller, stepped between the students and took LaDawna's arm. "I'm in the practice room down the hall. No spiders in there, I promise you. Come rehearse with me while Dr. Smith takes care of this."

I mouthed a thank you to the older woman.

The elfin dance teacher planted herself in front of me. "You have no right to touch a student."

"Or a teacher," I said sweetly. "Go to your room. All of you."

They went.

A middle-aged man in a blue blazer ran down the hall toward me. "I'm Dean Klimton. What's going on here?"

Fargo's father. "Your son played another of his potentially fatal pranks." I described what had happened, including the smirk.

Two red blotches appeared on the dean's pale cheeks. "What do you want me to do?"

I hadn't expected to be asked. "First, find out how many spiders he put in there. Second, lock him in until he finds all of them. Third, report this to the police. Fourth, expel him."

I heard a gasp. The dance teacher had returned to listen and, doubtless, to complain.

The father rallied at my last two demands. "I'm sure he had no intention of hurting anyone."

The man who'd gone to Annalynn's office because his son brought a loaded pistol to the audition surely didn't believe that. "Every first grader in Laycock knows the brown recluse can be deadly."

He gulped. "Only for small children."

"Or a young woman who's allergic to its venom." I spoke loudly enough that the dozen students clustered a few yards away could hear.

His shoulders slumped. He motioned to the guard. "Unlock the door, please."

When that was done, the dean opened the door about a foot but stayed in the hall. "Son, how many spiders did you turn loose in there?"

Silence.

"This is no joke. The young woman could have died from a spider bite."

"That's crazy," Fargo whined. "She'd just swell up a little bit. Besides, the spiders weren't meant for her."

The dean shuddered. "How many," he said softly, "did you put in there?"

"Two adults and three little ones."

The dance teacher gasped.

"When you've gathered them all up, knock on the door." The dean closed the door and motioned for the security guard to lock it. "My sincere apologies, Dr. Smith. His behavior was inexcusable." He pulled back his shoulders. "He was foolish and thoughtless, and as the dean and his father, I'll see that he's punished." He took a deep breath. "I swear to you that he didn't know the gun was loaded at the audition, and he didn't shoot at you Monday night."

I wasn't so sure. A little interrogation behind bars might give us the answer, and it would keep Fargo out of the way for a little while. "He's admitted he did this. Will you call the police or shall I?"

He licked his lips. "The faculty handles students' misdemeanors."

"This was a felony, not a misdemeanor." I was bluffing, but it sounded reasonable. "Call the police."

He looked at the students filling the hall and took out his phone. "Very well. While we're waiting, I'll make sure he finds *all* the spiders."

Except the one I'd put in my bag. Let the vicious brat keep searching. "I'll be close by."

Students parted like a denim sea as I strolled down to Nancy Alderton's practice room. When I opened the door, LaDawna was singing an exercise *a cappella* while the older woman, head cocked to one side, listened from the piano bench.

LaDawna stopped. "I'm teaching her the exercise you gave us. Did you learn it in Vienna?"

"Yes, I used to play it for a friend, an opera singer. Let me play it for both of you."

The minister readily relinquished her seat. She began well, but soon threw up her hands and left it to the girl to soar into the upper range.

Jim Falstaff opened the door. "Sorry to interrupt. I need to speak to you, Phoenix."

"Go ahead," Nancy said. "LaDawna and I can work together today."

I said good-bye to them and joined Jim in the hall. Only Klimton and the security guard remained. We walked away from them.

Jim scratched the whiskers on his right cheek. "I don't know whether a felony charge will stick."

"I don't really care. I want to scare the—uh—stuffing out of the little weasel and find out whether he shot at me Monday night. I'd love five minutes alone with him in a sound-proofed room."

"No way." He glanced down the hall. "His dad looks downright sick. If you're willing to go in there with a spider still on the loose, you can ask him for a brief private conversation with the boy."

"Okay, but you take him to jail after that."

Jim walked down the hall and spoke to the father in a low voice. He told the security guard to unlock the door and then motioned to me.

I had the guard open the door wide and checked to make sure Fargo was on the other side of the small room before I stepped in and closed the door behind me. I studied his contorted face but couldn't tell whether he was fighting fury or tears. "You've pointed a loaded gun at me. You've put venomous spiders in my clothes. Why?"

He took quick shallow breaths and clenched and unclenched his fists. "You're ruining my life!" He beat his fists on the top of the innocent piano.

A spoiled young ass. "Correction. *You* are ruining your life. If you don't want to become a cell block's new girlfriend, tell me exactly where you were Monday night."

He glared at me. "I don't have to tell you anything." Then he unloosed such a steady stream of profanities that he must have rehearsed it.

I doubted that Jim would do any better than I had. The kid was too egocentric to admit how much trouble he had caused others, and himself. I blew him a kiss and left. His curses—a rerun of his earlier performance—followed me down the hall.

Jim hurried after me. "Well?"

I thought a moment. "He thinks like a ten-year-old. He's

convinced his father will get him out of trouble. Can you charge him with assault with a deadly weapon?"

"I can threaten to, but the prosecutor will never go for that." Jim sighed. "I'll be lucky if I can host him overnight at the jail. Sometimes that wakes them, and their parents, up. I'll call you if he says anything I can believe."

"Thanks, Jim." I paused at the door and surveyed the campus and streets before stepping outside. Damn it! I'd learned nothing except that Fargo still belonged on my suspect list. He'd be out of commission for at least a few hours. Time to follow up on my hunch about Derek Gribble's reunion with his old pal Roscoe.

Chapter Twenty-Two

My priority was to find out where Derek Gribble had been Saturday and Monday nights. If he could have been helping Roscoe, I'd devise a way to track Gribble's pickup and his truck without tipping off him or law enforcement.

He'd hinted he was with a woman. Waiting for the car to cool, I called Connie to see if her cousin had come up with a name.

"Trudy's grapevine says Gribble brags about women flirting with him, but the only woman anyone remembers him mentioning is Boopsie Kobold. She's divorced."

Could this be a bad joke? "Kobold is German for goblin. The name sounds like a stripper's alias. Come to think of it, so does LaDawna McKnight."

"Not everyone has a common first name like, say, Phoenix," Connie shot back. "Boopsie sold furniture at the store where Gribble worked as a mover. Now she works at Liquors and Lariats. It's just off the square where Lee's Timepieces used to be."

"I remember. I'll go buy some wine."

Five minutes later, I opened the door to Liquors and Lariats. A *zaftig* bleached blonde who had breezed by sixty smiled a welcome. A piece of adhesive tape on her nametag had Boopsie printed on it in black capital letters.

I began with the mandatory comment: "Hi. It's good to come in out of the heat."

"Every August gets hotter. Either this global warming stuff is for real or hell is moving upward." She paused to make sure I appreciated her joke. "Either way, you need a drink. What can I help you find, honey?"

A gregarious woman eager for company. Good. "I'm not quite sure. I haven't been in here before, but I couldn't resist the name. Tell me about the ropes." Looped lariats hung on the walls above glass refrigerators loaded with beer. In the center one, a shelf held cheap scotch, vodka, and tequila.

Eagerly she launched into a long, funny tale of the owner's short career as a rodeo rider.

I listened and laughed, establishing rapport. "You're a born storyteller," I said when she finished. "Do you tell professionally?"

"Oh, no. But I do love the sound of my own voice. Now, what'll it be? Liquor or lariat?"

"I'm looking for a good Missouri wine, something to drink with chicken."

"Oh, dear. He doesn't carry much wine." She walked behind the counter and bent down to a low shelf. She pulled out a dusty bottle with a screw-off cap. "I don't drink myself and I work here only part time. I really can't tell you whether this tastes more like nectar or vinegar."

"Judging from the dust, it's aging in place," I said, making it clear we were sharing a joke. A bond established, I made my move: "Didn't you used to work at that furniture store over on Pershing?"

"Oh, yeah. I worked there for thirteen years. I bawled my eyes out when it closed. Seems to me Laycock ought to have enough business for one furniture store."

I studied the label. "It must have been like losing a family member."

"Oh, yeah. I'd worked with most everybody there for at least ten years." She sighed. "Four of us get together every other Saturday to play pitch or hearts."

Pay dirt. "Really? Even after—what—a year?"

"Oh, yeah." A light frown creased her forehead. "Well, most of the time. Three of us played Yahtzee last Saturday. Our fourth didn't show. He *claimed* he had to take his mother-in-law to the emergency room." She wrinkled her nose. "He fancies himself a card shark. I figure he got a chance to play for money somewhere."

Or to go gambling at a casino with an old friend. I handed the bottle back to her. "A married man comes on Saturday nights without his wife?"

Boopsie smiled ruefully. "Believe me, we're doing them both a favor. She cooks a special dinner, some eggplant thing he hates, for her mother every other Saturday." She tsked. "What ticked me off, he asked us to get together Monday night. Then he called at the last minute to say he had an out-of-town delivery. A likely story, I'd say."

Maybe not. Maybe he took supplies to Roscoe. Definitely worthwhile to watch Gribble. "I'd find another fourth. Or is he a personable guy who's fun to have around?"

"Not really." She laughed. "He's more a habit." She rummaged around and found another bottle of wine. "This comes from Hermann, that old German town on the Missouri River. It must be good. No dust on the bottle."

I bought the wine, a chardonnay, and chatted a minute about Missouri's resurgent wine industry before leaving.

Considering the low statistical probability that Gribble had been with some other woman both Saturday and Monday nights, I had to track his movements. In Vienna, I kept the tools on hand. A Langley friend could procure state-of-the-art trackers for me, but even a courier couldn't deliver those to me for a couple of days. I'd have to improvise. Laycock must offer trackers for regular people—parents of kids like Fargo, pizza places with delivery cars, pet owners.

My best hope for a civilian tracker was the town's small Radio Shack. I drove over and went in to browse.

A slender blond teenager rushed from behind the counter to greet me. "Dr. Smith, you were so right to make them arrest Fargo. He doesn't know the difference between teasing and harassment."

I recognized her as one of the dancers in the hall. Word of anything I bought here would be all over town before dark. "Thank you. I hope his parents will recognize that."

She frowned. "Our dance instructor doesn't. Could I help you find something?"

Think fast. "Do you have one of those invisible fences to keep cats from coming into the yard? They stalk the hummingbirds."

She whirled and walked toward the back. "You can buy things on the Web to keep your cat in your yard. I don't think we carry anything to keep them out."

While she was looking, I spotted a tracker to put on a dog's collar. Surely I could make that work, if I could buy it anonymously. I thanked the girl and left. I sat in the car and debated my next move. To go back in there under bright lights to buy the pet tracker, I'd need a really good disguise. Same for Connie. Forget the disguise. Use an asset. I dialed Vernon Kann.

"What's new, Phoenix?"

"I need a favor, a confidential one."

He said nothing for a moment. "Glad to do it—if you tell me why."

I'd anticipated that. "It will be obvious when I tell you what I need." With luck he wouldn't be able to figure it out and would be egotistical enough not to admit it.

"What is it?"

"An electronic tracker you put on a dog's collar."

"Why can't you buy it yourself?"

"The clerk in Radio Shack knows me." Surely that would tell him to stop asking questions.

A long pause. "Would you like for me to drop it off at the castle?"

"No. I'll pick it up tomorrow morning."

"I see." Another pause. "Is the collar for Spiderman?"

He'd already heard what happened at LCC. "No, of course not."

"I can be a lot more help if I know your target. Besides, it's a fair trade."

Telling anyone went against the grain. Telling a reporter repelled me. But I was operating in Laycock, not Eastern Europe. "I can't even give you the initials, doggone it."

He didn't respond. I tried again: "Doggone and dadgum, Vernon, you know the value of deniability."

He snorted. "Yes, I've watched plenty of politicians 'not know' or 'not remember.' " He fell silent for a minute. "I'll be doggoned. By the way, how's Mrs. T?"

He'd gotten the message. I confirmed: "Good. I'll go check on her tomorrow after I pick up the tracker. Thanks."

One tracker down, one to go.

My cell phone rang before I could pull out. Willetta Volcker, Tiny's deputy, from her personal phone.

She didn't waste words: "From the grapevine, not me: An Indian casino in Oklahoma—about a six- or seven-hour drive from here—deposited nine hundred-dollar bills from the Cleveland bank robbery this morning. The FBI has alerted airport security, highway patrols, and border guards from Texas to California to watch for the distinctive Cantree ears. They've made it clear investigating Roscoe's connection to Derek Gribble will receive a lower priority than investigating you and

Annalynn. They say she has serious financial problems."

Bloody hell! "Just the aftermath of her husband's death. She'll be in good shape as soon as she sells some investments." I wished that were true. How much to tell Willetta about Gribble? She'd stuck her neck out to call me. I mustn't endanger her by hinting at what I intended to do. "The Cantrees faked an air departure right after the robbery. This could be another feint. Gribble gave a false alibi, probably because he was helping Roscoe. Could you put out the word to watch for both of his vehicles?"

"Done." She hung up.

Friday morning during breakfast, Tiny called Annalynn. She motioned to me and turned on the speakerphone.

Tiny said, "The FBI says Roscoe is headed southwest toward Mexico."

She held up a silencing finger to me. "Do you believe he's gone for good?"

"The bastard's too dangerous for us to take a chance."

"I agree," Annalynn said. "Did the FBI see anything from the helicopter yesterday?"

He didn't answer for a moment. "Strictly QT, they found a campsite in some timber along a ditch about ten miles east of the old Cantree farmhouse. He'd hidden a vehicle among the trees."

Annalynn handed me a notepad. "Was he alone?"

"Yup. That surprised me."

I scribbled "NC's cars" on the pad.

Annalynn nodded. "Is he driving another one of Norval's old cars?"

"We don't know—wait a minute. How do you know about those cars?"

"From a source in Boonville."

Tiny sighed. "I sure hope Norval isn't mixed up in this. He claims Roscoe paid him to fix up that car and came by for it around eleven Saturday night."

Credible. I started to scribble.

Annalynn had anticipated my question: "How did he get there?"

"If anybody knows, they're not telling me," Tiny said. "Norval says Roscoe walked up while they—Norval and his wife—sat outside cooling off with a beer. If he's telling the truth, somebody gave Roscoe a ride."

Likely Derek Gribble. I had to get trackers on both his pickup and his truck.

The moment Annalynn left for the office I called Elena at the bank with my question of the day: "Has Derek Gribble made any large cash deposits this week?"

"Give me a moment." Keys clicked. "No, only checks from the expected source."

Damn. I doubted he would be smart enough to hold onto all of a payoff. "I suspect he's being paid for criminal activity. I don't have anything official, but could you ask your tellers to put any cash deposit he makes into a separate envelope?"

"That's somewhat . . . unusual. Is this related to the matter we discussed earlier in the week?"

She risked major repercussions if her boss found out she was helping me. She had the right to know why I wanted the information before she decided whether to give it. "He may be helping Roscoe Cantree."

She drew in her breath sharply. "I see. Let me look into that and call you back."

Two minutes later Elena rang me from her cell phone. "Every bank in the area is already watching for hundreds," she said, her voice low. “Can’t Mrs.—Sheriff Keyser give me something official?”

“Sorry. This is my hunch, not an official request.”

“I’ll do what I can, but I can’t guarantee anything. Got to go.”

Scheisse. Another legal limitation. I rounded up Achilles and headed for Vernon’s with the tools I’d need.

He sat on his front porch with an open laptop, a thermal pot, two cups, and a little brown paper bag.

I greeted him and handed him the cash to pay for the tracker.

“The thing’s pretty damned big,” he said, pouring me a cup of coffee.

“I won’t need the whole thing. Go ahead with your work while I take a look at it.”

When he turned his gaze back to the screen, I slipped on surgical gloves and opened the bag. Using it to obscure Vernon’s view, I cut away the tracker’s unneeded bits, messed up its ID, and roughened its surface to age it. Then I glued on the magnets that would hold it in place in a narrow opening between the pickup cab and the toolbox mounted in the bed. That done, I put away my tools, tossed the scraps in the bag, and began to set up the monitor on my iPhone.

Vernon closed the laptop. “I’m going to Columbia to research that elder abuse story today. I’ll also have lunch with some knowledgeable friends. I heard you have a rental car to return. I could pick you up at Avis about three thirty.”

“Thanks. I was wondering how I’d get a ride back.” I wrapped the tracker in a tissue, put it in my purse, and stripped off the gloves. “You realize that gratitude won’t compel me to answer any of those questions you’re itching to ask.”

He absentmindedly picked up the gloves. “Your resumé doesn’t begin to cover all your talents, Phoenix. If I didn’t know what a low opinion you have of the media, I’d swear you’ve been an investigative reporter."

I smiled, relieved his guess had gone so far astray. "You'd be surprised how hard it is to get accurate information from entrepreneurs and bankers through regular channels."

"Surely you don't mean you're versed in industrial espionage."

I said nothing, content to let him accept that explanation for my unusual skills.

He studied my face, obviously not quite sure what to believe. "Be careful, Phoenix. You're not dealing with bankers now."

Chapter Twenty-Three

I called Mrs. T and asked if I could bring by the *ouzo.*

"Come, come," she said. "You stay for little chat?"

"Of course." The longer I stayed, the better chance I had that Kiki would bring the pickup to me.

Parking beneath Mrs. T's maple tree, I noted that the lawn now had green patches amid the brown. I started to take Achilles around to the back, but the front door opened.

"Bring your friend inside," Mrs. T called.

"Come," I said, not sure he would. He hesitated, but he came, his nose twitching. "This is Achilles."

She chuckled. "Now I know for sure you are Greek."

He politely waited for her to settle in her chair and put aside her walker before offering his paw.

"A gentleman," she said, shaking the paw.

Maybe I should take him on all my informal interrogations. I showed her the bottle of *ouzo.* "This is the only one I could find. Is it a good one?"

She pulled it close to read the label. "Very good. Thank you, thank you." Tears welled in her eyes. "Many memories."

"Would you like for me to put it in the kitchen?"

"Please. Now we will have tea. Tonight I will sip a little *ouzo* and remember."

While the water boiled, I checked her cabinets and refrigerator. They were not as well stocked as they had been on my last visit.

The front door opened, and Greek words flew between Kiki and her mother. Kiki stormed into the kitchen with Achilles at her heels. She carried two plastic grocery bags.

"Good morning," I chirped. "Will you have a cup of tea with us?"

She turned her face away and put the bags on the table. Finally she said, "I brought Mom a lemon for her tea."

"That was thoughtful of you." Nothing as disarming as a little praise. I had to hold her here until I could get to the pickup. "She appreciates your shopping for her."

"I love my mother," she said, her voice low and fierce.

"I know you do." Makeup didn't quite cover a bruise on her left cheekbone. I had to do something about Derek Gribble fast. I'd ask Annalynn to request an official check of hospital records to see whether Kiki had suffered any suspicious injuries.

"Need to make a phone call," Kiki mumbled, hurrying out the back door. She came back in just as I finished putting our tea on a tray. She handed the phone to me. "My husband wants to talk to you." She grabbed the tray and hurried down the hall.

Intrigued, I smiled to warm my voice. "How are you today, Mr. Gribble?"

"You get out of that house now and don't come back," he snarled. "You bother that poor old woman again and I'll sue you for—for stalking."

What an idiot. Maybe I could surprise him without giving too much away. "An interesting idea. Did it come to you Monday night?"

"You can't pin that shooting on me," he screamed. "I was playing cards with my lady friends." He hung up.

His lie confirmed the need for the tracker. I strolled into the living room and gave the phone to Kiki.

She grabbed it and hurried toward the kitchen.

Time to apply a little more pressure. "Mrs. T," I said just

loudly enough for Kiki to overhear, "I'm a financial expert. Would you like for me to help you with your bookkeeping?"

The old woman frowned and motioned me to come close. She whispered, "I am old. I am not a fool. What he takes, I give. Better you go now."

My stomach lurched. Had I made the situation dangerous for mother and daughter? What I broke, I had to fix. I whispered, "Call me if you need *anything.*"

I let Achilles out first, checked the street, and reached into my purse for my keys, a tissue, and the tracker. "Achilles, find, please." I stared at the pickup.

He looked at me for more detailed instructions. "Find, please." He'd found marijuana in tires twice before. "Check the tires."

He trotted to the pickup's nearest rear tire, sniffed, and moved on to the front one. When he went to the street side, I called, "Achilles, come," and walked around the back of the pickup toward the cab. I slipped the tracker into place. Crude, but it should work.

One vehicle down, one to go.

During the night I'd come up with a simple solution for the other tracker, an untraceable cell phone. I drove home and set one up with a contact list giving numbers for a pizza place in St. Louis, a porn shop in Kansas City, and FBI headquarters. If the FBI found the tracker, those numbers should divert suspicion from me. And drive the agents nuts.

Now to locate the truck. I daren't risk doing it the obvious, easy way myself. Connie wanted in on the action. I called her cell and said softly, "Are you alone?"

"Just a sec." A mumble of voices. "All clear."

"Gribble lied about being at Boopsie's. I want to find out if he's going somewhere today to meet Roscoe." I checked the tracker on my cell. Kiki had returned home. "Could you please call his house from a phone at the college and disguise your voice? Ask whether he's available to make a delivery today. If he says yes, tell him you'll call him back as soon as you tend to some emergency."

"Got it. Does Annalynn know about this?"

"Strictly between us." I disconnected, confident Connie didn't mind keeping a secret if she thought that would protect Annalynn. On the other hand, Connie would crack if Annalynn frowned at her. Had to risk it.

I thought about the newspaper photo of the furniture store's old truck that Gribble had received in lieu of severance pay. Even if he'd painted out the signs on its white metal sides, the truck would be easy to spot, surely too conspicuous for him to risk using it to meet Roscoe. The pickup would be much safer.

The phone rang. Connie.

She spoke *sotto voce*. "He left about eight to take a couch to Moberly and won't be back until late afternoon. Sounds fishy. Who would hire a truck to deliver a secondhand couch? Besides, even with a long lunch, that's four or five hours more than that delivery should take."

"Right. He's up to something. Thanks."

Now what? I had nothing concrete. No, I had enough that I couldn't let it slide. I dialed Willetta Volcker's private number on my cell.

After several rings, she answered, "Hi, girlfriend, what's up?"

An FBI agent must be sitting in front of her. I kept my voice low. "The buddy left town in his truck on a suspiciously long delivery. He may head up your way."

"Thanks. Talk to you after work."

I hung up. Willetta and I were definitely on the same page.

Reassured, I called Annalynn. "I heard that Gribble took his truck out of town on a fake-sounding delivery. Could you have your deputies watch for it?"

She didn't answer for a long time. "Phoenix, did you put a tracker on his truck?"

Lucky she asked me that now. "No, I did not. If I had, I'd know where he's gone and wouldn't be asking you to look for him."

"Yes, of course. Sorry. I'll alert our patrol cars."

"One other thing. Could you dog-sit this afternoon? I'm going to drop off that rental car parked under the jail and get a lift home from Columbia with Vernon."

"Fine. You and Achilles can ride back with me after lunch. Pack up a chew toy and something else to amuse him. I'm not playing fetch with him in the hall anymore."

Vernon said little as he focused on navigating Columbia's modest early rush-hour traffic. He'd obviously lost his urban driving skills after years in Laycock, where dogs sometimes sunned themselves in the middle of the street. I remembered that he'd gladly yielded the wheel to me when we drove out to search for a rabid deer.

After he cautiously merged onto 63 North, I checked my business e-mail. My old boss at Adderly International wanted a contact with esoteric financial information. I debated a moment before sending a name from my private list. Then I peeked at the tracking app an instant before putting away my mobile. The pickup hadn't moved.

I kept quiet until Vernon loosened his death grip on the steering wheel. "Learn anything of interest from your 'knowledgeable' friends?"

"A little." He kept his eyes on the road. "They've known the players for years. The Cantrees were always pure trouble—drinkers, liars, petty thieves. The boys were good athletes and smart enough, but Norval was the only one who finished high school. The others got expelled for cheating or fighting."

His speed had dropped to sixty. Next time I'd offer to drive. "What about Derek Gribble's family?"

"Quiet, hard-working people who managed to buy a new car every few years. My friends barely remember Derek, but his sister babysat for them a few times. She left home the day after she graduated from high school and never came back. Not even for her parents' funerals. That could signal abuse."

"Any official reports of her father abusing her or her mother?"

"No, but the mother had lots of 'accidents,' the old code for beatings. Sons see, sons do."

"Kiki had a bruise on her face today." A school bus passed us. I reined in my impatience at Vernon's turtle speed. "What about the Glasgows?"

"The polar opposites of the Cantrees. No one could believe it when their youngest took up with Orson. Sheriff Towson—he was a rookie cop then—was fit to be tied. He dated a Glasgow girl and clashed with Roscoe in high school. Some thought he went out of his way to pull over or run in any Cantree."

"No wonder Tiny takes the old threat against him seriously." His history also might explain his holding out on Annalynn and me about Lily Glasgow Stringer.

"That's all I found out." He accelerated until the speedometer hit sixty-five. "How did your morning go?"

"As planned, except that Kiki called Gribble. He told me to keep away from Mrs. T." I'd give Vernon nothing more. "How's your article on elder abuse coming?"

"Really well, I say modestly. I had two great interviews after lunch, one with a nurse who works in respite care for the elderly and another with a cop who investigates domestic abuse. He cited both physical abuse and financial fraud. We'll run a long feature and a what-to-do sidebar Sunday."

We'd slowed to sixty. "Couldn't you have talked to them on the telephone?"

"I wanted nuances and personal anecdotes, not just information. Nothing beats a face-to-face interview."

Reporters work a lot like spies. That's one reason I don't trust them. That's also why I'd expected Vernon to give a more substantial report. He'd let me down. I needed a little nonjudgmental affection, the kind only a dog gives. I called to make sure Annalynn and Achilles were still in the office and asked Vernon to drop me there.

Achilles greeted me enthusiastically, obviously ready for a run. Annalynn declared herself ready for a whiskey and drove us home.

Achilles tore out of her garage to go check on his hummingbirds.

I needed a run myself, partly to work off my frustration. It wasn't quite six, but clouds had moved in and muted the sun. "I'm going to change clothes and take Achilles out for a run on shady streets before we eat."

Annalynn unlocked the door and punched in the security code. "Does that mean you think Roscoe has left the area?"

"No, but no one has followed me all day. I'll keep my eyes open."

"At least drive across town and run where no one expects to see you," she said, opening the liquor cabinet. "And wear the Kevlar vest."

I changed into shorts and a T-shirt, scooted out the front door without Annalynn seeing I didn't have on the vest, and whistled for Achilles.

He raced between Annalynn's house and garage to join me and ran circles around me as I walked toward my garage. When we reached my driveway, he skidded to a stop, grabbed my shirttail in his teeth, and pulled hard. I drew my gun and let him drag me backward. He didn't let go until we had crossed Annalynn's driveway.

Barking ferociously, he blocked me from going back to my garage. My heart rate jumped. He'd behaved much like this at the booby-trapped farmhouse.

Chapter Twenty-Four

Annalynn ran toward me with a Glock in her hand. "What's wrong?"

Achilles intercepted her, herding her back toward the house.

I holstered my gun and took a deep breath to steady myself. "Achilles won't let me near my garage." Annalynn didn't get it. "Like he wouldn't let me go into the farmhouse Saturday night."

The blood drained from her face. She pushed past Achilles to grab my arm. "Back inside. I'll ask the FBI to send its bomb squad."

Fine with me. I certainly didn't want to look for explosives. While she talked to Lester Wharton on her office phone, I slipped into the kitchen and dialed Connie's home number. She answered immediately.

"What are you doing in the next fifteen minutes?"

"Leaving for Macon to sing at an anniversary dinner. Why?"

Telling her about the possible bomb would scare her. "Could you please drive by the Gribbles' house and see if his truck is there as you leave town."

"What's happened? What aren't you telling me? Is Annalynn okay?"

"She's fine." Connie's imagination would frighten her more than the truth. "Achilles smells an explosive in my garage. We're calling in the FBI bomb squad."

"My God, Phoenix! This is way worse than Fargo's spiders. We've got to find that crazy Cantree before he kills you."

"That would be nice," I said. "Gribble may be key to that. Don't slow as you go by, and keep an eye on your rearview mirror all the way to Macon and back. Call nine-one-one if anyone follows you."

"Why would they? I'm not the one who killed a Cantree," she pointed out. "I'll call you about the truck in ten minutes."

Achilles pushed his water bowl in front of me. I filled it and poured myself a glass of lemonade.

Annalynn hurried in and emptied her scotch down the drain. "The bomb squad won't be here for a couple of hours. You check to see if the security cameras' motion sensors picked up anything. I'm going to talk to the neighbors. Someone must have seen something."

The guy could be lurking nearby to watch the fun. "No, don't go outside. Start checking this afternoon's camera footage while I get out of these running clothes. If need be, we'll all three go question the neighbors."

"You're not leaving the house without that Kevlar vest."

I ran upstairs and slipped into jeans and a blue T-shirt that matched the vest. As I strapped on my holster, Connie phoned to report the truck pulled up at the Gribbles as she drove by.

"Phoenix," Annalynn called from downstairs, "my front-porch camera picked up someone."

I ran downstairs to the entertainment room. "Can you tell who it is?"

"No. He's wearing a big-brimmed hat and a workman's uniform and carrying a clipboard and a backpack. He looks like he's checking meters. He went between my house and the garage and then your house and the garage at two thirty-five, but he never came out." She reran the tape.

"Check the camera in back from two thirty-five on."

At two fifty-two, the meter man walked behind my house and wormed his way through the evergreen trees bordering my yard.

Not a glimpse of his face or of his ears.

"Smart to have come in the front way," I said. "Anyone seeing the guy in person or on camera dismissed him as a meter man." I started for the front door. "He must have gone in through my garage window. I'm going to take a look."

"Phoenix, no!"

Her fear stopped me, for a moment. "I won't get close."

She shook her head violently.

"I'll take my binoculars. I won't go any closer than Achilles—advises."

She breathed deeply until she regained control. "We'll go in your house and look out the living room window. Right after I call Jim to block off my street. Now put on the vest!"

This time I obeyed.

Guns drawn, we went out the back door and crept toward the front. Achilles trotted ahead of us and gave an all-clear bark, but he insisted we go all the way to the sidewalk before walking past the garages and up to the front door of my little brick house. I had Venetian blinds on the side window, which was some eight feet from the garage. I left them down as protection from breaking glass and parted two slats at eye level. Even before I raised the binoculars, I saw what I hadn't seen coming into the house: All of the glass had been broken out of the small shoulder-high window. You had to be strong to hoist yourself up through that.

"He must have put it on the garage door," I mused. "If I'd have gone into the garage, I'd have noticed the window and not touched the car."

"Do you think he linked it to the door opener?"

"If he did, this could be a warning like the shots in the restaurant. I could open the door from several feet to the side and escape most of the force of the blast. If he intended to kill me, he rigged it to blow when I'd be close to the explosion."

I wanted badly to know which it was, but not badly enough to risk checking the garage myself. On the other hand, I was pretty sure our visitor had left the area either immediately or when we came out of the house with our guns. "Let's go talk to the neighbors about the meter man."

It took us more than an hour to go to every house on the block. Our only hit came from two ten-year-old boys. Playing in a tree house, they'd noticed a black motorcycle parked in a neighbor's backyard sometime between two and three. One remembered that the license plate was dirty.

Annalynn contacted the FBI, the highway patrol, and sheriffs from nearby counties to watch for the bike and a complaint about a stolen one. I pointed out that Gribble's truck would have provided a great hiding place for the rider to come into or leave Laycock, but she refused to say that with no evidence.

With darkness coming on, we sat in silence on the castle porch warning the curious to stay away while the LPD patrolled the block. When Wharton and a bomb expert finally arrived with a black Labrador, they ordered us inside.

The hall light showed me how pale Annalynn was. We needed fuel. "Defusing that thing could take a while. I'll scramble us some eggs."

"I can't eat." She headed into her home office.

I gave Achilles some water and poured lemonade for Annalynn and me.

Wharton came to confirm that the dog had smelled explosives on the garage door. He and the expert studied the security footage, asked for permission to cut an entry into the back of my garage, and called for more help.

Annalynn worked the phones with her colleagues while I made tuna fish sandwiches and tried to figure out how Roscoe knew I was gone. I concluded he didn't care. He'd counted on his disguise to enable him to move in and out undiscovered.

I gave Annalynn a sandwich and took mine upstairs to eat while I called Stuart. I gave him the short version of what had happened, talked it over with him, and, reluctantly, insisted he stay with his kids. We talked until the doorbell rang. I hadn't felt so comfortable with a man in years. Perhaps too comfortable. Was I responding to a friend or a potential lover?

Wharton came in with a computer hooked up to a camera on a small robot. First the camera showed me the device on the bottom of the garage door. Then the camera checked everything else in the garage. I noticed only one thing: The bomber had unlocked my car door. Wharton went back out.

A half hour later a small explosion interrupted our ten o'clock tea. We hurried onto the porch. Neighbors and reporters were taking photos of what had been my garage door from the street.

The bomb expert waddled toward us in protective gear. He pulled off a head protector. "Sorry. The bastard hid a second explosive, a small one, at the top of the garage door. It damaged the back of your car." He pulled off a giant glove and wiped sweat from his face. "We need to take the door and your car to the shop."

I nodded. Now I knew Roscoe intended to kill me. I hoped the explosion had destroyed the Maryland license plates in a secret compartment in my car's trunk.

Wharton climbed out of a dark-blue van and hurried up Annalynn's front walk. "Dr. Smith, we need to have a little talk—alone."

"Certainly. Come on in." I brushed aside Annalynn's objection and led the agent into the entertainment room. I chose the recliner and left the couch to Wharton.

Achilles planted himself between us.

"A smart dog," Wharton said. "Not many dogs trained to detect drugs also recognize explosives."

So he had investigated Annalynn, me, and Achilles. Not good.

I leaned back in my chair, relaxed, and waited for the interrogation to begin.

The agent took a recorder from his pocket and placed it on the petrified wood coffee table. "Take me through your day, Dr. Smith, starting with when you got up."

An easy request. Perhaps too easy. "Let's see. Up between six thirty and seven. I let Achilles out and fed him. A shower. Breakfast with Annalynn." He was taking detailed notes, something he'd not done the first time he came to the house. "She left for the office about eight thirty and I went to have another cup of coffee with a friend."

"Her name?"

"*His* name is Vernon Kann. He owns the local newspaper."

"And what did you talk about?"

How would Vernon answer that question? "Mostly a story he's writing on elder abuse. He went to Columbia today to interview some people and offered to give me a ride back. You'll recall that I rented a car for a friend Sunday."

"What's the relationship between you and Mr. Kann?"

Men always expected a sexual relationship. "Casual friends. We met in May while he was covering the first set of homicide cases that Annalynn solved. We became friends in June during the second set of homicides she solved." Just in case Wharton had ignored her record as sheriff.

"And where did you go after that?" His voice and face conveyed boredom, but he gripped the pen.

"Around ten I took a gift to an elderly friend. I came home a little before eleven. I answered e-mail, checked business news, played fetch with Achilles, ate lunch with Annalynn. About one thirty I rode back to the sheriff's department with her to leave Achilles and pick up the rental car."

"I'll need the name of the woman you visited."

The FBI would frighten Mrs. T. "She's fragile. I'd prefer you don't upset her with questions." Much better to upset Kiki. "Her daughter, Kiki Gribble, came by right after I got there and was still there when I left. Please confirm my visit with her."

He tapped his pen on his legal pad. "Is there a connection between the newspaper story on elder abuse and your visit to the woman?"

"Yes." He'd been paying attention. "Her son-in-law is trying to force her to leave her home and turn her finances over to him. I visit regularly to encourage better care."

He arched an eyebrow. "It didn't occur to you to turn the case over to the sheriff?"

"If we can handle it without involving the law or social services, Mrs. T and everyone else will be happier."

He smiled. "You like to handle things on your own. Do you have something against law enforcement?"

I smiled back. "Only the FBI. I find most agents self-righteous, officious, and unimaginative, not to mention proud beyond what their performance warrants. Missing a bomb in my garage is a good example."

Red crept up his neck. "I'm sorry you have such a low opinion of us." He ducked his head and pretended to write a long note on his pad. "Who do you think tried to kill you today?"

"Roscoe Cantree."

"Why?"

"Because I killed his cousin."

He tapped his pen again. "I can imagine another reason: He thinks you grabbed the gold coins and cash from the robbery."

Now we'd moved to the nitty-gritty. "I doubt anyone who can elude the FBI and local and state law enforcement for a week is that stupid."

"Let's look at it from his viewpoint." He studied me, his eyes unblinking. "Five officers took part in the shootout. Then a medical team arrived. Before they left, three Highway Patrol officers secured the scene. Shortly thereafter a full contingent of agents arrived. Right?"

"I wouldn't know. Annalynn and I returned to Vandiver County before the troopers arrived."

He bounced in his seat, his eyes gleaming in triumph. "Exactly. You two were the only officers to leave the scene before we arrived. No one else had a better opportunity to remove the Krugerrands."

"You know that. The officers and the medical team who saw us leave empty-handed know that. Unless the FBI has leaked information, Roscoe Cantree does *not.*"

He scowled. "He could have heard it. The medical staff certainly told everyone they knew what happened."

"They don't know you haven't found the Krugerrands, unless you revealed it to them in your questioning—as you did to me last Sunday."

A white line appeared on his upper lip. "We are compelled to investigate you, Dr. Smith, because you had the opportunity to remove the coins from the car and the expertise to fence them."

I knew I should hold back, but I wanted to make it clear he couldn't intimidate me. "No competent detective would need more than a few minutes to clear me."

He squirmed but didn't flinch. "This incident forces us to reexamine every possibility."

"Then look at the possibility that Derek Gribble, Roscoe's sycophant in high school, is helping him." I ignored the skeptical look Wharton gave me. "Gribble owns a moving van. Today he was out of town all day, supposedly on a three-hour delivery. He could have met Roscoe, brought him and the bike here in the back of the van, and transported him out of town to his hidey hole before we discovered the explosives."

Wharton puffed out his cheeks and blew out air. "I need

evidence, not—imagination. You're angry at this Gribble because you suspect he's abusing his mother-in-law. You *suspect* him of firing three shots at you in a restaurant. Now you *suspect* him of risking prison to help someone he hasn't seen in years."

"Someone is helping Roscoe. And by the way, Gribble didn't shoot at me. I met him in a bar the next night and he didn't recognize me. I don't know who shot at me. Considering the bomb, I have to suspect Roscoe."

Wharton threw up his hands. "You're obviously an intelligent woman, but you're out of your element. You could get yourself killed by not cooperating fully with us."

My actions hadn't put me in danger. Someone else—almost certainly Roscoe—had done that. "Is the explosive in my garage like the ones you found in the farmhouse?"

"So far as we can tell at this point." Wharton glared at me. "Understand this: He really, really wanted you dead."

"How flattering." I refused to show alarm. "I must be on the right track. Gribble must have told Roscoe I asked where he—Gribble—was Monday night." I thought about it. "Roscoe could have heard a news report that my dog smelled the explosives at the house and prepared a back-up bomb."

Wharton leaned back in his chair and studied me. "You've been very busy. Maybe that's why people keep trying to kill you."

Chapter Twenty-Five

"For your own protection," Wharton said, "I need a detailed account of every move you've made since the shootout."

I hated to admit it, but he had a point. Something I'd done had made me a target. I began with Annalynn and me going to Oak Grove Cemetery. My account went smoothly until I got to Fargo drawing the pistol from his holster. Flashing back to being shot in the Istanbul spice bazaar, I jerked back.

"Sheriff Keyser," Wharton called, jumping up. "Something's wrong."

Annalynn raced in. "Phoenix, what is it?"

I regained control as Achilles leapt onto my lap. "A shooting pain. An aftermath of that botched gall bladder surgery. It happens occasionally." Ashamed that I hadn't concealed my reaction, I hid my face in Achilles' chest.

Annalynn hovered over me. "You need rest. This can wait until morning."

No, it couldn't. I'd waded in way over my head. It galled me, but I needed the FBI's help. I raised my head and forced a smile. "I'll be fine in a minute. Could you please make a pot of strong tea and heat some milk to put in it? And wildflower honey would be nice. Would you like tea, Lester? Or would you prefer coffee?"

"Tea's fine," he said warily. He turned off the recorder. "Maybe you should lie down on the couch."

I must look like hell.

"Yes, lie down," Annalynn said. "Rest while I make the tea."

I reposed on the couch like a medieval maiden. Achilles, his body trembling, stretched out beside me and put his nose on my shoulder. I stroked him until Annalynn brought in the silver tea service and her fine china, a subtle display of her resources.

She served Achilles first, coaxing him to leave the couch with a little plate of roast beef so that I could sit up.

Fortified with tea and shortbread cookies, I gave Wharton permission to turn the recorder back on. Aided by Annalynn's recollections, I soon brought the agent up to date, omitting only my undercover visits and the tracker. Rather major omissions, actually.

A thought kept gnawing at me. When Wharton turned off the recorder, I edged into it. "The Cantrees couldn't have planned this robbery. The planner had to know that particular bank and how and why to get into a specific safe deposit box." I paused an instant to let him agree. He didn't. I needed specifics to get a reaction: "The logical conclusion: Someone—perhaps an embezzler Roscoe met in prison—hired the Cantrees to steal the Krugerrands and to deliver them to a fence or buyer. Yet you're sure the Cantrees brought those coins to Missouri. Why?"

He leaned back, his knees wide apart, his face triumphant. "Because we learned that instead of turning over the coins to an accomplice in Cleveland, Roscoe Cantree contacted possible buyers in Las Vegas."

Gambler's heaven, a natural for Roscoe. "He double-crossed the embezzler."

Annalynn nodded. "Who then offered evidence against Roscoe in exchange for not being charged with the murder in the bank." She looked to Wharton for confirmation.

He swore under his breath. "Something like that." He picked up his cell and read a text. "We've loaded your car onto a truck. I'll e-mail the transcript to you tomorrow. Please correct it and add anything you missed asap." He picked up the recorder. "Like they say in the movies, don't leave town."

As soon as I woke up Saturday morning, I set up our iPhones to monitor the motion-sensor cameras and planned the placement of another camera to cover the blind spot. I added that to my shopping list of tools I never thought I'd need in Laycock.

Annalynn was answering out-of-town reporters' calls when Achilles and I left the castle and walked past the tarp-covered front of my garage toward my house. I'd need a mason and a carpenter to repair the damage. I went on into my box-strewn living room and called Stuart to fill him in. He'd already talked to Wharton and learned the FBI had found Roscoe's prints on my car. As a bonus, he'd damaged my brakes.

My stomach knotted. Anyone so determined to kill me would try again.

Stuart echoed my thought: "When you've committed one murder, you don't have much to lose if you kill again. Phoenix, Wharton called me because he wanted me to press you on a crucial question: Why would this guy target you rather than Annalynn or Tiny Towson?"

"I wish I knew. The only thing I can think of is that he expects me to be more vulnerable. Choosing an easy target fits with his running an elderly farmer off the road." Not a satisfactory answer.

Stuart sighed. "We've been talking about this case in the office all week. Cantree's actions defy all logic. That's one reason the FBI keeps looking at you, the only person around who knows how to get full value for the Krugerrands."

Ironic that my day job made them suspicious. "They suspect me even after they confirmed Roscoe planted the explosives?"

"I'm afraid so."

That cheered me up. "Then they're watching me. Annalynn

will be relieved to hear that." I visualized our block. "A couple of agents in the upstairs of the old Windom house, I'd guess." A less happy thought. They'd be listening to our conversations, either through bugs planted at our houses or a mobile monitoring system. Both, if they had any sense. "I hope they're watching Gribble, too. He'd gladly help his old pal get rid of me."

"You and Annalynn both need to be very careful," Stuart said. Voices sounded in the background. "Remember that I'll be at Mom's in a couple of hours, only blocks away."

LaDawna and Ado Annie arrived on their bikes a couple of minutes before nine o'clock. Both wore jeans and blue LCC T-shirts. Achilles stayed at my side as I let them in and pointed out which boxes went to which rooms. I started them on an easy job: putting together two bookshelves to fit under the windows in my office. I retrieved an old boom box and a pile of CDs I'd given Mom from the basement and put on a CD of Birgit Nilsson singing Isolde. The late Swedish soprano's voice would mask our conversation on the FBI bug and let LaDawna hear what magic a voice could make.

I settled down on the old leather couch in the living room with my laptop to order some tools of my trade from merchants who never advertised.

Achilles cocked his head and listened to the music but didn't howl.

At the first pause in the music, LaDawna appeared. "Who is that singing?"

"One of the greatest sopranos of the twentieth century, Birgit Nilsson. I had the privilege of hearing one of her last performances."

Nilsson continued, and the girl stood transfixed, tears welling in her eyes.

Achilles licked the back of her hand and offered her his paw.

She shook it and then knelt and hugged him, turning her face away from me.

Homesickness didn't explain the girl's emotional tension. Thank goodness the minister had been there to comfort her both times that Fargo had acted out. I shut off the CD player. "You can borrow my CD and listen to it at home. I'll put on something more upbeat for you to work by."

A car pulled into my drive. Brandon, also in jeans and an LCC T-shirt, walked over to look at the garage before coming toward the door with a CD in his hand. LaDawna had disappeared by the time I opened the door.

"Hi, Dr. Smith." He held up the CD. "I brought an *Oklahoma!* cast album to play while we work, if that's okay."

"An excellent idea." I pointed to Achilles. "If he doesn't decide to sing along. I'd like for you to start with the conference table. It goes in the dining room."

All went well through the overture, but soon after the singing started, Achilles added his voice. "Come," I said, heading for the back door. "Time to visit the hummingbirds." I checked the security cameras on my mobile before letting him out.

For the next two hours the kids worked and sang along with the CD while I checked e-mails and visited assorted blogs to obscure which ones I used for covert communications. Annalynn forwarded Wharton's transcript of my interview. I made minor corrections and sent it to her and Wharton.

"I have to go now," Ado Annie said. "They can finish up in about an hour."

"Thanks for coming today. How much do I owe your company?"

She blushed. "Since this isn't a cleaning job, you can pay us separately. Thirty dollars would cover my part."

I gave her a fifty. "If you need any advice on entrepreneurship"—she looked blank—"on building a business, give me a call."

LaDawna and Brandon came in and spread out the pieces of a credenza for the living room/reception. Singing with the cast album had been useful. Their voices were blending better now than they had Thursday.

The mobile I used for local calls rang. La Vida Loca. I answered.

"Someone found . . . something," Mariela said. "Could you please come in your own car? Police cars scare people away."

Bloody hell! I didn't have a car. Brandon did. Was it safe for him to drive me? Why not? The FBI would be right behind us. "Yes, thanks for letting me know."

The CD ended.

I turned off my laptop. "A good stopping point. Please let me take you two to lunch."

LaDawna said nothing, but Brandon tossed aside the lengthy instructions and said, "I'm ready to eat."

"I'll tell Annalynn where I'm going while you wash up. Would you mind driving, Brandon? My car is . . . being repaired."

His eyes widened. "I heard about the bombs on the radio this morning."

LaDawna gasped. "What bombs?"

Uh-oh. Another meltdown coming. To cut it off, I said matter of factly, "No big deal. A murderer named Roscoe Cantree planted bombs on my garage door yesterday. Achilles warned me they were there, so the FBI took care of it." I picked up my laptop. "I'll be ready in five minutes."

I went to the castle, told Annalynn where I was going, and wrote a note saying the FBI had bugged the house.

She nodded. "You're not going anywhere without the Kevlar vest."

A sensible precaution. "Okay. I'll put on a roomier blouse." I went upstairs to change, and to load a spare magazine to carry in my purse.

Annalynn met me at the bottom of the stairs with a folder. "I printed out some information Russ e-mailed me this morning." She touched her fingers to her lips to remind me to temper my reply. "I made some notes in the margins. We need to go through this together before our meeting tomorrow."

"So much to look forward to." I took the folder and opened the front door. "I'll look at this while the kids finish up this afternoon."

Achilles met me on the porch.

"Stay with Annalynn," I said.

He turned and leapt down the porch steps.

Annalynn handed me his leash. "The bombs brought back his separation anxiety, Phoenix. Take him with you."

I took the leash. "Okay. Don't go out alone."

Brandon waited by his car, his hands jammed into his pockets and his shoulders hunched. "LaDawna's real upset about the bombs. She ran into the bathroom and didn't come out. I think she's crying."

Where was the minister when you needed her? This wasn't my line of work.

Achilles offered Brandon his paw, and the boy shook it.

"Brandon, please cool off the car while Achilles and I go get LaDawna."

She came out of the bathroom as we walked in the front door. Achilles went straight to her and barked a question.

"I think he asked you to sing." Her red eyes and pale face indicated her throat was too tight for that. "He insists on going to lunch with us."

She leaned down to stroke him. "He's really sweet." She began to sing "Oh, What a Beautiful Mornin'." He followed her into the back seat of Brandon's car.

No one followed us, but a dark sedan with two women in it pulled out of a street ahead of us and parallel parked in front of the used-furniture store a half block from the restaurant. No need for the agents to follow us when they'd heard me tell Analynn my destination.

Entering the nearly empty restaurant, I saw that plywood covered the broken window. I greeted Mariela with a formal smile. "Could we have a table in the back where my dog won't be in the way, please?"

She studied LaDawna and Brandon a moment. "We better check with the manager." She handed menus to the teenagers. "Take the table with the red flowers on it." To me, she said, "Please follow me, ma'am."

The child was incredibly quick. We walked past the booth and into the kitchen. "It's in a tree in the alley," Mariela said softly. She handed me a pair of tongs and a plastic bag and picked up a folding two-step stool.

"Lead the way."

Mariela opened the back door and sprinted past the Rose of Sharon bushes and down the alley, Achilles and I at her heels. She stopped under an oak tree with branches extending over the alley and unfolded the stool. "It's in a little pocket between the branches."

I climbed up the steps and saw a pistol, almost certainly the one that had fired at me. "Who found it?"

"A kid climbing the tree."

"Did the kid touch it?"

Silence.

"I'm not going to tell anyone, but I need to know."

"Just the barrel. When he saw it was real, he got scared and put it back where he found it." She took a deep breath. "I wiped off the barrel with a paper towel."

"A sensible thing to do." I gripped the gun with the tongs

and dropped it into the plastic bag.

A car turned into the alley.

"Behind the tree!" I dropped the tongs, pulled my Glock, and jumped down.

The driver stuck her hand out the window. It held an FBI ID.

I lowered the Glock. As the car approached, I recognized the young "mother" at the casino. "Do you have rubber gloves with you?"

She stared at the plastic bag. "I'll have to take that."

"You're welcome to it, but on behalf of the Vandiver County Sheriff's Department, I will inspect it first."

Uncertainty flitted across her face. "I can't permit that."

"You have no right to take a gun because it's in a plastic bag."

"I'll need a supervisor's reading on that." She closed her window and spoke into a Bluetooth headset.

I folded the stool and handed it to Mariela. "I'll have chicken enchiladas, please."

"Anything to drink, Deputy Smith?"

"Water. Please tell my guests I had a phone call. I'll be there shortly."

She picked up the tongs and stool and ran down the alley.

I holstered my Glock and opened the bag.

"Use these," the agent said, stepping out of the car and holding out an open box of white gloves. "What are you looking for?"

I handed her the plastic bag and pulled out a pair. "How good the sight is, how many bullets are left, any ID numbers." I finally got the tight gloves on and took the gun from the bag. "Some children found it and told the girl at the restaurant. She called me."

I couldn't be sure how good the gun was without firing it,

but the balance was good, the sight looked true, and it appeared to have been well maintained. The shooter could have fired two more rounds.

"A lot of criminals don't think to wipe clean the bullets," the agent said. "A partial print should be enough to tell us if Roscoe Cantree loaded the gun."

"I don't think a man who put two bombs in my garage would miss me with three shots or leave behind a pistol with two bullets in it. He's working with someone." I put the gun back in the bag. "Whom do I call if I need help?"

"Claudene Dale." She smiled and said softly, "Willetta speaks highly of you and Sheriff Keyser. Enjoy your lunch."

A friend of the pregnant deputy, a reasonable woman, and possibly a valuable asset. Progress. I removed the gloves and extended my hand.

Chapter Twenty-Six

Brandon sat rapt—but not too enthralled to shovel in warm tortilla chips and salsa—while LaDawna described singing as a paid (barely) soloist in a big Chicago church.

"Before that I sang with a girl band, a jazz combo, and a folk group. All of them said my voice didn't fit their style," she said. "A folk singer sent me to the church."

"Being alone in Chicago sounds darned scary," Brandon said.

"Only the first month," LaDawna said, a touch of pride in her voice. "After that I always found waitressing jobs and cheap rooms. A lot like here, actually."

She relaxed and became more and more animated telling stories of her small triumphs and misadventures as an aspiring singer. For the first time I could see her capturing Laurey's personality.

The stories ended when the meal came. Both Brandon and LaDawna cleaned their loaded plates in silence. Both accepted my recommendation of the peach milkshake for dessert. Claudene Dale sauntered in and joined an older and heavier blond woman at a table. I signaled Mariela to bring shakes for them, too.

LaDawna made patterns on the table with her finger. "I noticed that you don't have any desks, Dr. Smith. Are you going to buy big fancy ones?"

"No, expensive furniture is for corporations. The foundation's money goes to direct services. I want a couple of nice old desks, real wood." Inspiration hit. Placing the tracker in Gribble's truck had become a major challenge with the FBI looking over my shoulder. If I bought used furniture, I could hire Gribble to deliver it. "I'd like to take a quick look in that antique place down the street before we go back."

Another problem registered. Only a dozen people were eating lunch. That broken window made diners uneasy. When Mariela brought the shakes, I gave her a credit card. When she brought the bill to sign, I added $200 in the tip line.

A moment later her father hurried toward the table, his face a giant question mark.

I rose to intercept him. "To fix the window," I said softly. Had I insulted him? "You can pay me back in milkshakes."

Mariela stepped from behind him. "Thank you, Deputy Smith. We'll run a tab. Please come back soon."

LaDawna, Achilles, and I walked the half block to the used-furniture store while Brandon opened up his car to cool it off.

Children's furniture—cribs, high chairs, a rocking horse—sat out front, giving me little hope of finding anything anyone would expect me to buy. Inside the place was dark and crowded. "You take the left aisle and I'll take the right," I said to LaDawna.

The sign outside said antiques, but junk better described the faded sofas, rickety rockers, and painted coffee tables.

"Here's a nice desk," LaDawna called.

Saved. I hurried toward her.

She stroked an oak top partially obscured by dented office waste cans. "This is pretty wood, and the drawers are all here. It's beat up, but I could refinish it for you. My mother and I used to refinish discarded furniture and sell it. There's another one almost as nice behind it."

"Good eye. These are exactly what I had in mind."

I sent her to search for matching desk chairs while I bargained for the two antique desks that had probably served bankers.

Then I began the delicate process of prompting the owner, a grossly obese gray-haired man, to suggest Gribble deliver the desks. To that end, I asked for immediate delivery.

The owner shook his head. "My truck is busy until Tuesday."

"Surely you know someone who moves furniture. I'll pay an extra twenty-five dollars, fifty if those desks are in my house by three o'clock."

"Cash?"

Don't be overeager. "Only if he knows what he's doing."

"I know one guy who might be available, but it'll cost you seventy-five."

I pretended to think it over. He wanted a bigger tax-free cut. He obviously didn't recognize me as the sheriff's friend. "Okay. Call him."

I followed the shyster as he limped, wheezing, to his desk and watched him dial Gribble's number. I still had the touch.

Brandon left as soon as he and LaDawna finished putting the credenza together. While she cleaned up, I went to the castle to get the cell phone to plant in Gribble's truck.

Annalynn was on the hall phone when I came downstairs. She hung up. "That was Wharton. The prints on the bullets belonged to young Orson."

An unexpected development. "Obviously he didn't leave the ICU to shoot at me. Roscoe wouldn't have missed. It had to be the fourth member of the gang."

She finished my thought: "Or a local accomplice. Stay away from Gribble, Phoenix. Concentrate on setting up the office."

"It's almost ready. I ran across some nice desks at the used-furniture place. The store arranged to have them delivered in a few minutes."

Her phone rang again, and I hustled out the door. I had to hide what I was doing from her as well as Gribble, LaDawna, and my FBI shadows. First, get rid of LaDawna.

I found the girl in my childhood bedroom stuffing packing materials into a box. I unlocked the back door. "Could you please shove everything outside and sort the paper from the plastic for recycling?"

"Oh, shit. I should have thought of that. Sorry. I'll sweep up the mess, too."

A nice kid. Conscientious. "You've done a great job today. I appreciate it. After you get this stuff outside, take a break to watch Achilles' hummingbirds in the backyard next door."

I hurried to the CDs and found a Scott Joplin to play. It would drown out most exchanges with Gribble but not a call for help, if either of us made one. Ready.

A minute or so later Gribble's truck stopped out front. He backed it into my driveway in one smooth try. I propped the storm door open and went out as he opened the back of the truck.

"Hi," I said with a friendly smile. "Thanks so much for delivering today."

He swiveled his head to look at me. He grinned. "Well, if it isn't the pretty lady from Harry's Hideaway."

"And you're the master pool player." He still had no idea who I was. "Is there some way I could get up into the truck and make sure the store gave you the right desks before you unload them?"

"Sure." He punched a button and the truck's metal gate folded down and then descended. "You can ride on my private elevator."

Going into that covered truck with him was reckless, but the afternoon sun shone into it and I had my Glock hidden under my long blouse. I stepped aboard and we rode up together. I spotted an air vent on the side that might provide a hiding place for the mobile.

He smoothed down a cowlick. "You here all by yourself?"

His question hinted at trouble ahead. "No, a friend is here." I stepped off the lift and pulled back the corner of a cover cloth. "This one goes in the last room on the left." Play to his vanity. "I'm impressed that you can handle anything so large alone, even with a dolly. I'm afraid you'll have trouble getting the desk through the doors."

He flexed his muscles, released a bungee cord holding the desk in place, and gripped the dolly's handles. "Sweetheart, I can get anything smaller than this truck through a door."

I smiled. "I'd like to see that." I stepped farther back to look at the other desk. As he eased the dolly onto the lift, I reached up and wedged the phone into place. "Yes, this is the other one." I joined him on the lift.

He was good. He pulled the dolly up the steps and angled the desk through my front door in no time. He exhibited a weightlifter's strength at the bedroom door, taking the heavy desk off the dolly and carrying it into the room.

"Very impressive," I said. Not a guy I cared to go up against now. He'd have been a challenge even before my bullet wound. LaDawna had closed the back door. Achilles was no longer an instant away. "Were you a wrestler in high school?"

"I horsed around some. We didn't have a wrestling team." He picked up the dolly rather than rolling it out. "I'll get the other one."

I looked out my back window. LaDawna, hands on her cheeks, watched the hummingbirds sip from the feeder. Achilles, nose in the air, faced my front yard.

I went out to the truck. The sun didn't shine on the vent, but Gribble could see one corner of the cell phone if he happened to look at the right place. He didn't.

I followed him back inside but not into the bedroom, preferring the comparative safety of the living room. I stood near the open front door with a ten-dollar bill in my hand. "Thank you."

He leaned the empty dolly against the piano. "I could use a beer."

"Sorry. I don't have any." I didn't offer a glass of water. If I went into the kitchen, he could corner me.

The back door opened an inch.

He sauntered toward me. "How about a kiss to sweeten the tip?"

"I don't kiss married men."

He lunged toward me with his lips puckered and his hands extended. I gripped his left hand and used his own momentum to flip him, sending him crashing to the floor on his back with his feet out the door. He moaned. I grabbed the dolly and dropped it on top of him. He sat up and flung it out the door. I jumped back debating whether to pull my gun.

"You teasing bitch!" He twisted around and rose to his knees. His eyes and mouth widened in terror. He scrambled out the door, grabbed the dolly, and raced for his truck.

I slammed the storm door shut to make sure my snarling defender didn't go after him.

LaDawna stood behind Achilles holding a broom like a javelin. *Maple Leaf Rag* provided background music as Gribble's truck roared out of my driveway.

I waited in dread for the meltdown that violence had evoked in LaDawna before.

She lowered the broom. "Would you please teach me to do that?"

Chapter Twenty-Seven

Annalynn burst through the front door. "Are you all right? I saw Derek Gribble run to his truck." She closed her eyes a moment. "Of course. He delivered the desks. How dare you take such chances!" She shook her finger at me. "Phoenix, you promised me—"

I cut in. "Annalynn Carr Keyser, this is LaDawna McKnight, the lead in *Oklahoma!*. She's assembled our office furniture. Monday she's going to clean up and refinish our desks."

LaDawna stepped forward. "She was wonderful. She refused to kiss him and he jumped at her and she threw him down like he was a stuffed gorilla."

Annalynn collapsed on the couch, shaking her head. "Why on earth did he try to kiss you?"

"Because I'm beautiful." I struck a pose. I hadn't mentioned buying Gribble a beer to Annalynn and Wharton. "He fantasizes about women finding him irresistible."

My cell rang. No ID. "LaDawna, would you please show Annalynn the desks?" I didn't answer the call until Annalynn, after a withering glare, went down the hall.

"Did you forget my name?"

Claudene Dale. The FBI team had heard the scuffle despite the music. "I had back-up." Achilles was plastered against me, his body vibrating. I stroked his head.

He gave me a disgusted look and trotted down the hall after Annalynn. She would forgive me for taking on Gribble alone before he did.

"Gribble didn't recognize you or your address. Still think he shot you?"

At least the FBI could identify him by sight. Or they ran his license number. "No. I'm open to suggestions for another candidate." I glanced out the front window in time to see the agents' car back out of my driveway. "I still think he beats his wife and helped his old friend."

"You were damned lucky you didn't get hurt, and so were we," an unfamiliar woman's voice said. "Leave this to the professionals." She disconnected.

I'd done just fine, thank you. A discomfiting thought: His wife might not do so well. "Annalynn, what can we do to stop him from going home and beating Kiki?"

She stepped out of her new office and across the hall into mine. "Did you say 'we'? That word hasn't been in your vocabulary lately."

I couldn't believe her petty dismissal. "I need some help here." Add the magic word. "Please."

She came out of the room and walked toward me, her composure regained. "Do you want to file an assault complaint?"

If Gribble were in jail, he couldn't hit Kiki. He also couldn't lead us to Roscoe Cantree. "No. I'll have to think of something else."

"You're back to *I* again."

Big mistake. "*We* need to think of something else." She wouldn't let this incident go. "Please. I'm stuck."

She gazed up a moment in thought. "I'll call Jim and ask him to let Gribble know the LPD is watching him. You persuade Mrs. T to have Kiki stay with her tonight."

I clapped my hands. "Brilliant!"

"Only if it works. I have to get back." She smiled at LaDawna. "Don't let Phoenix intimidate you. She's steel on the outside, but she has a marshmallow center." She frowned at me. "Come straight home when you finish here."

I nodded meekly, biting my tongue to hold back a "Yes, Mother."

LaDawna skipped out the back door.

As soon as Annalynn went out the front door, I checked the trackers. The pickup was at Mrs. T's, the truck near the Gribbles' house.

Mrs. T answered her phone promptly and listened silently as I summarized what had happened and voiced my concern for Kiki.

"I do not want to buy magazines," she said. "I cannot talk more now. I begin to feel unwell. I will ask my daughter to stay with me. Good-bye."

Achilles and I went out back and found LaDawna stuffing pieces of plastic into a big plastic bag. "All is well," I said. "The man's wife won't go home tonight."

"Thank God for that," she said fervently. "Could you show me that throw now?"

"I'll be glad to." I wondered if fear for her own safety had produced those meltdowns. A teenager who tackled Chicago alone had to be tough, or escaping from a scarier place. Perhaps she had fled to Laycock, too. "I'll show you basic self-defense moves and how to fall so you don't break or sprain something. Let's pile up the boxes to cushion some real falls—in slow motion anyway."

My wound remained tender, limiting what I dared do. I started by demonstrating grips and positions that counter attacks and give you leverage. She caught on quickly. I was afraid to let her throw me, but I had her lunge at me as Gribble had and flipped her into the boxes.

Achilles, who had been watching with a wrinkled brow, barked in protest. She jumped up laughing to reassure him.

Connie ran over from the castle. "What are you two doing?"

"Self-defense lessons," I said. "Care to join us?"

"No way I'll let you throw me around."

"Phoenix," Annalynn called from her back door, "we have a meeting here in half an hour."

"Be there in five minutes." I made sure LaDawna understood how to do the throw and worried that she needed to know much more. I issued a warning: "If you're attacked, scream and run if you can, but never hesitate to gouge the eye, break the nose, hit the head with a brick. If an attacker corners you, you may have to kill him to survive."

LaDawna's mood changed before my eyes. She dropped to her knees and buried her face in her hands.

Connie glared at me and moved forward to give comfort.

Achilles licked the girl's face.

She hugged him and concealed her face on his shoulder.

Connie could handle this better than I. Her daughters were only a few years older than LaDawna. "We don't have any rain predicted for a couple of days. Let's leave the boxes here for now." I took LaDawna's pay plus a generous tip from my pocket and handed it to her. "I'll round up the supplies you need for refinishing the desks."

She brushed away tears and tucked the money in her jeans pocket. "Thanks. I'll come at one thirty Monday."

I handed Connie my keys. "If you don't mind locking up, you can take a look at what your stars accomplished today. You'll *hear* the difference on Monday. Laurey and Curly's voices are blending much better."

I hurried through the back door of the castle and into the kitchen with Achilles.

"We have time for turkey sandwiches and sliced tomatoes," Annalynn said. "Wharton wants to talk to us and Jim about the pistol."

I washed my hands and face at the sink. "Despite the Cantree boy's prints, I'm betting the shooter wasn't Roscoe or Norval or Gribble. Who else is in play?"

A half hour later I said the same thing to Jim and Wharton in Annalynn's entertainment room.

Wharton stared at the blank television screen. "What do you say, Sheriff Keyser?"

"I agree with Phoenix."

"Chief Falstaff?"

Jim squirmed. "All I can add is this: Whoever ditched that gun knew how to disappear fast and figured no one would suspect them if they didn't have the gun on them." He ran his hand over his five-o'clock shadow. "I'm here to find out whether to hassle Gribble to keep him from hitting his wife or to pull back and give him a chance to make a mistake."

Wharton turned to Annalynn.

She gave the answer we'd agreed on: "Leave him to the FBI."

Wharton shook his head. "Sorry. He's not a priority for us. We're concentrating on investigating possible accomplices scattered from Ohio to Nevada."

Annalynn signaled for me to keep quiet. "Are any of them in Missouri?"

"Possibly." He stood up. "We reassigned the two agents who've been guarding you, Dr. Smith. I strongly suggest you stay home and stop playing Nancy Drew." He stomped out.

Annalynn followed him. I wrote a note to Jim: "Don't say anything. They're probably still bugging us."

He nodded. "I'll be going, too. We're having a cookout tonight." He wrote a note, tore it off his pad, and handed it to me as he left. It said, "I'll send a car past Gribbles' every couple hours tonight."

The rest of the evening the FBI heard little in the castle but the television playing to an empty room. Annalynn caught up on paperwork from the office. I completed the research and writing required to finish the foundation papers.

At ten o'clock the trackers showed both the pickup and truck remained in place. I went to bed and set the alarm on my phone for midnight. They hadn't moved then or at two, four, or six, at which point I got up, put on the Kevlar vest under a T-shirt, and took Achilles for a run. To give the agents time to catch up, I ran in place on Annalynn's front walk while Achilles checked nearby bushes. I moved out at my standard leisurely pace. It took Claudene three blocks to draw within twenty yards of me.

Achilles circled back to challenge her.

"Tell him I'm a friend," she called, her voice anxious.

"Come, Achilles."

Instead, he circled her and barked twice, a warning signal.

"He smells your gun and doesn't trust you behind me. You'll have to move up."

She caught up to me. "That's not how we're supposed to do it. Besides, you don't run fast enough."

I maintained my pace, and she moved a few strides ahead.

At the next corner I turned right to go to Memorial Park for a game of fetch. She cut back and ran around the perimeter of the park while Achilles and I played. She didn't follow us when, in response to Annalynn's agitated call, we jogged back to the castle.

She had coffee and the foundation papers waiting at the dining room table. Even with the explanations, we both found understanding the legal language hard going. We didn't finish until after nine.

Annalynn practically threw two cereal bowls on the table. "We're running late. What are you wearing to church?"

"Nothing."

"That will make a good impression on Stuart's family."

I filled my bowl with something claiming to be nutritious.

"Phoenix D Smith, you're afraid of two teenagers."

I covered my boring cereal with blueberry yogurt. She was right. I'd sooner square off with Gribble again. "I can't be in a crowd. It's a threat to public safety."

"I see." She poured milk on her cereal. "If only your FBI guards hadn't left town, I'm sure they'd attend the ten o'clock service at the First Methodist Church."

"Especially if they knew it's the one with the white bell tower only three blocks north of here," I said sarcastically.

Annalynn smiled. "You always say how good the FBI is at finding things."

I choked swallowing a laugh.

"Really, Phoenix, saying hello after church would be so much easier than socializing over a meal."

Why hadn't I thought of that? A meaningless exchange of insincere courtesies and it would be over.

Annalynn added, "Besides, I'm sure LaDawna will appreciate seeing a familiar face in the congregation when she sings her first solo. Connie offered to give her private voice lessons in exchange for singing with the choir."

I thought of yet another reason to go to church: to ask Connie to rent a car for me from Clunkers on Call, the town's only car rental service. "You've convinced me. I'll go."

"Good. Wear the green pantsuit. Connie recommends the white blouse with green trim, but I prefer the light-green blouse."

I wore Connie's choice.

LaDawna's voice sounded above the others in every song. Connie would have her hands full making that powerful operatic soprano blend with the *Oklahoma!* chorus.

The Reverend Nancy Alderton's first sermon in her new church dealt with God's creating a diverse world for His/Her and our pleasure. She made an amusing and superbly argued appeal for appreciating, not just tolerating, others' opinions, habits, and faiths. What was such a talented preacher doing in a nowhere place like Laycock?

On the way to Annalynn's regular pew up front, I'd spotted the two FBI agents in the back row, one on the right and one on the left. Stuart and his sister's families occupied a pew halfway back on the right. They all would get to the door to greet the new minister long before Annalynn and I did.

"Go ahead. I'll say hello to LaDawna," I said to Annalynn after the last amen.

"Promise me you won't sneak out the back way, you coward," she said.

"I'll be a few feet behind you." I waved at Connie and LaDawna and edged my way toward the dispersing choir.

LaDawna smiled shyly and filed out with the rest of the sopranos.

I reached out to shake Connie's hand and pass cash for the car to her. "I need a ride like the one we had last May."

She tucked the money in her robe. "When? I'm leaving right now to go sing at an anniversary party in Shelbina."

Scheisse. "When you get back. No noisy muffler, no conspicuous colors or dents."

"Of course." She glanced at the back of the church. "You're due on stage right now. Break a leg."

Stuart waited for me at the end of the line filing into the vestibule to shake hands with our new minister. He had bags under his eyes and his thick hair looked windblown. He smiled and strode to meet me.

A tingling warned me to guard against romantic fantasies.

He invaded my space. "I thought I'd imagined how beautiful you are."

He meant it. Love really is blind. I leaned toward him.

"Dad! Hurry up," a young blonde in a curve-accenting purple dress with pink swirls called from the knot of people at the end of the line.

He stepped back. "Kaysi, Zeke, come meet Phoenix."

The tingling stopped.

The seventeen-year-old turned her back to us and shoved her younger but taller dark-haired brother toward the double doors as though she hadn't heard her father.

I could read her lips saying, "She's old!"

Zeke stared at me over his shoulder a moment before she pushed him out of sight.

Stuart sighed. "Sorry. Kaysi's mad at me because she missed a pool party yesterday. She's hounding me to get her back for a friend's birthday barbecue this evening." He edged closer and brushed a strand of hair off my forehead. "She'll come around. Mom says to be persistent, not insistent."

Annalynn shouldered her way through the people bunched at the door and waved her phone at me. "We have to go. Roscoe Cantree shot someone in Indianapolis."

Chapter Twenty-Eight

"Thank God Cantree left the area," Stuart said. "You're safe. Now you can join us."

I couldn't face contending with Kaysi all afternoon. "I have to help Annalynn check out this Cantree story." A damned lame, and obvious, excuse. "Then we have a big meeting with a *pro bono* foundation lawyer this afternoon."

Stuart's whole body sagged. "I know Kaysi will be a pain, but the sooner she gets to know you, the sooner she'll accept you. We'll be at my sister's until four. Please come by for at least a half hour or so."

He'd made a good point. Delay wouldn't make the first encounter any more pleasant. Besides, I couldn't let a teenager intimidate me. "I expect to be free by three."

His shoulders lifted. "Thanks. Call me and I'll pick you up." He leaned toward me for a quick kiss.

"Phoenix, this can't wait," Annalynn said. She disappeared into the crowd.

People turned to look, and Stuart stepped back.

I reached out to squeeze his hand before hurrying toward the door. To show Kaysi what the *old* woman could do, I muscled my way through the lingering churchgoers, leapt from the top step to the sidewalk, and sprinted after Annalynn, already approaching the SUV's passenger door.

The moment I turned on the ignition, she exploded with laughter.

I zoomed out of the parking space and stepped on the accelerator. "What's so funny?"

"You. You've been so careful to play down anything that would hint at—umm—your athletic ability, but you showed off for Stuart's teenagers." She patted my arm. "Give them a little time. Naturally they resent his dating."

I'd deal with them later. "Where are we going?"

"First, the sheriff's department. Then you can go home to take care of Achilles."

"No, no. You owe it to me to be there when Russ arrives. Otherwise he'll think I want to be alone with him. You can make calls and check online communications from the ladies' parlor."

She said nothing for a moment. "Okay."

Good. "Did the FBI call you about Cantree?"

"No, Vern. He saw an Associated Press bulletin." Annalynn fiddled with her phone. "Roscoe was caught on surveillance tape robbing an all-night filling station. He shot the clerk but didn't kill him. Here's the story." She read silently. "Nothing new."

"He drove six hundred miles southwest to Oklahoma, came back through Missouri, and drove another six hundred miles east. Toward Ohio." I checked my mirror. The two female agents drove up behind me, stopping only when I pulled into Annalynn's garage. "We have company."

"Surprise, surprise." Annalynn jumped out of the SUV. "Let me talk to them."

Claudene rolled down the passenger window. "What happened?"

"Good afternoon. I'm Acting Sheriff Annalynn Carr Keyser. And you are?"

"Claudene Dale." She flashed her badge. "We saw you tear out of church."

"Could I have a closer look at your ID, please?" Annalynn studied the slowly proffered badge. "I appreciate your keeping an eye on Phoenix. I hope you haven't been terribly bored by our conversations. Would you care to come in for a cup of tea?"

"Ummm . . . no, thanks."

"Good-bye then." Annalynn strode toward the castle.

Amused but mystified, I walked with her. "Why didn't you tell them?"

"I wanted to make a point: Their supervisors should have filled in us, and them, a couple of hours ago." She unlocked the front door and punched in the security code. "You hit the Web and I'll call the office and Tiny."

Before I went online, I checked the trackers. Neither Gribble vehicle had moved.

It took Annalynn and me an hour and a half to piece together the full story. Around midnight Cantree had stolen a car from an apartment complex at the edge of Indianapolis. He drove to a nearby truck stop, bought a change of clothes, took a shower, and came to the cash register with a cart half full of food and drinks. The clerk rang up the bill and bagged the items. Cantree handed him a hundred and, when the clerk opened the register, drew a gun and demanded everything in the till and the clerk's wallet. The clerk handed over the money and reached for a gun under the counter. Cantree shot him twice, narrowly missing vital organs and arteries, and ran out with the money and the bags of food. The Indianapolis police checked the surveillance tape, ran the license plate, and contacted the car's owner. Someone recognized Cantree from wanted notices and notified the FBI. A little before noon they found the stolen car in a neighboring apartment complex.

Annalynn and I went into the kitchen to fix a quick lunch and try to make sense of what we'd learned.

She threw together a Caesar salad. "Indianapolis is about

halfway from here to the bank they robbed. Maybe they stashed the Krugerrands near the bank and he's going back to pick them up."

I squeezed a lemon as I debated whether to air my theories for the agents' consumption. What did it matter? They were supposed to be our allies. "Roscoe wouldn't have been identified if he'd worn a disguise."

"The way he did at the bank and the casinos. He wanted to be recognized."

"I see no other explanation." I added juice and water to the lemonade pitcher.

"Not many robbers take a shower and load up on groceries. He's camping out, avoiding hotels and restaurants."

"I'm relieved that he hasn't moved in on some poor soul. That reminds me, have you heard how Mark Keller is doing?"

We filled glasses and bowls and moved to the dining room table.

"Tiny said Mark's recovering at his daughter's house. I don't know whether the FBI is still watching his farm." She'd raised her voice. "The FBI doesn't always share."

I gave her a thumbs-up. "Another thing, why rob a place for a few hundred dollars? Those truck stops surely don't keep much more cash than that at night. Besides, Roscoe had several thousand dollars in small bills from the bank job."

"Maybe he gambled it all away."

We ate in silence for a couple of minutes.

The doorbell rang, startling us both. Achilles yawned.

Annalynn jumped up. "That must be Russ. I'd forgotten about him."

So had I. My ex no longer loomed large in my firmament. I took a last bite and carried our half-empty bowls to stow in the refrigerator. Be casual, hospitable, I ordered myself. I stuck my head out the kitchen door. "Hi, Russ, would you like something to eat or to drink?"

He smiled and thrust back his shoulders. "A glass of that great lemonade, please."

"Of course." He didn't look as old as he had—when was that?—only last Tuesday. Probably I'd just become used to seeing him in his late fifties rather than as I remembered him in his late twenties. "Lemonade or coffee, Annalynn?"

"Lemonade, please." She motioned for Russ to go into the ladies' parlor. "Thank you for all the work you've done on this. Did you have a good visit with your brother?"

I must thank Russ, too, I reminded myself as I poured the lemonade. Whatever his motives, he'd accelerated our establishing the foundation. I had to treat this as one more of my hundreds of business meetings.

And so it was until Wharton rang the bell a little after three.

I let him in. He'd aged seven years in the last seven days.

"Sorry to intrude, Dr. Smith, but I need to bring Sheriff Keyser up to date."

"Of course, Lester." I used his first name deliberately. "I expect no less than openness and cooperation from the FBI."

"Well, you're getting it," he growled.

Annalynn shot into the hall. "Good afternoon, Lester. We can talk in the entertainment room. Phoenix, please settle those last details with Russ. And give him directions to Vern's before you meet your date."

Not subtle, Annalynn. She'd sensed an interest in something besides business from Russ. So had I, but I'd ignored him the way I had others in countless business meetings. I went back into the parlor.

Russ put down the paper we'd been discussing. "What in hell is going on? I heard some cockeyed news report about a bomb in your garage. Is that why the FBI is here?"

"Agent Wharton came because they can't find the Krugerrands the bomber stole. I'm one of three people in northern Missouri who knows what Krugerrands are. Ergo, I must have them."

He chuckled. "Fine, don't tell me. It's none of my business." He picked up the paper and we covered the final points.

It was three thirty. I directed him to the bathroom in the back hall and called Stuart. "Sorry, I got held up, but I'll be free in a couple of minutes, if it's not too late." The less time with Kaysi the better.

"I'll be there in five minutes."

Russ finally limped into the parlor, leaning heavily on his cane. "Playing basketball in the Congressional gym really killed my knees. I'll settle for golf when my substitute knee heals." He picked up his briefcase. "Do you play golf?"

"Only for business reasons. I prefer the piano." I took the heavy briefcase from him.

He smiled, flashing whitened teeth. "Classical for thinking, ragtime for relaxing."

Enough reminiscing. I wanted him gone before Stuart arrived. I should have told Stuart that Russ was the *pro bono* lawyer. I moved into the hall. "I'll walk you to your car and point you toward Vernon's house."

Russ didn't budge. "Phoenix, are you content with your life?"

"Content? That's not in my nature, but I have few regrets. I look forward to new ventures." I opened the front door for him.

His Adam's apple bobbed. "I have many regrets."

"As you should," I said, not letting him off the hook. "Don't add to the list."

He chuckled and followed me onto the porch. "That sounds like my Phoenix."

I took his arm to steady him on the porch steps.

Stuart pulled into Annalynn's driveway, parked behind Russ's rental, and stepped out of the car.

Dread paralyzed my tongue as Stuart walked toward us, a quizzical expression on his face.

Russ extended his hand. "Hello. I'm Russ Torrint."

"I remember you from the wedding," Stuart said, pausing and focusing on my face, not seeing—or ignoring—the hand.

I stepped away from Russ and regained my voice. "He's the *pro bono* lawyer. He's in Missouri visiting family."

"Sorry if I cut into your play time with Phoenix," Russ said amiably. "We had a lot to talk about."

Stuart's lips smiled. He moved forward and offered Russ not a hand but an arm. "Looks like you could use some help getting to your car."

"No, thanks." Russ tucked the shillelagh under his arm. "I'm at that stage of recovery where stairs are difficult. I'll be back on the tennis court by October."

Stuart turned to me, took the briefcase, and carried it to Russ's car. "That seems a little optimistic, sir, but then you probably rely more on spin than speed."

I chuckled at Stuart's apt gibe at Russ's tennis, politics, and life.

"I play with finesse," Russ shot back, moving toward the car with a bare trace of a limp.

"Finesse won't beat stamina, at least not when you play a committed opponent." Stuart put the briefcase down by the car door and took his phone from his belt. He glanced at the screen and grimaced. "It's Kaysi. I have to go." He strode toward his car.

I hurried after him. "You're going back to St. Louis right now?"

"Yes. I keep my promises." He got in, his face grim.

Was that barb aimed at Russ or at me? I grabbed the door before Stuart could close it. "I'm sorry the meeting ran so long. We talked business. Nothing personal."

He closed his eyes and shook his head. "If he meant nothing to you, Phoenix," he said softly, "you would have told me he was here." He pulled the door shut, turned on the motor, and backed out of the drive.

Chapter Twenty-Nine

"Should I remember that guy?" Russ shaded his eyes to watch Stuart's car race away.

"No, he was just a teenager at the wedding," I croaked out, my throat and my heart tight. I couldn't let Stuart leave Laycock without denying that Russ had any hold over me.

A smile flitted across Russ's lips. "Now that you're free, you can ride with me to Vernon Kann's house and meet with us."

"A smart man like you will have no trouble finding it." The bastard had stalled so he could meet my "date." I forced my muscles to relax and my lips to smile. I wouldn't let Russ know he'd hurt me. "It's three blocks south, two blocks east. A blue Victorian."

Annalynn and Wharton came out the front door. He ran down the steps and hurried down the walk. She called, "You go ahead, Russ. I'll be along in ten minutes."

A phone call to Stuart wouldn't do. I had to talk to him face to face. "Annalynn, I need to borrow your Mercedes."

"Of course, but let's talk first."

"Later." I punched in the code to open the garage door. Russ's rental car blocked the drive, and he didn't offer to move it. I had to go back and forth three times to maneuver the Mercedes around his car, but I wouldn't ask the man for anything.

I shouldn't have been so foolish. By the time I reached the house, Mrs. Roper was opening her car door. I parked behind her on the street and got out.

"Stuart left." She glared at me with the blend of ferocity and disappointment only a teacher can convey. "He's a sensitive, loving man, Phoenix. If he's not sophisticated or intellectual or successful enough for you, leave him alone. Don't toy with him."

I didn't want to leave him alone. "I'm very fond of him, Mrs. Roper. I certainly don't want to hurt him."

"But you have." She sat down on the car seat and dragged her legs in. She shook her finger at me. "Kaysi won't be half the problem that I will be if you hurt my boy." She slammed the door.

I stood speechless, feeling like I'd flunked a final, while she drove off.

A car pulled up beside me. Claudene lowered the passenger window. "Cantree robbed a convenience store near Toledo about dawn. He wore a disguise this time, but he used the same MO and left a clear fingerprint. Now that he's definitely out of this area, we really are leaving." She opened her palm to flash a phone number handwritten on a card as the car started to move. "Stay alert."

"Thanks." I slumped into the Mercedes and gathered my thoughts. Stuart couldn't talk to me while he drove his kids home. *Scheisse!* I'd gone off without Achilles. He'd panic. I called Annalynn.

She didn't pick up until the fourth ring. "Yes, Phoenix."

Why was she mad at me? "Is Achilles with you?"

He barked, four short explosions. He was scolding me.

Annalynn shushed him. "He's upset that you haven't spent any time with him today. I had to bring him."

"I'll be right over. Send him out. If I'm in the same room with Russ, I won't be able to control my temper."

"I understand. See you shortly."

Six minutes later I pulled into Vernon's semicircular drive.

Achilles raced toward me.

Annalynn followed more sedately. "Let's switch vehicles. The Mercedes doesn't have a riding pad for Achilles."

"Of course." I got out and knelt to comfort and be comforted.

Annalynn knelt beside us. "Roscoe moved on to Toledo. Wharton said law enforcement—local, state, federal—in Ohio and Indiana is on full alert. He thinks they'll catch Roscoe at one of his Cleveland hangouts."

"My shadows told me on the way out of town." I lowered my voice. "Be careful of Russ. He has a personal agenda."

"He always did, Phoenix. Always. We'll talk later." She rose and went inside.

I let Achilles ride up front even though his pad was in the back seat. We both needed to work off some stress, but I wasn't dressed for it. At home, I checked the cameras and the trackers, changed into shorts and a tank top, and strapped on my Glock.

Plain old fetch wouldn't make up for my neglect. I dug out a new Frisbee to placate Achilles. As usual, I flagged before he did, but he followed me inside.

I rewarded him with his favorite dog food and sipped a glass of water while he ate. "I'm better with dogs than men," I told him. "I held back too long and kept one secret too many. Stuart's mother's right. I have to love him or leave him."

But perhaps I no longer had a choice. Why had I been so arrogant as to think that I could, and should, control this relationship? I hated it when a man did that. Stuart had made it obvious he would give me considerable latitude. He'd been wrong in thinking I cared about Russ, but my secrecy, and Russ' spin, had fostered jealousy.

My mobile rang. Connie.

I needed to think, not talk. I answered anyway. I'd already offended too many people today.

"I got the clunker. The pool player got one, too."

"Damn!" That strengthened my suspicion that Roscoe had left a false trail and was headed back to Missouri. And my trackers rode on the wrong vehicles.

"It's a perfect evening for a ride."

To follow Gribble. Connie loved coded conversations. Amazingly enough, they usually worked. "How thoughtful of you." I didn't want to meet here. The agents had left, but probably their bugs or cameras remained. "I'm going to clean up and take Achilles for a walk in about twenty minutes." She knew you couldn't walk Achilles. He always went for a run. "We'll stroll by Mrs. Warner's elm." Both Mrs. Warner and the tree had died while we were kids.

"I always loved that elm. See you around."

I changed into jeans and a long-tailed navy-blue blouse. No point in concocting a disguise. I'd have to take Achilles, and even the best CIA makeup artist couldn't turn him into a poodle, at least not in fifteen minutes.

Connie wasn't at our spot. I paused with Achilles to watch squirrels in a maple.

She pulled up in an old blue Jetta. "Could you tell me how to get to the Hy-Vee?"

I played along. "I'd be glad to show you the street to take." I opened the back door for Achilles and got into the front seat. "Cantree robbed a store in Indiana last night and one in Ohio early this morning. My shadows left town. Where's the other clunker?"

"At Mrs. T's. It's a gray sedan. I drove by on the cross street on my way here. Gribble was taking a tire off the pickup."

A bad tire could serve as an excuse for the rental. "He probably punctured it."

"If we park by the school on Hilltop Street, we can watch and follow him when he leaves." She pulled out. "Should we call Annalynn?"

She'd send us home. "Not until we have something to report." I distracted Connie with details of Cantree's movement for the next few minutes. The second I finished, she asked me about Stuart. I hesitated to answer, trying to craft a reply.

"Oh, Phoenix. What happened?"

I spilled my guts. She nodded and prodded and, miracle of miracles, expressed no judgmental opinions. To my shock, I asked for her advice.

"I agree with his mother that you have to consider him. You have to think of yourself, too. I have no idea where that's going to lead you. You're on your own on this one, Phoenix. No matter what Annalynn may say, you're on your own."

I didn't need that reminder. Or did I?

"Don't rush yourself. If Stuart wants to put up with you for years, another day won't change his mind." She fingered an earring. "On the other hand, if you don't talk to him soon, he may be so hurt he'll refuse to listen to you."

I groaned.

"Look! Gribble is moving. He's turning onto Fillmore." She started the car.

"Go down and take a left on the parallel street for two blocks and then turn right. We should be able to see him."

She stepped on the gas. We came around the corner just in time to see him turn off Fillmore. With almost no traffic around, we followed a half block behind him for three blocks. He pulled over and parked on the street.

I ducked down. "Down, Achilles. Connie, drive past and see where he goes."

"Eight-oh-nine," she said softly a few seconds later. "Two other cars are there."

"That's Boopsie's address. They're playing cards tonight."

Connie's phone rang. She pulled over to answer it. "Hi, Annalynn." Pause. "I'm sitting here talking to Phoenix." She turned to me, eyes wide. "Yes, we're in the clunker. We took it for a little test drive. How did you know?"

I leaned close in time to hear "standard police work. Every officer in miles knows you and Gribble rented clunkers. You two stay away from him." She hung up.

"Annalynn is getting really good at this sheriff gig," Connie said.

And I had been reduced to amateur status. "Let's have dinner at La Vida Loca."

I drove the Jetta home and parked it in my garage behind the tarp door. Inside the castle, I tried Stuart's home phone and cell five times. Only fair. I'd not answered when I didn't want to talk to him. I'd hoped our relationship would stay as it was. Thanks to Russ—no, thanks to my keeping his visit secret—that couldn't happen.

Achilles watched lightning bugs through the upstairs hall windows while I paced the hall trying to crystallize my thoughts about Stuart. I'd taken chances all my adult life, risking discovery, imprisonment, and even death repeatedly during more than two decades under deep cover and, since retiring, occasionally on contract assignments. At the same time, as Annalynn had pointed out, I'd run from emotional risks.

Did I like Stuart enough to come to love him? I didn't expect the dizzy obsession and lust of my teens and twenties. In my forties, I'd shuddered in silence as friends settled for companionship or financial security. I demanded a deep connection, a blending of the intellectual, emotional, and physical. Even if Stuart and I developed that connection—fell in love—would it be strong enough to survive his daughter's hostility and his mother's wariness? Forget them. Accept the truth. My emotions, not theirs, would determine what happened to the relationship.

I needed to stimulate my thinking with one of Mozart's intricate masterpieces. I started to go next door to my piano, but the prospect of sitting in that now unfamiliar house alone cowed me tonight. I went upstairs and pulled up one of his piano sonatas on my iPod. By the time it ended, I'd decided to forget the telephone. Better to write to Stuart. I'd clarify my thoughts as I wrote, and I could edit them. I propped my laptop on my knees on the bed and opened a document file. I wouldn't take a chance on writing an e-mail and hitting Send prematurely. How to start? An apology never hurts. What could I say after I said I'm sorry? I'd written thousands of reports. Start with a recitation of the facts. Easy to delete the irrelevant or humiliating.

Annalynn came upstairs and leaned against my bedroom door an hour or so later. "The meeting with Russ was a bust. We can't possibly afford to hire his wife's firm. Vern suspects they're already working for someone else. To top it off, Russ claimed he didn't feel well enough to drive to Columbia." She held up her hands to staunch my curses. "Relax. I offered to book him a room in the Sweet Nights Motel."

I laughed. "A perfect place for one more cockroach."

"Vern found another solution. His grandson drove Russ to Columbia and another Mizzou student drove the rental car." She closed her eyes and rubbed her right shoulder. "I'm exhausted. Sorry about this afternoon. I tried to back Russ off by mentioning you had a date. It never occurred to me he would care enough to sabotage it. Do you want to talk about what happened with Stuart?"

"No, thanks. I talked it out with Connie."

She arched an eyebrow in disbelief.

"Really."

"Okay. Good night."

I shut out everything but my letter. By now I'd written several hundred words and deleted three-fourths of them. The grandfather clock struck eleven. So far I'd apologized and explained why Russ was here and how I preferred not to see him again. Now for the big finish. No circumlocution, no ambiguities, no deception. "I honestly don't know whether we can build a relationship that can reconcile my independent lifestyle and your desire for a full-time partner, not to mention receive your family's approval. Here's what I do know: I haven't enjoyed being with anyone so much in many years. It's a scary, unfamiliar feeling. Moving ahead is high risk–high gain for both of us. I'm willing to take the next step if you are."

I reread it three more times, stalling, avoiding writing the last line.

Achilles roused himself from his green blanket and propped his head on my knee.

I scratched behind his ears. "It's all or nothing," I told him. I typed, "Love, Phoenix." Five minutes later I hit Send.

Chapter Thirty

Stuart didn't e-mail or call by midnight. I went to bed. Still nothing Monday morning. I dragged myself downstairs to let Achilles out and followed the aroma of coffee.

Annalynn, in uniform, sat at the table reading the Sunday newspaper. "Hi, sleepyhead. Vernon's article on elder abuse is really good. I'm going to ask his permission to make copies for my deputies to carry and pass out."

Great. I'd offended Vernon yesterday, too. He'd expected my comments on his article. "Don't take it to the office until I have a chance to read it." I poured a half cup of coffee and added milk. After a moment I added some sugar. I needed more than caffeine this morning. "Roscoe rob anybody last night?"

"Not that I know of. Jim sent word that Gribble's rental car was parked at his house all night. He had his pickup towed to a repair shop this morning. Maybe Roscoe really is gone for good." She put down the paper, revealing a bowl of mixed fresh fruit at my place. "Do you suppose he intended for the shots and the explosives to draw the FBI here? Away from wherever he put the Krugerrands?"

"I don't know, but he definitely intended to blow me up."

My cell phone rang. I took a deep breath, expecting to see Stuart's number.

It was Mrs. T. "You are no Greek girl. You are hussy. You are not welcome to my home again." She slammed down the receiver.

"Mrs. T believed Derek's portrayal of me as a siren." Her rejection hurt.

"He must have finally figured out you're the one pressuring them to treat her better. Watch out for him, Phoenix."

"And for Kiki. She's the one with the target-shooting trophy." My gloom deepened.

Annalynn pushed back her chair. "I have to go to the office and divide too much work among too few people. What's on your schedule today?"

Waiting for Stuart's response. "Completing the foundation papers and setting up the office files."

"Good. I'm glad you're staying in."

Five minutes after she left, the cell phone in Gribble's truck started to move. I watched it travel out of town and onto a county road running east. My pulse quickened. He could be going to meet Roscoe. Could Gribble's clunker fit in the truck? Barely. You wouldn't be able to open the car doors. He'd have to roll, not drive, it into the truck bed and then pull it out. I'd arranged that several times, but it required planning. I put on the Kevlar vest under a blouse and took my special mini backpack from the closet shelf.

The truck turned where my map showed no road and stopped. The rendezvous? I opened my laptop and went to Google maps. In a couple of minutes I found the likely place, a farm with two big houses and several outbuildings. I'd driven by there in June when I was looking for a deer with a broken antler. I didn't recall the family's name, if I ever knew it, but my brain retrieved the number on their mailbox. Annalynn's admin assistant would have the name on file.

I dialed. "Hi, Diana. This is Phoenix. I need the name of a multigenerational family that lives on a big farm out east of town. They have an old house and a new one. Their ID number starts with two sixes." People freaked when I rattled off a long sequence of numbers. “Could you look it up for me?”

“I don’t need to. I went to a retirement picnic for Henry Rupp out there last week. He’s moving into assisted housing today and turning the place over to the next two generations.”

False alarm. A man was moving. “Thanks. Anything new on Roscoe Cantree?”

“Nothing definite. If he’s stolen as many cars as they’re investigating, he could open a used car lot. Sheriff Towson still swears Roscoe will come back here. You be careful.”

To do that, I had to be sure what was happening at the Rupp farm. I looked up the name online and found numbers for Henry and Hank. I blocked the ID on my phone and dialed Henry’s number.

He answered after five rings.

“Is this Hank Rupp?”

“No, that’s my dad. He’s outside helping load a truck. Want me to holler at him?”

“No, thanks. This can wait. I’ll call him later. Bye.”

So Gribble had a legitimate job. I went downstairs and read Vernon’s article and sidebar. An excellent blend of human interest and information. I called to tell him so.

“Thanks for the idea, Phoenix. We’ve had more response than I expected. I may write a follow-up in a month or so. Have you talked to Mrs. T about the article?”

“No. She told me not to come there anymore.” Which placed her in peril again. “I’ll have to recruit someone else to check on her.” This day kept getting worse.

“I have something else to add to your to-do list. We need to figure out what your ex-husband is up to. I’m worried that he met with us to get information on our plans for an opponent. Would he be that sleazy?”

“Why not? He worked on the Hill a long time. He learned from the worst.”

A long silence. "Or he could have a . . . personal motive for this visit. He talked about your college days and asked about what you're doing now. I can understand his curiosity about you, but he seemed, well, a little too interested. Do you think he wants to either help or hurt you through Annalynn's campaign?"

Obviously my day hadn't hit bottom yet. "I have no idea. His wife, and employer, didn't expect him to come to Laycock for any reason. I don't know this man. I fell in love with a brilliant, idealistic law student. I divorced an egocentric philanderer. Ask your political friends who he is today." A package delivery truck parked out front. "I have to go, Vernon. Bye."

The driver's dark skin assured me he wasn't Roscoe or one of his white supremacist buddies. I signaled the security system that the man with three small boxes wasn't a threat. Achilles joined me as I opened the door.

The man smiled. "Morning, Deputy Smith. Three packages, three signatures."

"Certainly. Would you mind carrying them to the dining room table?"

"Glad to." He put them down and handed me a small clipboard. "My wife always complains you can't buy anything in Laycock. I remind her that keeps my job safe. She'd give a month of *my* salary to bring in a Nordstrom's or a Kohl's." He tapped the top box. "I'd take Menard's over all of them."

"Thank goodness for Internet shopping." I handed back the clipboard. By evening a dozen people would think they knew the sources of my packages. "Would you like a glass of cold water or some coffee?"

"No, thanks. I'm all set." He paused at the door. "How's Annalynn doing?"

"She toughs it through one day at a time by working from breakfast to bed."

"Tell her we're praying for her." He hurried toward his truck.

I closed the door and ripped open the fake Kohl's box to equip myself for my morning venture. The smallest packet contained wraparound sunglasses with a chain for the earpieces. I walked over to the window and tried them on, focusing on a bird landing in a tree across the street. I adjusted the lens to bring every feather into focus. A larger package held a poufy white-billed cap and a strip of tiny batteries. The back band had two adjustable buckles, one behind the right ear and one behind the left. I inserted the batteries behind the buckles, put on the cap with the bill pulled low, and walked toward the kitchen. In the bill I could see the hall and Achilles' tail behind me. Not bad. I'd have to adjust the cameras for distance outdoors. The park would be a good place.

"We'll open the big one later," I told Achilles. "I bought you a Kevlar coat you're going to hate." I took the boxes upstairs and stacked them on the steamer trunk at the foot of my bed. Hide them in plain sight.

I checked the trackers. Neither the pickup nor the truck had moved. I put such necessities as water and Achilles' tennis ball in my backpack and jogged to the park on a circuitous route. Achilles ranged around me exploring new territory. I soon took off the sunglasses. Looking ahead through the binoculars and watching the rear in the bill of the cap at the same time gave me a headache. The park's giant oaks provided shade, so we played fetch until his ball was a ragged, soggy mess. As we left the park, I dropped it in a swinging-door trash can where he couldn't retrieve it.

We took the long way back, going by an updated dime store to pick up the supplies LaDawna had listed. I could have been running an errand for my mother on a hot August morning forty years ago. Except for the Kevlar vest and the Glock and the two cell phones and the cap with rearview cameras.

Back at the castle, Achilles went to check on the hummingbirds while I concentrated on completing the foundation papers to be filed with the IRS. Not having set up the desktop computers at our new offices, I worked in the ladies' parlor on Annalynn's desktop computer.

She came in before I could finish and looked over my shoulder. "That can wait. I only have a few minutes to eat and bring you up to date on Roscoe Cantree."

With nothing prepared, we settled for a childhood favorite, sliced tomatoes and cheese and crackers.

When Annalynn didn't begin, I knew she'd come home to give me bad news. "I take it Roscoe isn't in custody yet."

"We're pretty sure the FBI has no idea where he is. They certainly don't know where he hid the Krugerrands. Willetta has been monitoring the Cleveland news on the Web. Bank officials have been openly criticizing the FBI for not recovering the money from a 'gang of petty criminals.' The FBI is asking local police to follow up on every car theft between Ohio and Nevada."

"Then they're not discounting the possibility he's heading back here. Have they really let Wharton and the other agents take time off?"

Annalynn rubbed her right temple with her fingertips. "I don't know. They've cut Tiny and me completely out of the loop."

They'd never really let them in. "They suspect a leak."

"Could they be right? Tiny withheld information from us. Do you think he's lied about the Cantrees swearing to get him? About them being enemies?"

I considered and discarded the possibility. "If I'd opened that farmhouse door, he would've been hurt or killed in the explosion, too. They've been enemies a long time." Vernon's lunch conversation verified that. "What about other people in his department?"

"The FBI checked out all of his and my people and found nothing."

I remembered a loose thread. "Did they locate Orson's runaway daughter?"

"Not that I know of. I don't even know whether they tried. He hadn't seen her in years, not even after her mother and stepfather died. She ran away from foster care at seventeen and disappeared. The boy ran away in June and joined his father."

"How is Orson Junior doing?"

"Recovering. They moved him into a secure rehabilitation facility this morning." She sighed. "It was a relief to hear that. I didn't want his death on my head."

"If the agents cleared everyone on your and Tiny's staffs, why stonewall you?" I answered for her. "They still don't trust me, which includes you, because I could fence the Krugerrands. They still don't trust Tiny because he grew up with the Cantrees. That's what you really came home to tell me."

"I suppose so." She smiled. "I have one piece of good news. Wolf—you remember Willetta's husband—parked behind a rural church last night to eat a mid-shift snack. Guess who interrupted him."

"He caught the cemetery vandals!"

"Three juveniles, two boys and a girl, none from Vandiver County, all with parents anxious to keep it quiet. They'll pay for all repairs and maintain the cemeteries for two years. Case closed. We'll go pick up our cameras when things calm down." She pushed back her chair. "I have to get back."

Achilles sprang to his feet and barked for her attention.

"Sorry if I've ignored you." She stroked his head.

"Would you mind taking him to work with you this afternoon? LaDawna sings while she works. So will he. I don't enjoy their duets."

"Fine. But first have him check that clunker for bombs and then put it in my garage."

LaDawna arrived on her bicycle right on time. Again she wore all black, and the bags under her eyes matched her clothing. She chained the bike to a tree and lifted a large backpack from the basket.

I opened the front door. "That looks heavy. Do you carry all your textbooks?"

She swung it over her shoulder. "I have to—to meet someone. I won't have time to go back to my room for anything."

Saturday she'd been anticipating an unpleasant encounter with someone. I looked for bruises on her face and arms but saw none. "Would you like some lemonade?"

"Thanks. I'll drink it while I work."

She didn't want to talk. "Start with Annalynn's desk. A good cleaning and polish may be all it needs."

She nodded and went on down the hall, taking the backpack with her.

I brought her the lemonade in a big thermal cup and settled down on the couch with my laptop to check e-mail and business news. In a few minutes I heard her singing softly. "Feel free to belt it out," I called. "It won't disturb me. I enjoy hearing you sing."

Her voice did disturb me. This gifted young woman should be preparing to study opera in Vienna, not rehearsing a student musical in Laycock. Connie could teach her how to breathe and other basics, but musical comedy and opera require different techniques and regimens.

The girl finished "Many a New Day" and came into the living room. "Come see the top. It has some nicks, but the wood cleaned up really nice."

I went back for an inspection. "The nicks give it character.

You've done a great job. Do you have time to shine the rest of it today?"

She looked at her watch. "I'll try. I have to leave at three thirty."

I went back to my laptop. In the middle of her second time through "People Will Say We're In Love," I noticed it was three forty. "LaDawna, it's time for you to go."

"Oh, God! I'll come back tomorrow." She ran past me and out the door.

Her panicked exit alarmed me. Was she rushing off to face the person she'd feared Saturday? A few basic self-defense moves didn't prepare her for a close encounter of the worst kind. I closed my laptop and delved into my own backpack. I didn't have time for a disguise, but I could obscure my identity with a floppy straw hat, an oversized beige blouse, and red canvas slip-ons. I reached the sidewalk in time to see her turn right at the corner and head toward the downtown.

I ran to the garage and backed the clunker into the street. Instead of following her, I took a parallel street for three blocks and then cut over to the street crossing the one she'd taken. She was pedaling half a block away. I went straight across, drove around the block, and followed a block behind her. I pulled into a parking space when she stopped at the post office and chained her bike to the rack. She looked at her watch and went inside.

Why would she rush to the post office? The last collection was at five. It was now five minutes until four. If she was meeting someone she feared, the post office was a good place to do it. An elderly man came out and drove away. I surveyed the street. Two cars were parked between mine and the post office. Three cars and a pickup sat on the other side of the street. The downtown saw little action.

LaDawna came out of the post office. Her backpack no longer bulged, but she carried a bulky plastic grocery bag with the top tied shut. Instead of returning to her bike, she crossed the street and went into Sarah's Beauty Salon. Hmmm. That black spiky hair certainly needed a hairdresser's help, but I doubted the girl sought a styling.

I got out of the car and sauntered to the Chinese carryout directly across the street from the salon. LaDawna stood at the sign-in desk.

"Hi," I said when the carryout's owner bustled out of the kitchen. "I'd like a cashew chicken and a beef with broccoli, please."

"Sure. Fifteen minutes." She rang it up and rushed back into the kitchen.

I sat down at the table with the best view and watched as LaDawna took a seat by the window. I put on my new sunglasses to get a close look. A woman with short light-brown hair moved a bag similar to LaDawna's from a chair to the floor. LaDawna put her bag on the floor next to the other one. Bloody hell! They'd set up an exchange. They sat there two minutes, both looking straight ahead. I couldn't see the woman's face or any movement indicating they spoke. The woman's hand reached over and closed around LaDawna's for a moment, a gesture of affection and reassurance.

The girl stood up, spoke to someone in the salon, picked up the bag the woman had brought, and walked to the door. When she opened it, the woman turned her head.

LaDawna McKnight had switched bags with Lily Lou Glasgow Stringer.

Chapter Thirty-One

I sat stunned. LaDawna McKnight had to be Madonna Cantree, Orson's runaway daughter and the music teacher's niece. Lily had told me Junior wouldn't say where his sister was. The literal truth, perhaps. I replayed my visit to Lily's home in my head as the girl crossed the street and unchained her bicycle. Lily and Norval had said good things about the girl. She'd impressed me with her talent and hard work. I couldn't believe I'd been suckered by aunt or niece, but this secret exchange implicated them in the robbery. I remembered the broken wasp nest and LaDawna's saying she'd gone to the emergency room when she explained her fear of the spiders. She'd been the fourth person at the abandoned farmhouse. Maybe Roscoe had escaped because he drove her to the hospital.

LaDawna carried the bag as though it were light. It didn't hold the gold. Perhaps Lily had brought her niece a change of clothes. Be realistic. More likely, the aunt brought the missing cash. No. I couldn't have been so wrong in judging their character. I'd dealt with slime for years. I recognized it. I wouldn't call Annalynn until I knew for sure what these two were doing.

Dropping money for my food order on the counter, I called, "I'll be back in a few minutes." Or not. I picked up an old newspaper, held it in front of my face, and waited at the door until LaDawna placed the bag in her backpack and rode away. Across the street, her aunt rose, said something to a hairdresser, and walked out. Approaching the pickup, she dropped the bag in a trash can—an amateur's mistake to dispose of it publicly. She started the engine with a roar, pulled out, and turned left at the corner.

At the other end of the block, LaDawna turned right, pedaling parallel to the street Lily had taken. Hmmm. I hurried to my car and followed LaDawna. As I went around the corner, she paused at the stop sign a block ahead of me and went straight. At the end of the next block she went to the right. She wasn't going toward the college or the house she shared with Ado Annie. The only thing down this way was an old residential neighborhood. I pulled over and let her gain a block on me. Lily's pickup turned the corner and followed half a block behind her niece. Interesting.

"The park," I muttered. "LaDawna must be making a drop in the park." I let Lily get a block ahead before driving after them. LaDawna swung left on the street running by the near side of the block-square park. Lily drove on and turned left on the far side. I made my left a block before the park, stashed my car out of sight, and approached the park from the other side. I put on my sunglasses and strolled to a well-shaded bench.

LaDawna had leaned her bike against a shaded picnic table and removed the bag from her backpack. She glanced around, ducked her head, walked to a trash can a few yards away, and stuffed the bag through its swinging-door top.

Definitely a drop. For Roscoe? Another gang member? I preferred to aim with the naked eye rather than the binocular sunglasses. I took them off and let them hang around my neck by the cord. Using the newspaper to hide my right hand, I drew my Glock. No time to call for help.

LaDawna sat at the table and opened a textbook. Across the park Lily watched from her pickup. I put my sunglasses back on and focused on Lily. She had her arm on the window frame, and it cradled the barrel of a small pistol.

Could they be laying a trap for Roscoe? An extremely dangerous game. I scanned the park. A young woman watched three toddlers play in the wading pool. One ran over to the trash can and stretched to put in some paper. An elderly man walked an arthritic dog by the white crape myrtles. Two girls about twelve, one white and one black, giggled in the gazebo. A boy and girl a little older walked their bikes along the sidewalk on the far side of the park. He stole a quick kiss. She stole it right back. Whatever happened, I was the only one here to protect all these people. I took out my iPhone and debated whether to call Annalynn.

LaDawna looked at her watch, glanced around, and ducked her head again.

The old man bagged his dog's poop in a plastic bag like LaDawna's and dumped it in the trash can. A nice surprise for whoever came for the drop.

A black pickup pulled up near me. A man with a Halloween pirate's mustache, long body, and short legs walked along the edge of the park. Derek Gribble. He wore a long-billed cap and a workman's uniform much like Roscoe wore to my garage and carried several big black trash bags slung over his shoulder. His eyes swept the park, flitting past me and the other people and lingering on the trash can near LaDawna.

An iPhone video wouldn't be great at this distance, but it would be clear enough to convict Gribble of being an accomplice. I pretended to text to cover the videotaping.

He walked in awkward slow motion toward the trash can where I'd discarded the tennis ball that morning. He struggled to release and remove the lid and spilled some trash pulling out the bag. He put in a fresh bag and jammed the lid on. His mustache came loose on one side.

I put my sunglasses back on and surveyed the park. No one

new here or anywhere in sight.

Lily watched Gribble do his slow-mo walk toward the other can with a perplexed look on her face. She'd expected Roscoe. She gasped and her lips formed, "Derek."

I dropped the sunglasses and focused the iPhone to film the climax of my movie.

Gribble fumbled with the top of the can. He paid no attention to LaDawna, sitting motionless nearby. The mustache fell off and he stuffed it in the trash bag he'd yanked out. He felt around inside the bag and then pumped his fist in the air. He threw a clean bag into the can and set the lid on top without securing it. No more slow-mo now. He moved toward the pickup like a race walker, threw both trash bags in the cab, and took off with squealing tires.

A dramatic ending for my production. Cut and print.

Neither LaDawna nor her aunt moved.

I didn't want the FBI confiscating my business phone, so I e-mailed the video to my local cell and then forwarded it to Analynn with a note: "I happened across Gribble collecting trash in the park. He must be up to something."

LaDawna sat still for five minutes. She glanced at her watch, folded her hands in a brief prayer, and buried her face in her arms. Her shoulders shook for a long time. Finally she raised her head, wiped the tears from her face, and gave a thumbs-up.

Lily responded with the same gesture and drove off.

The tracker showed Gribble had reached home.

My local cell phone rang. It was Mrs. T's number. I answered.

"Come see me tomorrow, Greek girl," she said. "Kiki and that man go on a trip." She hung up.

A trip financed by a payoff. Not from LaDawna and Lily but from Roscoe. He must have blackmailed the women by threatening to reveal LaDawna's identity or to kill them.

LaDawna and Lily had worked together secretly. Maybe not

so secretly. Maybe Tiny knew about LaDawna and was working with them for a cut of the robbery. Hard to believe. I certainly didn't want to believe it. Maybe he was protecting them. Brandon had stayed at his mentor's house after Roscoe ran Mark Keller off the road. Had Brandon helped LaDawna hide out at Laycock Community College? Couldn't be. The kid wasn't that good an actor.

I had to find out more before I told Annalynn and, inevitably, the FBI who left the package for Gribble. I could coax or force LaDawna to talk. But not out in the open.

She put her book in the backpack and mounted her bicycle.

I waited to see which street she took and jogged back to my clunker to follow her. She pedaled faster this time and I had a couple of bad minutes locating her. Two blocks later I realized where she was going. I pulled over and watched her turn into Connie's driveway. LaDawna had nerves of steel to go for a voice lesson now.

My phone rang. Annalynn. I made a U-turn and headed for the carryout place before I answered. "Did you get my video?"

"Yes. Where are you?"

"On my way to pick up cashew chicken and beef with broccoli. I ordered them right before I went to the park."

"Were you following Gribble? Give me the absolute truth."

"I was not following him." People tend to believe a quick answer more than a delayed one. I went on the offensive: "When I went to the park, I had no idea he would be there. What do you suppose he expected to find in those trash bags?"

"Did you see anyone put anything in that trash can?"

"I put Achilles' old tennis ball in the first one this morning. I saw an old man put his dog's leavings in the other one right before Gribble got there."

"Bring me your receipt for the meal. I need the time stamp."

"Sure. I'll be there shortly." She thought more like a cop every day.

I left on the floppy hat and oversized blouse to pick up the food and returned both to the backpack when I got in the car. Unfortunately, I hadn't put my shoes in the car and had to leave the red canvas pair on. Even though Annalynn was upset, she might notice the atypical footwear. Couldn't be helped.

I parked in a visitor's slot and took in my food. The receipt was stapled to the bag.

Diana, Annalynn's admin assistant, met me at the door and took me straight to an interrogation room, or possibly *the* interrogation room. The size of a walk-in closet, it contained a small metal table and two metal chairs. I noted an inconspicuous wall-mounted camera.

Annalynn came in, went through the official rigmarole, and said, "Please confirm that you agree to the videotaping of your statement for use by law enforcement agencies."

Was she making that up? "Okay."

"Please tell me what time you arrived at Memorial Park."

I clasped my hands in front of me on the table and sat up straight. "I didn't check my watch. I estimate that I arrived at the park six to eight minutes after I ordered dinner. Whatever time's on my carryout receipt."

"When did Mr. Gribble arrive?"

"About one minute before the time stamp on the video I took with my cell phone, which was about three to five minutes after I sat down on a bench on the northwest corner. His appearance attracted my attention. As I'm sure you noticed, he was wearing a generic work uniform much like Roscoe Cantree wore when he visited my garage. And that Halloween mustache." I paused. "That's why I started to film him."

She kept her face noncommittal. "Who did you see in the park before he arrived?"

Give the literal truth. "A group playing at the wading pool, a young teenage couple on bicycles, an older girl reading at a table, two adolescent girls talking in the gazebo, a man about eighty walking a dog." Lily hadn't been *in* the park. "That's it."

"Did either trash bag appear to be heavy?"

A good question. "No. He's a strong man, but I doubt that either bag contained twenty pounds of Krugerrands."

For a moment she let her public face slip, but she put it back on to be the grand inquisitor: "Did you see anyone put anything in either trash can?"

"Yes." The truth, almost the whole truth. "Three people went to the trash can near the shelter. I don't know what the reader and a wader put in. The old man left a bag of dog poop. I appreciate it when people pick up after their animals."

She kicked my ankle, a reminder to take this seriously. "What do you think was in those trash bags?"

I debated for a moment whether to say what we would all assume. "Cash. A payoff for helping Roscoe Cantree either in the past or future. Perhaps both. A little after Gribble left, his mother-in-law called to invite me to visit her tomorrow. She said her son-in-law will be going on a trip."

Annalynn pushed back her chair. "That will be all for now. We'll contact you later with more questions."

The camera light went off.

She opened the door a couple of inches, letting Achilles stick in his nose. "Invite Connie over to share the Chinese food. I won't be home for hours."

"Are you going after whatever Gribble picked up?"

She let Achilles squeeze through to me. "What do you recommend?"

"Wait and give him a chance to lead you to Roscoe."

She smiled. "You're starting to think like the FBI."

Hmmm. I must be missing something.

Chapter Thirty-Two

Leaving the sheriff's department, I assessed the situation. I had little time to convince LaDawna to confide in me, the person who'd killed her father and wounded her brother, before someone in the park gave a description that led Annalynn and the FBI to the girl. In an interrogation room, she'd clam up. No one would learn anything from her. I'd coaxed or bullied information out of many tougher people. Fear and greed had been my major allies as a covert operative. LaDawna had acted afraid of me at the college but not at the house. I'd do better with a soft approach.

I drove straight to Connie's and cheered when I saw the bike chained to a tree.

When I opened the car door, Achilles' ears perked up. He leapt over me and raced to the door barking.

Connie opened the door. "What's wrong, Achilles?"

He trotted past her and into the room that contained her grand piano.

I threw up my hands. "He heard LaDawna's voice and wants to sing with her."

The girl laughed. "He likes 'People Will Say We're in Love.' Do you mind if we end the lesson with that, Ms. Diamante?"

"I can hardly wait to hear this," Connie said.

"You'll find the soprano a lot more melodious than the tenor," I warned, assessing LaDawna. The only time I'd seen her so relaxed and happy had been when she told her Chicago stories at the restaurant. She thought the drop had solved her problems. I took the Chinese food into the kitchen to microwave and stuffed napkins in my ears to cover the sounds of the duet. I'd not get a better chance to question her. I set three places at the dining room table and turned on the microwave. As the duo began the final chorus, I went to join them.

LaDawna, her face joyous, dropped to her knees with the final note and hugged Achilles. "You're a wonderful tenor."

She barely resembled the sleep-deprived girl who'd polished furniture or the tearful young woman who'd mastered her fear in the park.

Connie laughed heartily and reached out to stroke Achilles. "Phoenix, what do I smell in the kitchen?"

"Dinner for three is served."

LaDawna jumped up, her face shy. "Oh, but I couldn't intrude."

"Of course, you can," Connie said. "One of the first things you learn in show business is never to turn down a free meal. You can wash up in the powder room at the end of the hall."

As soon as the door closed, Connie hustled me through the dining room into her small kitchen. "What's going on? She looked like hell when she got here. I couldn't get her to loosen her throat for twenty minutes. Does this have something to do with her wanting self-defense lessons?"

I put the last bowl in the microwave and whispered, "That's what I'm here to find out. Whatever I say, follow my lead."

Connie opened the refrigerator and took out a pitcher of iced tea. "Is she in serious trouble?"

I nodded. I didn't hesitate to take a chance on becoming ensnared in this myself. I had no right to involve Connie. I'd soften up LaDawna during dinner and bag her when we left.

She came to the kitchen door with Achilles. "Can I help?"

He was my secret weapon. "Would you mind giving the tenor

a drink and a couple of those treats that Connie keeps in a bag under the sink? His bowl is there, too." I took the rice and cashew chicken to the table. "Did you have a dog as a child?"

"No, we moved too much, but I used to play with neighbors' animals."

Ease into it with idle chatter. "Did you know that Connie grew up in this house? I used to take piano lessons here from her mother." I looked to Connie for help.

She poured the iced tea. "And then we both left for college and marriage and careers. I made music in five states and Phoenix made money in Eastern Europe. Neither of us expected to come back to Laycock."

The microwave dinged and I took the beef and broccoli to the table.

LaDawna followed. "I'm never going back to where I came from," she said fiercely. A blush crept up her neck. "I don't have any family there anymore."

I saw an opening. "Listening to you sing this afternoon, I wondered where you plan to study after LCC. Connie can teach you a lot about singing and stagecraft, but you need to begin your training for opera as soon as possible."

She stared at me. "Opera? You think I can be an opera singer?"

"Of course." How could she not know this? "Your range and vocal quality are ideal for opera. Surely Connie and I aren't the only ones to tell you this."

Her face lit up. "The only ones who know what they're talking about." Her face fell. "I can barely afford LCC. It will take years to make enough money to go to a place like Juilliard."

Not if you rob a bank. I decided to be straight about her singing. "You won't be ready to audition for Juilliard for a year or two. A good school demands more than raw talent. That you have in abundance. When you've polished it, scholarships will come."

"She's right," Connie chimed in. "Phoenix can help you find the right place to study and the scholarships. She knows a bunch of opera singers."

We'd set the bait. Now to guide LaDawna/Madonna into the trap. "We'll help you work out a course schedule here. You need to study Italian and German, for example. When Connie thinks you're ready, we'll find the right teacher for your voice."

Tears came to the girl's eyes. "You're so wonderful."

Connie's phone rang. She rose to go answer it. "That's not something Phoenix hears very often."

"And never from you," I said. "LaDawna, you have a rare talent. Please don't throw it away."

Her lips trembled. She ducked her head.

Connie came back in. "Phoenix, Annalynn says the FBI wants the phone you used to take that video in the park this afternoon."

Bloody hell! What rotten timing!

LaDawna moaned and slid off her chair.

Connie rushed around the table. "She's fainted! LaDawna?"

I brought a glass of water from the kitchen and sprinkled some on the girl's pale face. "Let's get her onto the couch." And get Connie out of the house.

The girl moaned again and tried to get up. "I'm so dizzy."

Connie put an arm around LaDawna's waist and half carried her into the family room to collapse on the old floral couch. I trailed along behind and switched on a lamp.

LaDawna searched for me. "You were in the park?"

"Yes." No time for subtlety. "Connie, LaDawna needs some high-energy food. Please go to the Dairy Queen and get her a hot-fudge sundae."

Connie whirled around. "You're keeping something LaDawna did from Annalynn."

Scheisse. "Yes, and you don't want to know what it is. Get out of here." When she didn't move, I added, "I have only a few minutes before Annalynn or the feds show up. Go."

LaDawna buried her face in a cushion. Achilles whined and licked her arm.

Connie took a deep breath. "I'm staying. You may need me. LaDawna, I have no idea what's going on, but you'd better listen to Phoenix and do what she says." She motioned for me to sit by LaDawna.

Play the mother. Comfort her. Not my usual role. I edged onto the couch and put her head in my lap. "You aren't on the tape, Madonna. Neither is your aunt. The problem is, someone else may have seen you put that bag in the trash can."

LaDawna wiped her eyes. "When did you find out who I am?"

"Right before I followed you into the park. What was in that bag?" I signaled Connie, mouth agape, to keep quiet.

LaDawna sat up. "I had nothing to do with the robbery. I swear it. I can prove it. I waitressed all that day at Riga Far West in Chicago. Dozens of people saw me."

I patted her hand. "Good." I wondered if the FBI had traced her to Chicago and learned that. "I would have told Annalynn immediately if I'd thought you are part of the Cantree gang." She had to know about the robbery. "I need the complete story, starting with what was in that bag and why you left it there."

She bit her lip and said nothing.

Connie sat down on the other side of LaDawna and put an arm around her shoulder. "Trust us." She handed LaDawna a tissue. "You have no other choice."

The girl nodded. "It was money from the robbery. My brother hid it in the trunk of the car they fixed up for me. I didn't even know it was in there until yesterday."

Make her think I knew more than I did. "In the old Mustang. Did Roscoe drive you to the emergency room when the mud dauber stung you?"

She started in surprise. "No, I drove myself. The doctor made me stay to see how I reacted to the antidote. That's where I heard about a shooting out in the country. They said . . . they said the sheriff killed the father and wounded the son and everybody was looking for the money." She covered her face with her hands and sobbed.

Connie rubbed her back and made soothing noises. Achilles licked her hands and whined.

I made an educated guess: "You went to your aunt for help. She knew if you stayed with her, you'd be identified and accused of taking part in the robbery."

LaDawna nodded and uncovered her face. She sniffed a couple of times and said to Connie, "Aunt Lily wanted me to work with you. When Brandon called all excited about auditioning, she said that I should enroll in LCC as if nothing had happened."

That didn't explain the drop. "What about the bag of money?"

LaDawna turned from Connie, the good fairy, to me, the devilish deputy. "Junior gave me a cell phone with his number on it. He said he might not stay with Uncle Norval after all. Roscoe called me on that phone and said he'd kill Aunt Lily if I didn't give him the money Junior gave to me."

That explained the exchange at the beauty salon. "You hid the Mustang on Lily's farm. And what did you say?"

"I told him I didn't want money with blood on it." She swallowed several times. "I thought once he had the money he'd go away and leave *all* of us alone."

I needed more. "Did Roscoe have a car at the old farmhouse?"

"I didn't see one, but he must have. He walked off right after I got stung."

The doorbell rang.

The FBI couldn't have come that soon. "Connie, give Annalynn the small phone—not the iPhone—in my bag and tell her—

something."

"I'm good at improv," Connie said, rushing from the room.

I hoped the drama queen didn't overplay it.

"Hi, here's the phone," Connie said at the front door. "Did you check on Mrs. T?"

"I didn't know I was supposed to," Annalynn said. "Has something happened?"

"I don't know, but Trudy asked me about her. One of the neighbors said it looked like someone had ripped off the front storm door. Could you swing by on your way back to the office?"

"Yes, of course. Sorry to interrupt your dinner. Bye."

I applauded as Connie came in and then turned back to LaDawna, who had stopped cringing when the door closed. "What instructions did Roscoe give you?"

"Put the money in a trash can at ten minutes after four. Watch to be sure nobody took it before a man in a green uniform came to collect the trash. Then wait five more minutes and leave."

Even if LaDawna had talked to the police, Roscoe would have been safe. "Did you recognize the courier, the man who picked up the trash?"

"No, I was afraid to look at him."

Connie clapped her hands. "I'll bet it was Gribble! Am I right?"

"You're right." Seeing LaDawna didn't react, I said, "The man who delivered the furniture. He's an old friend of Roscoe's. Your aunt recognized him."

LaDawna gasped. "Did he see her?"

"He saw nothing but the trash can. If you're lucky, no one else noticed you either. Annalynn might recognize you from a description." I thought about it. "I told her a girl reading a book put something in the trash can. Nothing, at the moment, proves you put the money in there."

Connie held up a cautionary finger. "Phoenix, Annalynn isn't going to believe you didn't recognize LaDawna. You better have an answer ready." She touched the girl's knee. "Your real name is Madonna?"

"Not anymore. There can be only one singer named Madonna. I used several different stage names when I first went out on my own, but I had to use my real name, Madonna Johnson, for jobs. So I changed it legally." She turned to me. "What should I do now?"

"Follow your regular routine." I gripped her shoulder. "If Roscoe contacts you or your aunt, call me immediately. Promise?"

She crossed her heart. "Aunt Lily's scared to death he'll come after both of us. That's why she brought the money. What do I do if the sheriff or the FBI comes?"

Tricky. "It will arouse suspicion if you call me."

Connie snapped her fingers. "Call the Reverend Nancy Alderton. She won't let them run over you. Have her call me, since I'm your director. I'll call Phoenix to get you a lawyer."

I nodded. "A good plan."

Connie gave a slight bow. "Now, LaDawna, wash your face so we can finish supper."

She blinked and wiped away tears. "You know, I'm really, really hungry."

Connie waited until the girl was out of hearing range. "Is Annalynn going to pick up Gribble and grill him, or will the FBI handle it?"

"Neither. Gribble and Kiki are going on a trip tomorrow. He'll lead the FBI to Roscoe." I tiptoed over and checked that LaDawna wasn't in the hall. "Do you believe LaDawna's story?"

Connie fingered an earring. "You had just offered her the world she's dreamed about. She won't risk her chance. Like *you,* she may not have told the whole truth, but yes, I believe her." She rose. "We'll have to reheat our food."

When LaDawna joined us at the table, her eyes were red, her expression calm. "Dr. Smith, I've been wondering and wondering about something. Why did Roscoe try to blow you up?"

Chapter Thirty-Three

The question caught me off guard. I opted to tell the truth and face the consequences head on: "Roscoe wants revenge. I fired the shots that killed your father." Don't be a coward. "And that wounded your brother. I heard he's recovered enough to leave the hospital."

A tear rolled down her right cheek.

"The Cantrees shot first—assault rifles," Connie said. "Phoenix and Annalynn had no choice." After a moment of silence: "Do you understand that, LaDawna?"

She twisted her fingers together. "I didn't at first. I do now. I don't understand why Roscoe would take chances to avenge my father. When Junior brought the Mustang to me in early August, he said Roscoe and Dad couldn't be in the same room more than two minutes without fighting. That night at the farm, he told me he thought they might kill each other. He asked me if Uncle Norval was mean like them."

Interesting. "Everyone says your Uncle Norval is a good man. Was he going to give your brother a home?"

"Only until December. He turns eighteen then. He planned to join the army." She threw back her shoulders. "I planned to live with Aunt Lily until I could find a job and a place I could afford in Laycock. We found both on the LCC website."

"And she cut and dyed your hair." Lily Stringer was a resourceful person.

Revenge had always seemed a weak motive for blowing me

up. I needed to play some Mozart and figure out Roscoe's real motive.

Driving back to the castle after following LaDawna to her cleaning job, I realized I'd outsmarted myself by giving my local cell phone to Annalynn. Now she or the FBI would receive any call or text from Stuart. Could I move the tracking apps from my iPhone to my laptop without losing the connections to the devices in Gribble's vehicles? I had several other things on that iPhone I didn't want the FBI to see, too.

A newish red Ford Mustang was parked in Annalynn's drive. Not an FBI car. I parked my clunker down the street.

Achilles raced ahead toward the backyard as I walked toward Annalynn's front door. He'd been cooped up since lunch and wanted to play. He deserved a few minutes outside before dark. I followed him into Annalynn's backyard.

He met me with his Frisbee in his mouth.

Between throws I found the number for the restaurant LaDawna had given as her alibi for the day of the robbery and called. It rang six times before a woman answered.

"Sorry to bother you during dinner rush," I said. "LaDawna McKnight has applied for a job. Do you recommend her?"

"Definitely. She's a good worker and very reliable."

"When did she leave?"

"A week ago Friday was her last day. She worked a double shift to make gas money to drive to some college. Tell her Ineta says hello." She hung up.

I was relieved to hear LaDawna had a strong alibi for the day of the robbery.

Annalynn opened the French doors and stepped out onto the patio. "Phoenix, Stuart called."

My heart rate jumped. "Did you talk to him?"

"Yes. I explained why I had your phone."

"Could you toss a few for Achilles while I call him back?"

"He was at the airport, going somewhere on a special assignment. He'll be incommunicado for several hours." She walked over to stand beside me. "He gave me a message for you. He prefers to talk face to face Saturday morning."

What did that mean? Was he picking me up for our holiday weekend or coming to say good-bye in person? "How did he sound?"

"Hurried. Worried." She reached down to take the Frisbee from Achilles. "Connie gave me the wrong cell phone. The FBI wants your iPhone."

"Those nosy bastards can't have it." Watch the temper. "I have business contacts and proprietary information on that phone. They better damned well give back my other cell phone, too. That's private property. While they're at it, they should return my car."

Annalynn gave a slight nod toward the house and threw the Frisbee.

"Scheisse!" I turned around. Claudene Dale carried a tray holding glasses of lemonade toward the patio table. Willetta, grinning, walked behind her. Both wore dark capris and floral blouses, but Claudene's fit snugly and Willetta's ballooned out over her baby bump.

"Calm down," Annalynn said, taking my arm and guiding me to the table. "Claudene and Willetta were on their way to La Vida Loca when you sent in the video. Claudene's supervisor asked her to check it out."

"I'll make a deal with you," Claudene said, placing her iPhone on the table. "Show me the video on your iPhone, e-mail it to my iPhone, and I'll return the other phone."

"Deal," I said instantly. I pulled up the video so she could watch it, and then e-mailed it to the number she had flashed at me.

Her phone rang.

Willetta laughed. "I told you she'd remember your number. Pay up."

Claudene took me over the same ground I'd covered with Annalynn, who went inside to take a call halfway through.

When she came back out to join us, she turned on the patio light. "No one noticed who put the bag in the trash can. They couldn't even describe anyone in the park, with one exception. The old man remembered Phoenix. He usually sits on that bench."

LaDawna was home free. So was I.

Willetta had said nothing during my interrogation. She broke her silence: "Gribble looked too happy for that trash to hold anything but a payoff. I've been collecting facts and rumors about Roscoe Cantree for a week. He would *not* pay an accomplice for services already received. Gribble still has to earn that money."

"Agreed." I told them how I had learned about his trip.

Annalynn fiddled with her glass. "I wonder whether Mrs. T told you because she wants you to visit or because Kiki ordered her to say they're leaving town."

Why hadn't I, the cynical one, thought of that? "I'll call Mrs. T right now. She shouldn't have gone to bed yet." I dialed the number and put the phone on speaker. She didn't answer until the sixth ring. "Mrs. T, it's Phoenix. I'm worried about making Kiki and Derek angry with you if I come to your house."

"No worries, Greek girl. Kiki can't find a friend to come if I have problems. She says, 'If big trouble, let that Phoenix woman help you.' You want to come drink *ouzo*? I have plenty."

I laughed. "Not tonight. Is there anything you want me to bring you tomorrow?"

"Yes. Bring your Greek dog. Maybe he likes *ouzo*."

"I don't think so. Tomorrow I'll bring you a special tea.

Goodnight." I disconnected. "What do you think, Annalynn? Did Gribble set her up to tell me he's going out of town tomorrow?"

"Impossible to tell from that. Claudene, are you watching him now?"

She grinned. "No, I'm sitting here talking to you. Phoenix, as far as I know, you've never had any direct contact with the FBI. Why do you dislike us so much?"

I scrambled to come up with an answer. "Could be agents' refusal to answer local law officers' valid questions."

She grimaced. "A large, powerful organization has to follow precise procedures."

Willetta shook her head in disgust. "One reason I prefer local law enforcement is that I dare tell you the FBI is on Gribble like syrup on pancakes. We lowly locals are to back away and pretend he doesn't exist." She rose. "Now I need to take my fetus home to bed. When you two figure out what Roscoe is up to, please let me know."

Annalynn was stretched out on my bed asleep when I came back from an hour at the piano. I'd started with Mozart, but that didn't work. I kept thinking about Stuart. I tried Brahms, Chopin, and Gershwin to no avail.

Annalynn desperately needed to rest. So did I. I tiptoed to the dresser and eased my pajamas out of the drawer.

Annalynn sat up. "I thought we'd relax with some music." She pointed to the bed and turned on the radio. Dolly Parton's voice provided cover for our conversation.

So the FBI was still listening in. I stretched out beside Annalynn.

"You didn't happen to wander into that park at exactly the right moment," she whispered. "Give me the rest of the story. Now."

Bloody hell! Deny it? Give her a tidbit? Tell all? None of the above. "I can't tell you anything else. I promised secrecy to a source, an innocent person the FBI would destroy. A person we'll need to protect if Gribble doesn't lead the FBI to Roscoe."

She raised up on one elbow and glared at me. "Don't give me that nonsense. You're forcing me to tell the FBI you have more information."

A bluff. "And how would you prove that?" Mistake. She was furious. "Believe me, this is something that, for now and possibly forever, you don't need to know."

She thumped me on the top of my head with an open palm, something she hadn't done since we'd argued during sleepovers as pre-adolescents.

Her rare loss of control alarmed me. And her. Neither of us had realized how much strain she was under. I turned off the radio and patted her hand. "We'll be okay. If need be, we'll listen to music after we see what Gribble does."

She closed her eyes several seconds, nodded, and rose from the bed. "Stuart has no idea how maddening you can be. Good night."

Her phone rang about five o'clock. I picked up the receiver to eavesdrop. A squad car had broken down. Annalynn told the deputy to replace it with the department's pickup, which was usually reserved for off-road duty or carrying equipment.

After she hung up, she came to my door. "We have to work together, Phoenix. You threw a fit when you thought I interfered in your love life. Now you're interfering with my work."

Not a bad argument. "I know nothing that affects your work."

She came to my bed to whisper: "I don't believe that. Roscoe tried to kill you. What if Gribble is a lure to draw the FBI away from here, to make us think you're safe? You risk your life when you keep secrets."

"Not this one. Believe me, I'm not endangering myself."

She went back to bed.

I couldn't go back to sleep. Was I endangering myself and others? Roscoe's only emotions appeared to be hatred and greed. LaDawna and Lily certainly feared him. He'd double-crossed whoever masterminded the bank robbery and fought with his cancer-ravaged cousin. I tossed and turned for an hour, going over the same unfathomable information. When I heard Annalynn turn on her shower, I threw on shorts and a tank top and went downstairs to let Achilles out and to make a pot of Irish breakfast tea. My stomach couldn't tolerate the strong coffee I loved this morning. I prepared a packet of loose tea to take to Mrs. T while the tea brewed. Then I poured a cup for myself and put the pot and a cup for Annalynn on the dining room table.

She came down in her robe a minute or two later. "I'm glad you were upset enough to have trouble sleeping. Sometimes you control your emotions far too well."

"That's the pot calling the kettle black. Tea?" I wouldn't have survived as an operative, or in the financial world, if I'd not acquired self-discipline. I'd let my standards slip here. She'd hidden her emotions behind a public face since kindergarten. "Any word on the Gribbles yet?"

She took her seat, poured some tea, and wrapped her fingers around the china cup as though to warm them. "They haven't left. I asked Vernon about their newspaper delivery. Kiki called late yesterday afternoon and stopped the paper until Sunday. Gribble had the brakes fixed on the pickup yesterday and put on new back tires. They've made the motions of a real trip. Maybe it's his makeup gift to her for flirting with you."

"I hope for Mrs. T's sake that Kiki isn't in on this." So much for shutting out all personal feelings. "Are any of your deputies or the LPD involved, or is this all FBI?"

She poured a dab of milk in her tea and stirred and stirred. "I believe that information falls under your need-to-know rule. You don't need to know."

"You're quite right," I said, refusing to take the bait. "I'm tired of cereal. How about eggs-over-easy for breakfast?"

She frowned. "Are you fueling for a busy day?"

Enough of this. "I hope not. I hope Gribble drives to a rental car company in St. Louis, parks his pickup where Roscoe can take it, and rents a car."

"Ahhh, I see." Her shoulders relaxed. "He returns the rental Saturday, reports his pickup stolen, and collects the insurance money. Meanwhile, Roscoe drives off to Las Vegas in a legal vehicle."

Right after he came after me again. I had to be on high alert.

After returning from following Annalynn to the office, I put on my rearview-camera cap and took Achilles for a run. Every few minutes I checked my trackers. At nine o'clock the pickup drove out of town and I lost the signal. The dog tracker had a limited range. I continued to monitor the cell phone in the truck. My conviction, fed by experience rather than knowledge, grew that Roscoe had set up Gribble as a lure or a fall guy. Maybe Roscoe sat in Mrs. T's house waiting for me to walk in. Unlikely. So were two bombs in my garage. Changing after my run, I put on the Kevlar vest under a long, oversized blouse. To play it safe, I'd go to her back door through the alley behind her house. Achilles would know if a stranger lurked there.

I parked the car on the side street in deep shade and strolled down the alley. Through a break in the hedge I could see a man in a red T-shirt. I drew my Glock.

Achilles wagged his tail and stuck his nose through the hedge.

"Phoenix?" The man had drawn his gun.

"Hi." It was one of Annalynn's deputies. "What are you doing here?"

He holstered his gun and exhaled loudly. "A friend and I came to fix the front door and do a little clean-up back here." He pushed a section of hedge to one side for me to come through. "Annalynn and Jim sent us," he whispered. "The old lady's alone."

"Glad to see you. Achilles can stay out here with you."

Mrs. T waved to me from the back door. She must have seen him pull his gun.

I waved back. "Good morning. I hope you like Irish breakfast tea."

She nodded and opened the door. "The nice sheriff sent two men to fix my door. Maybe they can make water come to my fountain, too." She stepped back in her walker to let me in. "You ready to make baklava today?"

"Thinking about it makes my mouth water, but I only have time for tea today. If you tell me what we need to make it, I'll bring those ingredients and anything else you need next time."

"Good." She filled the kettle and placed it on a burner. "I apologize I insult you. Kiki wants to believe her husband. Then Trudy tells Kiki's friend you throw him down because he wants to kiss."

Amazing. "How on earth did Trudy find out?"

"She heard chorus girl say to minister." She chuckled. "Trudy hears all, sees all, knows nothing."

We chatted and planned our baklava morning. I didn't mention Kiki again until I was ready to leave. "By the way, where did Kiki and Derek go?"

"Nashville," she said. "I give Kiki birthday money so she can eat at nice places."

"I hope she has a great time." I went to the door. I had to call Annalynn to pass on what I'd learned.

"Greek girl, why do the police come here?"

Careful. "It's part of a community relations program."

"You insult me with this lie."

"My apology." If I didn't tell her a semblance of the truth, she wouldn't call me when she needed help. "A dangerous criminal has been hiding out in this area. One of the places he likes to hide is in the homes of . . . people who can't fight him."

"You mean old people." She considered this. "Many old people live in Laycock. Why would he come to my house?" She shook a crooked finger at me. "No lies."

She'd know when Derek was arrested. "You must promise to tell no one. Not Kiki, not Derek, not anyone." I waited until she crossed her heart. "The man knows Derek. They were friends many years ago. He may know Derek left and you're alone. We don't expect the man to come to Laycock, but he may."

She threw up her hands. "That Cantree boy! He stole socks from our store. I have a cowboy gun and bullets. You load it for me."

Awful idea. "Mrs. T, if you don't handle guns regularly, you're more likely to shoot yourself, or me or Kiki, than an intruder."

She pointed to a cabinet drawer. "Under tea towel. You load it. I will carry it in my basket today. I will put it by my bed tonight." She smiled. "Don't worry. I am one tough dame. I sleep with a gun to shoot German soldier during the war." She pointed to my concealed holster. "You are one tough dame, too. We tough dames will make wonderful baklava."

I laughed. "Yes, we will." I inspected the small six-shooter, an old model I'd never seen. It was oiled and clean. Kiki probably took care of it. I loaded it and put it in the walker's basket on a tea towel.

If Roscoe showed up here, she'd have a chance. Once he was caught, I'd remove the bullets.

★ ★ ★ ★ ★

The day dragged on. I finished the foundation papers and mailed them. The truck didn't move. LaDawna completed work on both desks—singing with Achilles until I put him outside—and went to LCC for a rehearsal. The Gribbles arrived in Nashville in their pickup. Roscoe's whereabouts remained a mystery.

About five thirty I gave up searching for information about Roscoe on the Web and tilted my head back to make sure the Sword of Damocles didn't hang over me.

I had to be lacking some key fact that would account for him trying to kill me. Willetta said she'd dug through every possible source for information on him. I called her private number.

She answered the phone with a question: "You hear anything?"

"Nothing. You?"

"Zero. Tiny thinks Roscoe sent the FBI on two wild goose chases and is hiding out somewhere around here again. Lily Stringer refuses to leave her farm, so he's sleeping out there until Roscoe is caught."

Good. "I'm calling to ask what you found out about Roscoe that's not available on the Internet."

"Not much. In prison, he sold protection services to white-collar types, or anybody else with money. That's how he connected with the embezzler who planned the bank robbery."

She was good. "What about other prison pals?"

"He had toadies, not pals. Claudene says the FBI checked on all known associates and came up empty."

"That would explain his recruiting his dying cousin." LaDawna had said Roscoe and Orson fought. "Any reports on how well they got along?"

"A neighbor remembered them yelling at each other a couple of times this summer, including the weekend before the robbery. Just a sec." Only her muffled voice came through for a minute or so. "Claudene says he'd have a lot better chance of hiding out in an urban area than a rural area. People here notice a new face in a store or restaurant. Farmers notice if an unfamiliar vehicle drives by."

"How well do you know Claudene?"

"Pretty well. She's my cousin. As you can tell from our names, we're both daughters of fathers who wanted sons. She's spending her days off with me and going back to the Kansas City office Thursday. We've been trying to figure out why Roscoe has it in for you."

Her statement was really a question. "So have I. Early on, I assumed he wanted revenge. The FBI suspected that I took his Krugerrands. That was a bad guess. If I had the coins, he would have tried to kidnap me to lead him to them, not to kill me." A new theory began to form. "I'll let you know if I figure it out. Bye."

Work my way up to it. Use the information I had to think through the robbery and escape from the thieves' viewpoint.

Start with the mastermind, a guy dumb enough to get caught embezzling from a bank. He's sentenced to several years in prison. He's disgraced himself and lost any chance to make a decent living when he gets out. He knows a bank patron, probably a crook, hid a small fortune in a safety deposit box. The embezzler would be a suspect if someone takes it, but being in prison gives him the perfect alibi. He needs a flunky, someone bright enough to rob the bank but not knowledgeable enough to sell the coins. The convict providing muscle to protect the mastermind completes his sentence. He's a gambler willing to take a chance for a big score. Just the guy the mastermind wants.

Roscoe takes the job. He has no record as a bank robber so suspicion won't automatically fall on him. The mastermind gives him a blueprint, literally and figuratively, on how to get to the coins. Roscoe uses his skills as a car thief to add his own wrinkles to the getaway. He has trouble finding a crew either because the job carries high risk or no one trusts him. Roscoe recruits a driver, but he needs guns in the bank lobby to help him get out of there. He turns to family.

Orson is dying. He's alone and scared. He contacts the son he's ignored for years. The boy, bitter and desperate, runs away from a foster home to join his father. Father and son share a love of cars. They work on Orson's old Mustang together and begin to bond. The boy contacts his sister, probably the only person he loves, to tell her he's with their father. Orson agrees to give LaDawna the car. Or the son trades participation in the robbery for it. Or he drives it to Chicago on his own. Orson agrees to the bank robbery so he can pay for painkillers and care. Maybe he wants to leave something for his son. Orson and Roscoe argue about the boy becoming part of the crew. The boy wants to do it. Orson tells Norval about the cancer and asks him to give the boy a home for a little while.

Probably not quite right. Close enough. Now came the part I knew least about.

Orson and Junior don't trust Roscoe to pay them. Or they want cash to spend, not coins to fence. The two Orsons rob the tellers and flee to Missouri to give the boy a new start. The father doesn't really care if he escapes. He's dying.

Meanwhile Roscoe has to escape from the police and the accomplice expecting the Krugerrands. He figures neither will be after him for a day or two. He drives, or rides a motorcycle, to Missouri to pick up the rebuilt Chevy waiting in Boonville. He meets Orson and Junior at the abandoned farmhouse. Hmm. Roscoe got away in another vehicle after he used the rebuilt car to force Mark Keller off the road. Roscoe must have stashed that vehicle earlier and caught a ride to the farmhouse with the Orsons. They booby-trap the farmhouse doors, planning to lure their old enemy there after they leave for Norval's.

But they fight. Maybe it's because they know Orson left fingerprints that enabled the FBI to identify him and point them toward Roscoe. They definitely fight over dividing the spoils. Orson takes two-thirds of the cash, half of which Junior puts in LaDawna's car. Roscoe takes off with a third of the cash and all of the coins. He calls his old stooge, Derek Gribble, and arranges for a lift to Boonville and his next car. Sunday Gribble finds out he helped a wanted man escape and stays mum out of fear of both Roscoe and the law.

I paused to evaluate my scenario. What I'd guessed fit what I knew.

That left the question of why Roscoe, in disguise, went to the casino in Boonville Sunday rather than heading for the big payoff in Las Vegas. Gambling lust could have held him a little while, but surely he'd heard Orson had died at the farmhouse and knew Tiny and the FBI would be hunting for the missing cousin. And for the missing gold. If the law found Roscoe with the coins, he'd never beat a murder charge.

Facts and educated guesses converged and pointed to a good reason for Roscoe to stick around. He no longer had the coins.

Chapter Thirty-Four

If Roscoe didn't have the coins, who did? Not the mastermind or his cronies. The FBI had verified that. Not the Orsons. The FBI had searched all around the abandoned farmhouse. I ticked off possible candidates: good cousin Norval, talented second cousin LaDawna, childhood victim Lily, high school stooge Derek, old enemy Tiny.

Achilles dropped the chew toy he was destroying and trotted out with his tail raising a breeze. The front door slammed.

"Phoenix," Connie called, "I brought a rotisserie chicken for supper. Annalynn will be home in about five minutes."

"Thanks. I'll be down shortly."

I reviewed my candidates one by one. Norval honored family, but he'd rejected the Cantree criminal lifestyle. LaDawna had met the fugitives at the farmhouse, but she had worked hard to support herself and become a singer.

I reined in my emotions. I liked the girl, but that drop in the park looked bad. It implicated Lily, too, but she despised and feared Roscoe. My visit to her home indicated that she had helped LaDawna out of love for the lost little sister and guilt for not taking in the orphaned niece and nephew.

Derek was too damned dumb for Roscoe to trust with the coins.

That left Tiny, but he'd hounded the Cantrees years ago and trapped them at the farmhouse.

Damn it! Who had the coins?

Connie tapped on my door. "Would you like corn on the cob?"

No one! I jumped up, elated that I'd found the answer. "Roscoe hid the coins! He hid them Saturday night after he found out Orson was a person of interest in the robbery. Roscoe's still here because he hid the gold somewhere in plain sight and hasn't been able to retrieve it!"

Annalynn appeared behind Connie. "What are you talking about?"

I went through my thinking, ever more sure I was right, and ended, "Roscoe hid the Krugerrands in some public place. With Tiny's staff and FBI agents looking for him, he couldn't risk going back to get them. That's why he left blatant clues he'd robbed those places in Indianapolis and Toledo. And why he sent the Gribbles off to Nashville."

Connie cocked her head. "Okay. I'll buy all that. Why would he try to kill you?"

She and Annalynn waited expectantly.

My brain sputtered. "I haven't worked that out yet."

"*We* will work it out," Annalynn said. "I'll pass on your theory to Tiny. Maybe he'll know of possible hiding places." She whirled and ran down the stairs.

Connie tiptoed into my room to whisper, "Surely the FBI already knows who LaDawna is. We have to tell Annalynn before Wharton does."

Scheisse. "I called the restaurant. Her alibi is absolute. We'll have to tell Annalynn LaDawna is Madonna without saying what happened in the park."

"She'll suspect you of holding back. Better if I say a student confided in me. Do you think she's safe from Roscoe? He knows she's in Laycock."

I'd worried about that earlier. "My guess is that she's served his purpose, that the only things on his mind are retrieving the gold and selling it." The worry line didn't disappear from Connie's forehead. "Besides, he had that cell number, but he doesn't know where she lives. He probably doesn't even know her new name."

Connie tugged on a turquoise earring that matched her blouse. "I want that poor girl in a safe place. Tonight. One of my voice students is a freshman at Truman State. I could take LaDawna to Kirksville to stay with Emma a couple of days."

"A wise precaution. Where's our Isolde-to-be now?"

"Cleaning city offices with Ado Annie. They finish at nine."

"She's safe for a couple of hours."

The second step on the stairs squeaked. "What are you two doing up there? I've put on the corn."

Connie winked and pirouetted to go downstairs. "We were talking about the girl playing the lead in *Oklahoma!*. Phoenix says she should begin her operatic training."

"Is she that good?"

"Achilles thinks so," I said, following Connie. "He drove me nuts singing with her while she polished our desks this afternoon. What did Tiny say?"

"He's intrigued." She took a deep breath. "Let's take a thirty-minute timeout from this case while we eat."

We chatted as we ate, but in my head beat a constant refrain: Why did Roscoe want to kill me? By the time we carried our coffee into the ladies' parlor, I had a possible answer. I waited until we'd each taken our usual seat to test it on Annalynn and Connie. "End of timeout. Roscoe didn't try to kill me for revenge. He thinks I know where he hid the Krugerrands. He expects me to go after them when the FBI takes off in the wrong direction, which they did today."

Connie twirled her finger in the old crazy sign. "You're living in Theory Land, which is right next door to Fairy Land."

Annalynn raised a skeptical eyebrow. "The major flaw in this theory is that you have no clue where they are."

"But he doesn't know that," I pointed out. "If we can figure out *why* he thinks I know, we'll have the *where.*"

Connie shook her head. "How on earth did you earn a doctorate in economics? No, that's the wrong question. Did studying economics warp your brain?" She slapped her forehead. "God help me! I see what you mean. You went wherever he hid the coins. He saw you there."

"Yes!"

"Where were you?"

Annalynn jumped up and brought a file folder from her desk. "I printed out your statement on everywhere you went last week before the bombing." She pulled it out.

I didn't need to read it. "He saw me in two places, at Lily Stringer's house—well, he saw my car—and at Oak Grove Cemetery." Facts I'd misinterpreted fell into a whole new configuration. I thought of a way to confirm my new interpretation. I went to Annalynn's desk and dialed Vernon.

Voices chatted in the background when he answered.

"Vernon, can you search your online morgue? I need some information urgently."

"I can search headlines and a few hundred specific names or terms. Does urgently mean tomorrow morning?"

"Urgent is stop-the-presses immediate. If I'm right, you'll need to write a whole new front page."

"I have to excuse myself from my dinner guests and get my laptop. I'll call you back in a minute."

I hung up. Could the hiding place possibly be so obvious? "Vernon may find information that proves me wrong." Annalynn and Connie were literally breathing down my neck. "Keep reading my statement."

Neither one moved.

The phone rang. I put it on speaker.

"What do you need to know?" Vernon's high tenor voice sounded like that of an eager young reporter, not a retired publisher.

"The last time a child, or anyone else, was buried at Oak Grove Cemetery."

Annalynn gasped and clutched my shoulder.

"You're full of surprises," Vernon said. "Oak Grove isn't in my search base, but I can get you an answer with old-fashioned reporting. Give me a few minutes." He hung up.

Connie pulled off an earring. "What's a burial got to do with this?"

Annalynn stepped away and stared out the window with her back to us. "I stumbled over a new grave, a little one, right after the shootout. Phoenix thinks maybe it wasn't a grave after all."

Connie's eyes widened. "Oh."

I motioned for her to keep quiet. When the phone rang, I answered and hit speaker.

Vernon said, "According to the minister, the last burial was an eighty-year-old man. It snowed that day. What's my headline? We have to start printing at midnight."

Annalynn took over. "I can't promise we'll meet your deadline, or even guarantee the story. You can't tell anyone else. You can't come near Oak Grove."

A long, long silence. "You have my word. I need yours that you'll call me as soon as possible."

"You have it. Prepare to write about Roscoe Cantree hiding a half million in gold."

Chapter Thirty-Five

Annalynn sent word for her two deputies on duty and Tiny to take an urgent conference call in ten minutes and spread out the county map on the coffee table.

I had to tell her about LaDawna fast. "I don't think the FBI is still watching Orson's daughter. Do you want me to ask Claudene whether we should put the girl into protective custody?"

Annalynn circled three intersections on the map. "Use your own judgment."

Connie winked at me. "I think you should, Phoenix. She's terrified of Roscoe."

I picked up my cell phone from the hassock.

Annalynn reached over and grabbed the phone. "Who are you talking about?"

"LaDawna McKnight, Orson Cantree's daughter. I assume the FBI stopped shadowing her because she had nothing to do with the robbery."

"My Lord, Phoenix!" Annalynn raised the phone as though she were going to throw it at me. "What have you done? How long have you known who LaDawna is?"

Connie put a restraining hand on Annalynn's arm. "LaDawna confided in me yesterday afternoon after her voice lesson. Didn't the FBI tell you about her?"

Annalynn handed me the phone. "Call Claudene. Connie, please call my dispatcher and tell her to call an off-duty officer in to monitor the Oak Grove camera."

I dialed Claudene.

She answered not with hello but a question: "What's the conference call about?"

"Mapping out the strategy to catch Roscoe tonight. Annalynn will explain. She assigned me to find out whether agents are guarding Orson Cantree's daughter. If not, we better put her in protective custody."

Dead silence for several seconds. "Where is she?"

The FBI, or at least this rookie agent, had no idea of LaDawna's identity. "She's in the mayor's office." Absolutely true. "She's terrified of Roscoe."

"Was she involved in the robbery?"

"No. I checked her alibi myself, since no one shared the information with us."

"Bring her in immediately." She hung up, doubtless to call her supervisor.

That had gone quite well. I hadn't even had to reveal that Madonna Cantree had become LaDawna McKnight.

Annalynn pulled me over to look at the map. "It will be dead dark in about forty minutes. Right after that we need to have officers on foot at the cemetery and squad cars here, here, and here to watch the roads and block escape routes. The main problem is getting everyone in place without being seen by Roscoe."

"You have another problem," Connie said. "You don't have anybody available to monitor the camera. I volunteer."

"Thank you. I hereby deputize you. Go on over." She stood up. "Phoenix, you take the extension in the hall. Please don't say anything unless I ask you to. We don't have time for anyone to argue. They have to accept that I'm in charge."

"Agreed." I followed Connie to the front door and whispered, "Pick up LaDawna on the way. Don't let her out of your sight or near a phone. That will protect her if he's thinking of taking a hostage and us if she's helping him."

"Phoenix! Do you distrust her?"

"No, but I have on rare occasions been wrong. We can't take the chance. Go."

I hurried to the hall phone.

"Pick up," Annalynn said.

In a minute or so she had Tiny, two deputies from each county, and the FBI agent on the line.

"Please listen and don't interrupt," Annalynn said. "We have to move immediately. We believe Roscoe Cantree is hiding nearby because he buried the Krugerrands in Oak Grove Cemetery."

Everyone on the line except me said something.

"Quiet," Sheriff Keyser ordered. "He may attempt to retrieve them tonight. I need eight people altogether. How many can you field, Sheriff Towson?"

"Three—me, Wolf, and Claudene Dale."

"Four," Willetta said. "I'm not too pregnant to handle communications."

Annalynn hesitated a moment. "Okay. That gives us eight. We'll work in pairs. If we don't see him coming in, our motion-sensor camera at the back of the cemetery will pick him up. Our goal is to arrest him there. Unit One will conceal a civilian car in the timber about a quarter of a mile southwest of the cemetery and walk to the field across from the cemetery."

"That's my post," Tiny said.

"Yes," Annalynn agreed. "You and Claudene. My deputies, Spike and Chester, form Unit Two. Conceal your vehicle—use the pickup—along the county road that runs about half a mile behind the cemetery. Odds are he'll come in that way. Unit Three, Willetta and Wolf, conceal your vehicle near the first intersection east of the church. That's about two miles away."

No wonder she'd let Willetta come. That was the least likely place to see action.

"Unit Four, Phoenix and I, will be between the church and the first intersection on the west. We'll maintain radio silence and keep in touch by phone until the action begins. Can everyone be in place within twenty-five minutes?"

A chorus of yeses came over the line.

Claudene said, "An excellent strategy until we can bring in an experienced FBI team. That may take three or four hours."

"Meanwhile," Annalynn said, "take no chances. Roscoe's smart and he's ruthless. Good luck."

I drove like a NASCAR driver most of the way to our spot, the stack of hay bales where Roscoe parked to wait to run Mark Keller off the road. We pulled into position right on schedule. The other three units reported that they were in place within two minutes.

Annalynn discussed alternative actions with them while I strapped Achilles into his new Kevlar coat. He didn't like it, and our tension frightened him. He stayed so close to me that I could hardly walk the thirty yards or so to the road's grassy border. It had no shoulder. I sat down in the tall grass to get a close view of any traffic.

The last light had faded. Clouds meandered overhead, threatening to block out most of the light from the stars and moon. With nothing but crickets and an occasional inexplicable rustling in the grass to distract me, I had a chance to think. Roscoe had lured Mark Keller out of his house and run him off the road so he wouldn't see Roscoe in the cemetery. A few minutes before that Roscoe had come to Lily's house but driven on. Probably he'd expected to find LaDawna and the cash there.

Lily had to be warned. I dialed her number.

She answered immediately.

To keep her from recognizing my voice, I raised the pitch and spoke rapidly: "This is Vandiver County Deputy Phoenix Smith. We suspect Roscoe Cantree is in the area. Please lock up and turn on all your outdoor lights."

"Thank you. I did that as soon as I came home. I also keep my telephone and my pistol at hand."

I heard a car coming from the east and said a quick goodbye. The headlights came into sight. I flattened out and put my arm over Achilles. I raised my head as the lights flashed by and saw an indistinguishable blur. I heard Brandon bellowing out the opening of "Oh, What a Beautiful Mornin'."

I walked back to the SUV and leaned on the open window on the driver's side. "That was Brandon, Connie's Curly. He lives near here. Anything happening?"

She covered her Bluetooth's mouthpiece. "Claudene and Tiny are hunkered down in the pasture across from the cemetery. Spike reported a Travis Farms pickup went by pulling a horse trailer. He checked. No report of it being stolen. Willetta and Wolf saw Brandon and a van with far too many people in it. Connie says she's glad LaDawna is there to help her keep awake."

I marveled at Annalynn's apparent calm. Trusting in my judgment, she had risked her rising reputation in setting up this stakeout. What we knew indicated Roscoe had buried the gold in the cemetery. I could be wrong. I didn't think I was. I felt less certain he would come for it tonight, and that our hastily organized team could catch him if he did. Events tonight could jump-start or throttle her political campaign.

"We set the camera on constant feed," she said. "I want Connie off the units' conference call. Please call her on your cell and keep in touch with her."

A reasonable measure. We didn't want LaDawna following the operation. I put on my Bluetooth headset to free my hands.

Connie let me know she resented being cut out of the action. "You realize that we're doing nothing but watching silhouettes of gravestones. In black and white."

"Send out for popcorn. I'm putting my phone on mute. Turn yours down to minimum until you have something to report." Maybe LaDawna would tell Connie more if no one was eavesdropping. And I wouldn't have to hear their prattle. I welcomed the silence. "It's so quiet out here you could hear a car a half mile away."

"Don't fall asleep," Annalynn said. "How far are we from the cemetery?"

"About a mile and a half. Out of hearing. Why?"

"I wish we were closer. He's had a week to figure a way in and out of the cemetery, and to buy another assault rifle. He could have gone into the cornfield sometime today while the FBI trailed Gribble to Nashville."

Partly at my suggestion. "Maybe I should walk to Mark Keller's house and sneak through the corn to the edge of the cemetery."

"Forget it. We stay in pairs, and everyone stays in place. That way no one gets shot because they're mistaken for Roscoe. Get in the car and tell me about LaDawna."

Annalynn was going to make sure I didn't go off on my own. I told her everything except that LaDawna had made the drop in the park.

At ten thirty-five, Annalynn whispered, "I'm going to look ridiculous if we're wrong about this."

"It's still early. Farmers just turned off the ten o'clock news and went to bed."

We sat in silence for several minutes.

"Mayday! Mayday," Connie yelled. "I see something moving."

Annalynn inhaled deeply. "All units, full alert."

I took my phone off mute. "What and where, Connie?"

"Rear center of the cemetery. It could be a dog or fox. There's no light."

"It's him," LaDawna screamed. "I saw a spade handle by the stone that looks like the Washington Monument."

I knew exactly where Roscoe was. "He's about thirty feet from the cornfield. Halfway between it and the fake grave."

"Tiny, don't approach for three minutes," Annalynn said. "If he hears you, he'll run and lose himself in the corn. Give him time to get to the gold and start digging. Wolf, head for the cemetery in three minutes. Spike, in four minutes drive down the road and find his vehicle." She turned on the department radio. "Units Two and Three, break radio silence as needed but keep your phones on."

I put the key in the ignition, itching to turn it.

"Willetta," Annalynn said, "notify and maintain contact with medical personnel, the Highway Patrol, and the FBI."

That should keep the pregnant cop occupied. I spoke softly into my phone: "Connie, as soon as this goes down, call Vernon and tell him to hold the press. Nothing else."

"I can see a tiny glow on the ground in the middle of the cemetery," Connie said. "He's standing now."

"Tiny, he's digging," Annalynn said softly. "Cease voice communication and go." She put a round in the chamber. "Roscoe must have been in that Travis Farms pickup."

"Yes, and a horse trailer could carry a motorcycle. A minute until we go."

"We go in thirty seconds, Phoenix. I want Roscoe to hear our motor, not Tiny and Claudene running into the cemetery. I also want to get there before Wolf and Willetta."

Brilliant. She should've been a general. I turned on the engine and the parking lights and drove slowly over the rough ground to the road. No sign of traffic.

"Go!"

I put on the dims and stepped on the gas.

As I hit seventy, Connie said, "Two people are moving along the west side of the cemetery. I wish this camera had sound."

We were halfway there. "Siren, Annalynn?"

"No, Roscoe will run if he knows it's the law."

A few seconds later I could make out Mark Keller's roof. Then I heard gunfire, at least two guns. I braked to slide into the church's parking lot, hit the high beams, and drew my Glock.

A man with a cloth bag over his shoulder bolted into the corn. I fired three times as he vanished into the dense green.

Claudene Dale fired as she raced between the tombstones toward where Roscoe had vanished.

"Tiny's down," Annalynn said, opening her door.

"We lost the picture," Connie yelled.

Wolf and Willetta roared past us and along the edge of the cemetery toward the cornfield. Wolf spilled out of the driver's side and plunged into the stalks close behind the FBI agent.

Willetta turned off the car's headlights and shone its searchlight above the corn.

A good try to light the officers' way without making them targets, but it wouldn't show them Roscoe. They'd never find him in there.

Willetta got out of the squad car and trotted toward the cornfield. She dropped to one knee at the edge. "I found four coins."

Maybe one of us had hit Roscoe, or at least the bag. He might double back later to get the coins. I jumped out of the SUV to go help Annalynn with Tiny.

"Over here," he called. "He got me in the thigh. I'm bleeding pretty bad."

"I'll bring the kit," Willetta said.

Blood stained his trousers from hip to knee. My keychain

tool kit included a small but sharp blade. Annalynn held a flashlight while I cut off the cloth to expose the wound. Willetta arrived with a first-aid satchel. I gave way to her and wiped the blood off my hands on the grass as best I could. I drew my Glock and ran toward the break in the cornfield.

A motorcycle engine started deep in the corn and moved away.

All four of us swore.

I holstered my gun and stepped into the corn with a flashlight to search for the coins. I found a half dozen and tossed them onto the grass.

Annalynn said, "Roscoe blocked the road with the horse trailer. We've lost him."

Then he had only the motorcycle. He'd want a car.

Willetta trotted back to the squad car. "The bullet went through Tiny's leg. It missed the main artery but he's losing blood. Help us get him in the car. I'm going to take him to meet the ambulance." She drove around the edge of the cemetery to him.

He fainted while the three of us were hoisting him into the back seat.

Wolf burst out of the corn. Claudene followed a moment later.

"Wolf, you go with Willetta," Annalynn said. "We'll stay here in case Roscoe cuts back for the gold he dropped."

As the squad car roared out of the cemetery, a terrible thought hit me: Roscoe knew a place a few miles away to get a vehicle and a hostage. I sprinted toward the SUV with Achilles at my side. "I'm going to Lily Stringer's."

"No," Annalynn shouted. "You're not going anywhere alone!"

"I have Achilles." I opened the door, followed him in, and turned the key. "It's only seven or eight minutes away. I'll call if I need help. Achilles, on the floor."

"Phoenix? What's happening?" Connie hadn't hung up.

"I can't talk now but stay on the line." I backed out of the parking lot and drove as fast as the roads and the SUV would allow until I turned onto Lily's road. Then I dropped down to fifty-five, the speed a neighbor would drive on the way home.

I couldn't remember how far it was to her house, but I knew her lights would be visible when I topped the next rise. No lights. But she'd left her lights on. *Scheisse!* "Connie?"

"Here."

Mustn't let LaDawna know her aunt was in trouble. "Tell Annalynn and Claudene I need backup. The more the merrier. I'm going to drive past and walk back to assess the situation. Good-bye."

A quarter of a mile or so beyond the house I saw a tree-lined lane. I killed my lights and pulled in, stopping to avoid hitting something in the road. I waited for my eyes to adjust to the darkness. A motorcycle.

A pain shot through my bullet wound. Purely psychosomatic. Nothing to fear but fear itself. That was plenty. Planning my strategy, I ejected the magazine from my Glock and jammed in a full one. I had to try three times before I could force myself to open the door and step out. I stuck the phone in my pocket.

Achilles didn't follow.

"Come, boy, quiet," I whispered.

He didn't move. He'd already assessed the situation.

I left the door open and felt my way to the motorcycle's front tire. I punctured it in four places.

Achilles grabbed the hem of my vest and tried to pull me back into the SUV.

I got in front of him to close the door and lock it. I had no time to waste. Rather than stumbling through the undergrowth, I ran up the side of the road toward Lily's house. I hoped Roscoe was hotwiring her pickup. I feared he was taking her hostage. Nearing her yard, I slowed to a jog to regain my breath and watch for trouble. A light went on in her kitchen. A few seconds later it went out.

I tried to visualize the room. I'd come in through the back door, on the far side of the house. The only other outside door I'd seen was in the living room at the front. No vehicle had been parked in the driveway lined with yellow roses. She must keep the pickup in the big shed at the end of the drive. I cut cater-cornered across the yard toward the back of the house.

Something touched my left leg. Deputy Dog was on duty.

I heard metal on metal—the shed door rolling open. I crept around the back corner of the house.

"Get in there," a man snarled. "You're my chauffeur."

Two car doors opened. I dashed to the row of rose bushes and dove under the fragrant blossoms as the engine sputtered and the headlights went on. Pain from my souvenir of Istanbul made me gasp. Definitely not psychosomatic this time.

The headlights made it impossible for me to see Roscoe. The engine roared and died. She'd stalled it.

A good tactic. I squirmed forward until I found a good view between two clusters of roses.

He screamed curses at her that Fargo would have loved to add to his repertoire. Roscoe ended the curses with, "No funny business!"

The engine roared. I used its noise to put two bullets into the radiator or, I hoped, some other vital part.

The engine revved, sputtered, and died. The headlights stayed on.

"Goddamnit," he yelled. "Release the hood." He threw open his door and yanked her out with him. They were so close together I didn't dare shoot. He shoved her ahead of him to the front of the pickup. The lights went out. He slapped the front of the pickup, probably searching for a hood release.

I could see her light blouse, but he was a dark blob. I waited for him to turn on a light or flashlight and give me something to aim at.

"Hey," he said, "what the hell?"

Uh-oh. He'd felt the bullet holes.

An instant later the light blouse stood in front of the dark blob.

She grunted. A shadow now covered her left shoulder and ran across her upper chest.

"You out there! Throw me your car keys or I'll kill her," he yelled. "Tell him I'll do it, Silly Lily. Tell him."

"He'll do it," she croaked.

Even without seeing I was sure he had his left arm across her throat and held a gun to her head with his right hand.

"She takes a bullet in the head on the count of three unless you throw me your keys. I don't mind driving a cop car."

She'd never survive if I gave him the keys. She'd die if I shot and missed.

"One!"

I aimed an inch above the dark blob on the right shoulder of her light blouse and fired.

He screamed and the white blouse sprang away. I fired at the center of the blob.

He staggered.

A pistol popped like a firecracker. He stumbled forward. The pistol popped again. He fell. The pistol popped four more times and then clicked and clicked and clicked.

Chapter Thirty-Six

After I made sure Roscoe's heart had stopped, I led Lily away from the body to her back steps, where her knees gave way. I pried the empty revolver from her hand and went inside to turn on the porch light. As I came back out, the red Mustang whipped into Lily's drive, braking barely in time to avoid running over the body.

Claudene jumped out with her gun ready and crept toward him.

"He's dead," I assured her. "Your crack FBI team is a little late."

Annalynn ran to Lily and me. "Are you hurt?"

Lily dropped her head between her knees. "I shot him. I shot him six times."

Claudene rose from examining the body. "I see four wounds: his right hand, his chest, his shoulder, and his upper thigh."

Thinking about my shot in the dark, I joined Lily on the steps. "I take credit for the hand. That's probably the best shot I ever fired." I drew Achilles close. We were both trembling.

He stayed at my side as Lily and I told our stories to Claudene and Annalynn. I refused to go through it again when agents, troopers, and deputies converged. A few snarls from Achilles enabled me to keep the swarm of cops-come-lately at bay long enough to call Vernon. I gave him the bare bones of the story—mainly the two-county and federal operation Annalynn organized in minutes and Roscoe's death at the hands of his hostage. I slid over his eluding us at the cemetery. Instead, I played up Lily's ingenuity in stalling him and in secreting the small pistol that she pulled out of her pocket when an unnamed Vandiver County deputy distracted him.

To mollify the FBI, I credited Claudene with playing a major role on Annalynn's team and with identifying Roscoe Cantree's body. I sent Vernon one iPhone photo—Lily Stringer sitting on her porch steps sobbing while Annalynn knelt in front of her offering a consoling hand. A picture of the compassionate crime fighter should come in handy when Annalynn campaigned for Congress.

Willetta and Wolf Volcker arrived a few minutes later to report Tiny had no serious damage and to represent their sheriff's department. The action had ended out of Annalynn's jurisdiction.

She said nothing as we walked down to the SUV. She let Achilles get in front with her and lie on her feet. She didn't answer when I asked if she wanted the air conditioner turned on.

When we were halfway home, she said, "If you were a real deputy, I would fire you. You disobeyed orders. You put yourself at mortal risk. I was so frightened for you tonight. Now I'm so angry—no, so mad—I can't talk to you."

"That's okay. You can thank me tomorrow."

She slapped me on my right leg, hard.

Achilles barked his disapproval.

"I'm sorry, Achilles," she said, reaching down to hug him. "You're quite right. We have to accept Phoenix for what she is. Let's have some nice music." She went through the dozen CDs in the car and chose a Dolly Parton album. I speeded up in anticipation of a duet.

Somehow Annalynn bore Achilles singing in her ear. I had a splitting headache by the time we reached the castle.

It was well past one, but Vernon and Connie waited for us on the front porch with wine glasses in their hands.

Vernon raised his glass to me. "Great reporting, Phoenix. I ran it almost word for word in eighteen-point type. Unattributed, of course. Now, Annalynn, I need to interview you so that I can write a follow-up scoop for our website."

"Oh, Vern, I'm exhausted. Can't it wait until morning?"

"No," he said firmly. "You promised me the story. It has to run before that press conference you'll hold at, say, eleven tomorrow. That's priceless exposure. You'll gain thousands of votes at that one appearance."

Connie rose, wine glass in hand. "Let's give them some privacy, Phoenix."

As soon as we were inside, she put a finger to her lips and motioned for me to follow her to the kitchen.

Achilles went straight to his water bowl.

She leaned on the kitchen island. "I can't tell you."

I ran fresh water for him. "Can't tell me what?"

"I can't tell you." She waited.

Another of her coded conversations. She'd stayed around for a couple of hours to have it. The sooner I figured out what she wouldn't tell me the better. I saw one obvious subject, but I didn't dare mention LaDawna in case a bug was listening. "Laurey told you something in confidence."

"I can't tell you." She motioned to me to go on.

"Laurey contradicted something she told us earlier."

"I didn't say that."

That was a relief. I couldn't think of anything else. My head and half a dozen other places hurt. "I'm too tired for guessing games, Connie."

She fingered an earring. "It's now or never. I'll think better of it by morning."

What would LaDawna tell Connie and make her promise not

to tell me? The girl must have done something illegal. "She helped her family."

"Come on, smartass. I didn't say that."

What else was left? I'd tied up all the loose ends. Except one. Dreading the answer, I struggled to phrase the crucial question: "She found a second gift, a small, noisy one."

Connie raised her arms in triumph. "I can't tell you that."

"Bloody hell!" LaDawna had shot at me in La Vida Loca with a pistol her brother had left in the Mustang. I remembered the bullets went well above my head. I remembered her tears when I'd threatened Fargo and her unease when she realized I was going to help her practice the next day. She'd been in shock. But she could have killed me. It's hard to shoot accurately in the dark.

She hadn't hit me. I hadn't hit her aunt.

Connie tossed an earring on the island. "Well?"

"Give me a moment to digest this." The kid had passed through hell repeatedly in her short life. For the first time she had a real chance. Her remarkable aunt would provide love and support. Connie and I could guide her toward a fine career. If I stopped her now with a felony charge, even this tenacious, talented girl might never recover. I wouldn't add that to the heavy weights already on my conscience. "Thank you for not telling me anything. I'm going to forget this whole conversation."

Connie smiled. "You're a real pain, Phoenix D Smith, but you're worth the trouble. I hope Stuart knows that."

That remained in the back of my mind through all the folderol Wednesday about our beating the FBI to Roscoe and the gold. I suppressed my tension while making baklava Thursday. Kiki interrupted us with pleas to Mrs. T to hire a lawyer to guide Derek Gribble in trading information for a lesser charge. I reexperienced the agony of my teenage years Friday as I packed and repacked for the Labor Day getaway—or breakup—with Stuart.

Saturday morning after breakfast with Connie and Annalynn, I brought my weekender downstairs. Then I thought how humiliating it would be to have it there if Stuart wanted to call the whole thing off. I took it upstairs and put it in the closet.

I returned to the dining room where Connie and Annalynn were lingering over coffee. "We're not in high school anymore. Don't you two have something boring to do somewhere else?"

Connie grinned. "You wouldn't deny us a little vicarious pleasure."

Maybe I could shame them into giving me some privacy. "Don't you mean voyeuristic pleasure?"

Annalynn poured more coffee for both of them. "The important word is pleasure. Don't forget the baklava you saved for Stuart. It demonstrates your domesticity."

"Ha ha and ho ho." I went to the kitchen to get it.

Achilles dropped his chew toy and trotted to the window wagging his tail. Stuart always brought a present, even if only an old tie. Achilles loved to shred Stuart's ties.

I hurried toward the front door, hoping to step outside, and out of sight, to greet Stuart. Connie beat me there and welcomed him in.

He looked good. Really good.

He didn't have to tell me I'd need my weekender. He'd brought Achilles five Frisbees. For me, he'd brought one red rose.

ABOUT THE AUTHOR

Carolyn Mulford decided to become a writer while attending a one-room school near Kirksville, Missouri. After earning a BA in English at Truman State and an MA in journalism at the University of Missouri, she received a different kind of education as a Peace Corps Volunteer in Ethiopia. She worked as a magazine editor in Vienna, Austria, and Washington, D.C., and then became a freelance writer and editor. She changed her focus to fiction with her return to Missouri. Her first novel, *The Feedsack Dress,* was honored as Missouri's Great Read at the 2009 National Book Festival. Her first mystery novels, *Show Me the Murder* and *Show Me the Deadly Deer,* came out in 2013. She blogs about her writing on her website, http://Carolyn Mulford.com.